For Mary Ann Grossmann

thanks for your time!

Sincerely

John J Bah

THE MISSING ELEMENT

A James Becker Mystery

by

John L. Betcher

Published by
John L. Betcher
Red Wing, Minnesota
john@johnbetcher.com
2010

ISBN: 1451512716
EAN-13: 9781451512717

Available for direct purchase at:
www.johnbetcher.com

For Lynn, Anne and Kate

CHAPTER 1

To avoid security, he entered the building through a service door. Accompanying him were two, broad-shouldered men in denim jeans, navy jackets, baseball caps and leather gloves. They were hired muscle. He wasn't the type to dirty his hands with this sort of business.

The threesome climbed the back stairs to the seventh floor. After a quick check for anyone who might be present in the hall, they exited the stairwell and proceeded to her apartment. He extended his gloved hand and rapped on the brass knocker.

Inside the condo, a middle-aged woman slept. It had been a difficult day at the office. She'd left work early with a headache and was hoping a short nap would help shake it.

Awakened by the knock on her door, she glanced at her watch . . . 6:30. Who would come calling, unannounced, at this time of evening? She arose and left the bedroom. At the entrance door, she pressed her cheek against the cool wood . . . checking the peephole.

She hadn't expected to see *him* tonight.

Nevertheless, after a short pause, she unchained the door, unlocked the deadbolt, and turned the knob to allow him inside.

No sooner had she cracked the door, than the two thugs shouldered their way into the apartment – shoving her roughly to the hardwood. The fall left her unable to catch her breath. Moving quickly, the men jammed a terrycloth rag into her mouth, stifling her feeble attempts to scream.

She had never dreamed that her caller was capable of physical violence. Yet there he stood . . . looking down at her with satisfaction.

She gagged as the rag brushed the back of her throat.

The hirelings picked her up by the arms and dragged her farther inside the apartment. Being slight of build, and knowing the limits of her own physical abilities, she did not resist.

He secured the door and followed behind.

When they were all well inside her home, the two henchmen stood her on her feet, and released their grips. They continued to block any hope of escape.

She reached to pull the cloth from her mouth. But one of the thugs jerked her hand away, then secured the rag in place with lengths of broad, grey tape.

Now the man spoke to her. His voice was calm, but cold . . . cold in a way she had never heard any voice sound before.

He advised that she leave the rag in place and cooperate fully. He didn't intend to do her permanent harm, he said. But she must do as she was told.

She saw little choice in the matter.

He directed her to sit at the dining room table – which she did. Then he produced a pen and some linen stationery, placing them on the table in front of her. She was going to write a note.

As he watched over her shoulder, she began to write. Could she include some subtle clue in the text? She wrote slowly, pausing after every sentence to rub out a "kink" in her writing hand.

She had chosen her words with care. Would they pass his scrutiny? He was no fool, after all. Even if he approved the note as written, would anyone understand the sub-text of the message?

She could only hope.

When she had finished writing, she signed at the bottom and put down the pen. He removed the paper from the table, and with a further brief perusal, pronounced it, "just fine." The man nodded toward one of his accomplices.

The thug grasped her from behind, closing a muscular arm around her chest and shoulders. Then he clamped a chemical-soaked cloth over her rag-stuffed mouth and nose.

She recalled a momentary and futile struggle before blackness took her.

*   *   *

When she awoke, the blackness remained. But she wasn't blind. This place was just incredibly dark.

Getting up from the cold, damp cement floor, and with her arms extended for balance, she turned in a circle. In one direction, she could barely make out a thin line of light . . . and she stumbled toward it.

CHAPTER 2

Saturday, October 17th, 7:45 a.m.

The navy blue Mazda 6 had been following at a distance of about two hundred yards ever since I made my swing past the Red Wing YMCA and onto Levee Road. This was my usual running route for a Saturday morning, and anyone with an interest would know that. I kept my eyes forward, maintaining the steady seven-minute-per-mile pace that had proven appropriate to providing a good aerobic workout for a forty-something man in my condition.

Ten years ago I would have been running five-minute miles. You do what you can.

With the river on my right, and the city to my left, my feet pounded a steady rhythm on the gravel road shoulder. I continued past the main barge dock and the Consolidated Grain terminal. These two structures marked the hub for commercial traffic on the Mississippi River at Red Wing. As I ran by, wafts of coal dust from empty barges gave way to the dusty-sweet smells of early harvest that filled the air around the terminal. Eighteen-wheelers spewed acrid blue plumes of diesel exhaust as they lined up to dump their loads of shelled field corn, adding variety to the aromatic smorgasbord.

I chanced a quick glance behind me. The Mazda was still there. But it kept its distance.

It was a beautiful morning for a run. Sugar maples and aspen were just beginning to show a bit of yellow foliage. The sun shone brightly from the southeast, its rays barely clearing the tree-covered bluffs of town, too early in the day to brighten the roofs of the stately, turn-of-the-century homes closer to the river.

At this latitude, the highest temperature the weak, October sun could encourage was a damp forty-five degrees Fahrenheit. But it was warm enough for me to wear my black jogging shorts and a red T-shirt, and cool enough for me to stay comfortable, even at this pace. It would be a shame for an intruder to interrupt my exercise routine on such a day.

A couple hundred yards farther along, I passed the boathouse village on my right. The village was a sheltered harbor where garage-like structures, made mostly of red or silver metal, floated up and down on poles sunk deep into the river bottom. The boathouses were buoyed by empty, plastic fifty-gallon drums, situated strategically beneath their floorboards. The poles, called "gin poles" by the locals, kept the houses aligned along several stretches of wooden dock. Each boathouse-lined dock extended about 250 feet from the shore into the harbor bay.

The boathouses were quaint. But I imagined the local artists who painted watercolors of the boathouse village were better able than I to appreciate its artistic character on this particular morning. Having an unknown vehicle on your tail heightens awareness of many things, but bucolic beauty isn't one of them.

Another hundred yards along, I left the roadside, continuing onto the concrete running path that led away from Levee Road and toward Baypoint Park. The right-angle turn in the direction of the park proper gave me another opportunity to surreptitiously check the status of my pursuer.

Still there. Still keeping his, or her, distance.

Baypoint Park was originally a landfill for the City of Red Wing, Minnesota. The entire area was located below the flood plain, and nearly surrounded by the waters of the Mississippi. Accordingly, it had seemed the perfect spot for a dump – it never filled up. Every ten years or so, a flood would come through and carry the landfill's contents away downstream.

That was before the world became aware that not everyone lived upstream. And people began to consider the environmental impact such activities had on the river, and on the communities down its course. When the fog of egocentrism lifted, the City removed the remains of the potentially friable dump contents, and established the spacious and lush recreational area toward which I now ran.

The jogging path through the park formed a circuit around its perimeter. Three laps of the circuit equaled two miles.

Continuing into the park and onto the lap circuit, I knew my follower would either need to remain on Levee Road, some seventy yards distant, and watch from there, or pull into the Baypoint parking lot, conceding me a closer look.

As I rounded the downstream end of the park path, I saw that the Mazda's driver had chosen to park in a spot about twenty feet from the far side of the jogging path. I guess they were going to wait for me to come to them, instead of the other way around.

Continuing along the river side of the loop, I overtook two women exercising their dogs at a more leisurely trot. I noted that the park was otherwise deserted.

Looking over my shoulder to offer the two joggers a "Good Morning," I grabbed another quick peek at my tail. The Mazda had darkly-tinted windows. I couldn't tell if it held one or more occupants.

I had three choices. I could jump into the river and swim downstream, evading my uninvited pursuer entirely. I could keep on running as I had been, waiting to see if the Mazda's occupant would take the initiative. Or I could face the situation head-on.

I elected the last option.

Leaving the concrete trail, I cut across the thick, dewy-wet grass, past the children's play area and the sand volleyball court, and directly up to the Mazda driver's window. The car engine was turned off and the windows were up.

I stood there for a moment.

Nothing happened. No gunfire. No descending car window. No door locking or unlocking.

Hmm.

Facing the rear of the car with right hand on hip, breathing steadily despite my run, I rapped the knuckles of my left hand against the driver's window – three times.

I gazed into the distance and waited.

Presently the window slid silently down into the door frame.

"Gunderson!"

It was Ottawa County Chief Sheriff's Deputy, Doug Gunderson. He and I were friends – more or less. I mean, he was a good guy and all. But his rigid adherence to rules and regulations, and my penchant for regularly ignoring them, created some friction. Most people knew the Chief Deputy as "Gunner."

"How d'ya like the new car?" Gunner asked with a grin on his face that implied more than the question he had just asked.

"You're lucky I didn't just shoot first and ask questions later," I said, turning to look the smirking deputy in the eye.

Gunner knew that I had good reason to be cautious of suspicious activities, and that the world harbored a number of individuals, gangs, corporations and even countries who might want to do me harm. He also knew that, despite my attire, I might be wearing a gun. But he trusted, correctly, that I was not the sort to shoot first, and regret later.

"So, besides being a prick, is there some reason you have been following me since I passed the YMCA?" I asked politely.

"A prick? I'm hurt," he said, still grinning.

"Yeah . . . so sorry to bruise your tender ego."

Gunner paused . . . his smile fading.

"Actually, there is a reason I've been on your tail." His face turned a deeper shade of serious. "Can we grab a park bench and have a chat?"

Now he had piqued my interest. Gunner was not the type to want to chat. Usually when we had a visit, it was I who interrupted his routine – not the other way around. This situation presented an anomaly. And anomalies interest me.

"Sure. Let's grab one on the other side of the park, facing the river," I said. "More peaceful and more private."

"Good idea."

I stepped away from the car door, allowing Gunner to climb out. Reaching back inside the car, then withdrawing and turning toward me, he produced two convenience-store coffee cups, complete with napkins, and offered one in my direction. I nodded my thanks and accepted the steaming cup.

Gunner was about my age, six feet, 180 pounds and in pretty good shape. Though there was a hint of a belly, his body was mostly muscle. Gunner's round face, light complexion and short, reddish-brown hair were typical of many fourth-generation Scandinavian immigrants to this area of Minnesota. He was not in uniform this morning. Instead, he wore soft-soled deck shoes, tan khaki shorts and a black-patterned golf shirt, covered by an open, black cotton jacket. I knew he also carried a gun in there somewhere.

Neither of us spoke as we trod through the thick, wet grass toward the river.

Eventually, having reached an appropriately-secluded, green wooden park bench, we stopped. Using the tiny paper napkins that had come with our coffees, we each wiped the dew off our portion of the bench before sitting.

We sat quietly for a long while. Gunner was taking his time starting this conversation.

I waited.

The sun continued its ascent in the sky behind us. The occasional late-season pleasure boat idled through the vapor rising from the main channel of the river, observing the "No Wake" zone adjacent to the park.

While I continued to wait for Gunner, I thought about the Mississippi. The river here – the river Gunner and I were watching flow by our feet – was not the expansive "Father of Waters" that rolls past St. Louis and on toward New Orleans and the Gulf of Mexico. Near Red Wing, a half-decent golfer could hit a three-iron across the Mississippi's main channel.

Had Congress not committed the Army Corp of Engineers to maintaining a minimum channel depth of nine feet the entire length of the river, it wouldn't have been possible for powerful tow boats to push great flotillas of barges from the Gulf port of New Orleans all the way to St. Paul. Even at this corner near Red Wing – the narrowest on the navigable length of the Mississippi – the main channel was wide enough to accommodate a raft of fifteen barges and their tow.

It is true that, on occasion, the barges did get stuck on the mucky river bottom while attempting to negotiate the Red Wing corner. It was, after all, a devilish challenge pushing a thousand feet of barges, more than a hundred-fifty feet wide, safely around this narrow bend – especially headed downstream, and in the dark. But groundings happened rarely, and only when the tow's pilot strayed outside the colored channel marker buoys. (Red – Right – Returning from the sea. Green was the other side.)

In many ways, the river slowly slipping past the green wooden park bench accurately mimicked life here in Red Wing – a relaxed meander. Not the east coast hustle and bustle and always-late-for-something that I had once considered the norm.

Now that I had stopped running, and was sitting here on this damp bench, patiently awaiting the beginning of Gunner's "chat," the morning chill had begun to penetrate my perspiration-dampened jogging attire. I decided to move things along.

"So I hope your goldfish didn't die. That would really suck," I offered, as a conversation starter.

We both continued to gaze out over the water.

"No." A pause. "But I'm sure not comfortable doin' what I'm about to."

More silence.

"Gunner. If you plan to arrest me, you should've just called my cell and I would have surrendered myself peacefully. I'm that kind of guy." Maybe a little humor would loosen him up.

He didn't seem amused. "Aw hell! I need to ask you a favor," Gunner finally choked out, still eyeing water below.

"Now, now. That wasn't so bad was it?" I said with faux sympathy, patting him on his near shoulder.

"Okay. Enough!" He shrugged my hand off his shoulder, turning his gaze my way. "This is serious. At least it might be. So can you stop cracking wise for two minutes? I'll try to bring you up to speed." Once his glance had confirmed the seriousness of the matter, Gunner again faced the river.

I waited some more while the Chief Deputy organized his thoughts. A sip of coffee staved off a bit of the cold. But I began to wonder whether the chill I was experiencing was entirely due to the temperature.

"Beck," he began, "my wife has this friend from college. A guy named George Whitson. Lives in Minneapolis. She hasn't seen or heard from him since her last class reunion, maybe three years ago. And they're not really that close. But she knows him, right?"

Gunner glanced my way and I nodded.

"Anyway . . . Whitson calls Connie last night and wants to know if she can get me to help him with a problem."

"What sort of problem?" I prompted.

"Jesus! Give me a minute to tell the story, will ya!" A steely stare.

"By all means," I said, hands up, palms out. "Please proceed."

Sheesh! Gunner was owly this morning.

"According to Connie, it seems that Mr. Whitson's wife is missing."

"Kidnapped?"

Gunner gave me an impatient look. I gave him one back.

"Unsure at present," Gunner replied. "Last time Whitson saw his wife was two days ago when he left for work in the morning. At that time, he says she was at their condo and everything was hunky-dory. The next thing he knows, he's coming home after work and his wife is gone. She left a note saying she'd had enough and was bailing on the marriage."

"That's too bad, but not all that rare," I said.

"Yeah . . . but here's the weird part. She also left her cell phone, keys and credit cards behind."

"Now that is weird," I agreed.

Gunner continued. "By the time a wife calls it quits, she usually has already emptied the bank accounts. And when she leaves, she takes the car, the credit cards, the family jewels and anything else worthwhile, with her. I've never heard of a spouse of either gender leaving the car, the money and the credit cards behind.

Anyway . . . Connie feels sorry for this guy and wants me to try to help him out."

"She take in stray dogs, too?"

Gunner ignored my question and continued speaking to the river.

"Look . . . I tell her it's not my jurisdiction and that Minneapolis isn't going to help me out. I tell her the Twin Cities cops are going to think I'm a small town shit-kicker who should mind his own business and not tell them how to do their jobs.

But she still wants me to try to do something." He faced me again. "What can I say?"

Gunner paused for a moment, allowing me an opening.

"Is this the part where you ask me for the favor?" I smiled.

Gunner looked down and shook his head. "I know I'm gonna regret this . . . but I'm bound by loads of bureaucratic baggage like jurisdiction, legal procedure, chain of command and all that stuff. You, on the other hand, are hampered by no such burdens."

He had been watching the river the whole time, but now turned my way. I was still smiling.

"It's probably just what the wife's note says it is," Gunner went on. "She probably just left him. But as a favor to my wife . . . as a favor to me . . . would you mind looking into it?" A pause. "Please?"

When he said the "please," I knew I had to do what I could. From Gunner's perspective, he was groveling.

"Gunner," I said. "I've always been a sucker for a love story. You're trying to honor your wife's special request, even though you think it's probably silly – which I do, too, by the way.

But for the sake of marriage and chivalry – and because I am an altruist at heart – I shall accept your challenge and take on your quest, relieving you forever thereafter of its onerous responsibility."

I was on a roll.

"Therefore, never send to know for whom the lawyer works; he works for thee. And even though we stand here on an island – or almost an island – no man is an island. Every man's death diminishes us. As if . . ."

"All right, all right! Enough!" Gunner looked a bit as though he wished he had kept silent about the whole affair. "I suppose I'm going to owe you forever for this."

I ignored the statement.

"How about I go home and shower and we meet for breakfast at Smokey Row in an hour? Then you can give me more details – at least what your wife has told you so far."

"That's good by me." Gunner sounded relieved.

I wasn't sure if his relief stemmed from my agreement to help, or from the cessation of my soliloquy.

"See you at . . . " he checked his watch, "9:15."

We both stood. Gunner didn't wait for me as he started back across the park toward his car. After a few steps, he stopped and turned back toward me. "And Beck?"

"Yeah?"

"Thanks."

"Never let it be said that I didn't do the least I could do," I replied.

CHAPTER 3

An hour later, Gunner and I had ordered our breakfasts and were seated in a booth by the front window at Smokey Row, my favorite morning and noontime restaurant in Red Wing. Smokey Row is equal parts bakery and coffee shop. The atmosphere oozes fresh bread and Colombian Dark Roast. Each of us held a bottomless cup of gourmet coffee on the Formica booth-top in front of us.

The run home, and a warm shower, had erased all memory of the dampness and chill I had begun to feel in the park. It was a beautiful day and I was actually excited to have something interesting to do.

I decided to start the conversation.

"So what do you make of the 'Dear John' note?" I asked. "Is it legit?"

"Husband swears it's her handwriting."

Gunner blew on his coffee.

"Did he report her, ah, absence to the police?" I continued.

"He told Connie that he tried filing a missing persons report. But the local cops, Minneapolis that is, seemed pretty convinced that she'd just walked out on him and would eventually turn up looking for some of the money and plastic she'd left behind. They told him to hold off another couple days before filing a report. She'd likely check in at home by then."

"Sounds logical. Any kids?" I asked, sipping my freshly-ground, French Vanilla.

"No kids," Gunner said. "Both husband and wife work all the time and apparently never got around to starting a family."

"How much do we know about Whitson and his wife? What's her name, by the way?"

"Sorry . . . Katherine," Gunner said. " S h e   h a s   a high-level computer job at an international tech company named ComDyne, headquartered in Eden Prairie. She's got a bunch of education – has a couple PhDs in something or other."

"So she would be Dr. Whitson?" I asked.

"I guess," Gunner replied. "Oh, yeah . . . she's supposedly kind of a big deal in computer circles. Other than that, I'm afraid I don't know much."

Gunner paused for a moment, rotating the coffee mug in his hands.

"I was hoping you and I could maybe pay Whitson a visit this afternoon?" he asked finally.

"Without Connie?" I suggested.

"She'll probably want to come along; but I'm gonna do my best to convince her otherwise. Whitson might be more, ah, forthcoming without her there. We'll have to see how successful I am at persuading her."

I knew that sometimes Connie could be . . . what's the best word . . . determined.

Our food arrived.

Gunner had a fried egg sandwich on wheat with a side of hash-browns. I had opted for the oversized pecan caramel roll, which I intended to drench in butter – maybe not a healthy choice; but I had just finished a run and deserved a reward.

CHAPTER 4

As I drove my dark grey Honda Pilot home from Smokey Row, I wondered what I was getting myself into. Even though my law practice didn't include divorce work, I had been around enough of my clients' family disputes to know that marital issues were likely to be messy and unpleasant. I worried a little about what Gunner and I would find out, and how that information would affect Connie.

That was all the thinking time I had in the ten block trip home from breakfast to my Jefferson Avenue home. I know . . . I should have walked. But I had just finished a run after all.

As I entered our kitchen through the sliding glass door from the back porch, the outer wooden screen door slammed shut behind me. I really should update the screen door closer with something more twenty-first century, eliminating the slam. But there is something sort of authentic, and small-townish, about the old-style spring approach. It makes you want to call out, "Honey, I'm home."

"Honey, I'm home," I called as I passed through the kitchen in search of my wife, Elizabeth.

Beth and I had been married for nearly twenty-one years and were parents of two grown daughters – Sara and Elise. Both girls were living away from home, attending separate colleges out of state.

We had come to Red Wing upon the occasion of my retirement from twenty years of sub rosa military and intelligence operations. At that time, Beth and I had decided that the cessation of bullets, hand grenades and rocket launchers provided an opportunity for more settled lives for ourselves and our, then teenage, daughters. So about six years ago, we had all picked up our lives and come here to live in my childhood hometown.

Hearing no response to my greeting, I surmised that Beth might be working in her attic studio, and therefore, would be out of earshot of my call.

I wasn't the only Becker family member to have a secretive government past. Beth had done a variety of extremely sensitive computer work for the CIA during our time in Washington. I didn't know all the details. But the Agency still contacted her occasionally on a consulting basis. So I knew she had skills that folks on the Agency's current payroll lacked.

Even though it was my hometown and not hers, Beth had actually made a better adjustment to small town life than I. She'd gotten much more involved in the community. Church, fine arts organizations, book clubs, coffee groups. I liked Red Wing well enough. But from time to time, I craved the adrenaline rush of international intrigue. There was a definite dearth of that in Red Wing.

I jogged up the stairs, two-at-a-time. I had some caramel roll to burn off.

Two-and-a-half flights up, my head emerged just above attic floor level. Beth was working at one of her sewing machines, creating art from cast-off attire. The stairwell in which I had paused was behind her, so I took a moment to appreciate the view through the spindled railing.

She sat with impeccable posture on the wooden sewing stool, her sleek lines pleasantly silhouetted against the light from the arched dormer window. She wore a black cashmere top that clung nicely to her trim shape. Fine, sandy-blond hair hung loosely across her shoulders. The faintest touch of her perfume hung in the air. I breathed deeply. I could just stand here on the steps and watch her indefinitely.

Dragging myself out of my reverie, I called cheerfully over the hum of the sewing machine, "Hi, Beth. How goes your morning?"

She stopped sewing and rotated to face me.

"Oh, hey . . . what's your name again?" She grinned. "I thought I heard the screen door."

I climbed the rest of the steps to the attic and entered Beth's studio. Approaching my lovely wife, I bent over and gave her a gentle kiss on the lips. When I pulled away, her eyes were closed, and her full lips formed a satisfied smile. I felt my breath catch and my heart skipped a beat.

"Care to visit?" she asked cheerfully.

"No thanks. I'm just here for the view. You keep on working. I'll sit and watch a while. It always amazes me how you can do that stuff – rags to richness."

"I think it's 'riches.' But suit yourself, Shakespeare," she said.

My word had correctly described Beth's activities. She was just being playful.

I took a seat cross-legged in a smallish, tan club chair, while Beth returned to her clothing work.

Besides creating unique clothing pieces, Beth also designed jewelry and painted with colorful acrylics on canvas. The studio held an area for each of these activities. The attic was Beth's artistic sanctuary.   I always tried to respect the separateness of this space – to insulate it from distractions of our daily lives. I didn't want to talk about Gunner's problems here.

After I had watched Beth work for a few minutes, I asked, "What's your timetable for creativity today?"

"Actually," Beth replied, while still maneuvering a denim jacket around the sewing machine, "I was about to finish up here and see what you were up to."

"Okay," I said. "I'm going down to the back porch to read the paper. I'll catch you when you're through up here."

"See ya in a few."

I uncrossed my legs and stood up. "Love ya," I said.

With that, I walked reverentially across the attic and headed down the stairs.

About half an hour later, as I sat on the back porch swing reading the local and metro newspapers, Beth's face appeared in the sliding doorway from the kitchen. "May I get you anything on my way out?"

"No, I'm good, thanks."

I put the papers on a wicker chair and Beth joined me on the swing.

I could now see that, to complement the black cashmere, she was wearing slim-fitting denim jeans and black boots with moderately spiked heels. Her legs looked a mile long.

"I saw Gunner this morning on my run," I said, looking directly at my wife. "He's got a new car. We had breakfast. Connie's good."

She knew there was more and waited patiently.

"Uh, Beth. Gunner asked me to do him a favor."

"What sort of favor?" she asked, giving the swing a small push with her feet.

"It's kind of a long story; but in short, he'd like me to check out a runaway wife situation in the Twin Cities. It involves some guy Connie knew in college, and he's not getting any help from the metro cops."

"Are you thinking it's something more than a family in distress?"

"Actually, I don't know what to think yet. But Gunner asked for the favor, and I'd like to accommodate him. It'll probably involve a few trips to the cities, asking some questions, being told some lies – the usual stuff. I will need to impose on some of our personal time to help Gunner out. But of course, I'll use office time for any heavy lifting."

Beth waited patiently.

"Anyway, I think I'm going to take this thing on and see what happens. Maybe it'll spice things up a bit . . . get some juices flowing. Do you have any opinions?"

"If it's what you want to do, I think you should do it. When do you need to start?"

"This afternoon?" I offered, smiling apologetically.

"Of course." Beth returned my smiled across the swing. "Actually, the timing works out quite well. I've got some errands to run anyway. Some artsy stuff I don't think you would care for. Go do your thing. Definitely."

"Thanks, Beth."

We leaned together and exchanged a quick kiss.

"Gunner is making arrangements for a meeting time and place. Feel free to go about your artsy stuff business and I will call or text you when I know the details."

"Roger Wilco." She offered up a lame salute. "See you later."

Beth abandoned me on the swing, gathered her purse and car keys from the kitchen, and headed for the garage. A moment later, Beth's silver rag-top Mitsubishi Spyder pulled out of the driveway and purred slowly down the alley.

Beth always tried to be supportive of my extracurricular activities. She knew that small-town lawyering was never going to meet my need for adventure. And I loved her for that.

CHAPTER 5

Saturday, October 17th, 1:30 p.m.

Gunner had arranged for us to meet with Mr. Whitson at the Whitson's condo in downtown Minneapolis. He and I had driven separately in case I wanted to start working on the 'case' right after our visit.

I located the address, parking in a pay lot nearby.

The condo was a recently-renovated space in an ancient brick building in the warehouse district – two blocks from the heart of the city. It was a seriously upscale development. I would probably need to trade three of our homes on Jefferson to buy a one bedroom flat in this joint. No wonder the Whitsons both worked so much. They had to make the mortgage payments.

There wasn't a doorman. A uniformed security guard manned a desk in the entryway. I announced myself to the guard. He said Mr. Whitson was expecting me and gave me directions to the Whitson residence.

This building had seven stories. The Whitson apartment was number 701. I took the elevator and got off on seven. Arriving outside Unit 701, I rapped twice with the brass knocker on the heavy oak entry door. A thin man with salt and pepper hair answered my knock. He was about five feet ten, 170 pounds, and wore a solemn expression on his pallid face.

"Mr. Becker, I presume?" he said, offering his hand in my direction. His voice and face were both sad. There was liquor on his breath.

"A pleasure to meet you, Mr. Whitson," I replied, accepting the handshake.

His hand and wrist wilted as I tried to get a grip. It felt like I was trying to hold onto something slippery. I shook hands the best I could, given his weak participation.

"Please come in," he said.

As I entered, I could see that this had to be one of the premiere units in the building. It was a corner, three-bedroom apartment with an open design that merged the spacious kitchen with a living/dining area so large, and a ceiling so high, that it seemed as though it would be hard to avoid an echo.

In all, I estimated the condo held, perhaps, 3,500 square feet. But I hadn't actually seen all the rooms. It could be bigger. The price tag on this home would be well into seven figures, even in Minneapolis.

The whole place smelled of pine cleaner and furniture polish. There wasn't an un-dusted flat surface anywhere. And no magazines or newspapers were evident. It looked like no one lived here.

Gunner and Connie were already seated on one of the leather sofas in the great room. Mr. Whitson beckoned me toward the Gundersons with a wave of his arm. "Please have a seat anyplace that looks comfortable," he said. "May I serve you a beverage?"

"No. Thank you very much," I responded as I crossed the vastness and sat in a formal upholstered chair in the general vicinity of Connie and Gunner. I waved hello to the Gundersons, seated on the couch to my distant right. For me to have detoured over there just to shake hands would have made Connie and Doug feel like they were part of a funeral receiving line.

Apparently, Gunner hadn't been successful in persuading Connie to stay home after all. We would have to work around her presence a bit. But we should still be able to get enough information for a solid start.

Mr. Whitson followed me into the room and sat to my left in a chair matching mine. He was holding a crystal lowball glass filled about halfway with brown liquor, no ice. From the odor on his breath in the doorway, I guessed it to be scotch.

As soon as Whitson was seated, Gunner started the discussion.

"Mr. Whitson . . ."

"Please call me George," Whitson interrupted.

"Very well, George. Please relay to us all the details of your wife's disappearance, beginning with Thursday morning, the day she, er, vanished."

Whitson relayed the same story that he had already told Connie, and that Gunner had passed on to me. Things were fine that morning. She was gone when he returned home after work. The note, phone, credit card and keys had been left, arranged neatly, on the bed.

"And what have you done so far to try to locate your wife?" I asked.

"She doesn't have any family. Her parents died a while ago. And she is an only child," he said. "So I tried contacting people from her work. Her supervisor, co-workers, other names I recognized from Katherine's discussions of her work day. Her only real friends are at work. We both work at least sixty hours a week. There's not much time for a social life outside of business gatherings."

He took a large swallow of the scotch and stopped talking.

"And what did they say?" I prompted.

"Oh. Yes. Of course." Another swallow of liquor and the glass was emptying fast.

"Her supervisor, a gentleman named Dr. Allister, told me that she had been at work until around five Thursday afternoon. Then she had told him she was leaving for home a bit early with a headache. One of her co-workers, Jim or Sam or Don or something like that, also said she had been at work Thursday. He had left work before five, and Katherine was still in the office at that time."

Whitson paused for another drink of scotch. His glass was now empty.

"Would anyone care for a beverage?" George asked somewhat casually as he started to rise from his chair.

"Mr. Whitson," I interrupted, "if we are going to find your wife, we need you to be coherent to help us. Would you mind postponing a further drink until we have finished our visit?"

Whitson sat back down. "Of course. It's just been . . . well, I'm not quite myself today."

"I think we all understand," I said.

Then I continued. "So if I am hearing you correctly, your wife was at work until five Thursday and left with a headache. Had anyone else seen Katherine on Thursday besides her co-workers?"

"There's no one that I know of," Whitson answered.

"And what is the next thing you know about Katherine's whereabouts on Thursday?" I prompted again. It appeared I was going to need to pry the information out of him.

"The next thing I know is that I came home about 7:30 that night and she was gone. When I went into our room to change clothes, I found the note and the other things on the bed."

"Are any of her personal effects missing? Jewelry? Clothing? Makeup? Perfume? That sort of thing?"

"I didn't think to look. I'm sorry."

"How about suitcases? Any of those gone?" I continued, trying to remain pleasant.

"I . . . I didn't check that either." Whitson's head was hanging and he stared at the floor.

"But you did contact the Minneapolis Police," I said. "When and how did you do that?"

"I called them Friday morning," he said. "I had hoped Katherine was just upset about something and would come back on her own Thursday night."

His head was back up and he was trying to focus his attention on me.

"I asked for Missing Persons. They connected me to a man who said I shouldn't worry and she would probably show up soon. He wouldn't accept a formal report. At least, I think that's what he said."

Whitson was fading.

"And on Friday night when Katherine was still missing, did you call the police again?" I asked, fearing that I already knew the answer.

"Why, no. I didn't think it was right to bother them again so soon," Whitson said, sounding surprised at my suggestion.

"So you called your old friend, Connie, who you knew had a cop for a husband. Is that right?" I asked.

"Yeah. I couldn't think of who else to call . . . what else to do. I don't really have any friends who would help me. And I remembered Connie telling me at our reunion about the exciting police work her husband does. I knew she lived in Red Wing and I found her number in the book. I may have disturbed a few other Gundersons before I reached Connie. But she said she would get her husband to help."

His gaze had, once again, dropped. But now, he looked up from the floor and across at Connie on the couch. "Thank you so much."

I could see why Connie wanted to help this guy. He was totally lost and he had no clue what to do about it. I could also understand why his wife might want to leave him.

Connie spoke up. "George. I know these guys will find Katherine. They're very good at this kind of stuff. You'll see. It'll all work out okay."

I knew Gunner had some experience with runaway spouses. But those hadn't resulted in happy endings for the couples involved. And neither of us had any experience at all in kidnappings. They just didn't happen very often in Ottawa County. And even if one should occur, jurisdiction for such matters would fall either to the FBI, if the kidnapping was interstate, or to the BCA, if authorities believed the victim remained in Minnesota. The BCA is the Minnesota Bureau of Criminal Apprehension – in other words, the state cops.

With her sunshine and roses outlook, Connie had written a check to George Whitson that Gunner and I might not be able to cash.

"Thanks again, Connie," Whitson managed before hanging his head on his chest.

"Don't worry, George. It'll be okay." Connie may have been comforting to Whitson, but she was making me nervous as hell.

I was going to ask Whitson some more questions, but I could see his eyes were closed and his breathing was slow and even.

He had fallen asleep.

CHAPTER 6

As long as we had access to the Whitson apartment, I couldn't see why we shouldn't have a look around. Maybe something would jump out at us. It happens.

I motioned to Connie and Gunner with right forefinger at my lips to indicate that Whitson was asleep. Then I rose and waved for them to follow me into one of the adjacent rooms.

As luck would have it, I had entered the master bedroom. I recognized it because the note, and Katherine's keys, credit cards and cell phone, were neatly arrayed on the bed. The Gundersons followed me in. Gunner closed the bedroom door behind them.

I turned to Connie. In a kind voice I said, "I'm so sorry your friend is in this situation. And I will do everything I can to help him find his wife. But you need to understand a few things about what might happen.

First of all, it is entirely possible that his wife may have left him voluntarily, in which case, the best outcome here is that we find her, and George realizes that she really does want out of their marriage. There's nothing your husband and I could do to make that scenario any happier for George."

Connie nodded.

"But worse yet," I continued, "we may find out that George gave her good reason to leave, or even that he has been involved in some illegal or immoral activities. Once we start digging, there's no way to know what we will find.

Do you still want us to do this – to look into Katherine's disappearance?"

It was obvious to me that Connie hadn't really given thought to these possibilities, and especially not that George, himself, might be in some way culpable.

She paused before answering.

Finally, Connie looked me in the eye with resolve and said, "I hadn't thought of all that stuff you just mentioned. Doug tries not to bring his work home. But if there is any chance of you helping that poor man out, I hope you will still pursue the investigation, regardless of where it leads."

"Okay," I said. "But please try to be prepared for whatever may come."

Connie nodded again.

I turned to Gunner. "Okay, Deputy. We need to give this apartment the once-over."

"Right. But don't disturb any evidence – just in case this thing starts to look hinky."

"Certainly," I said. "You check for missing personal items; I'll take a closer look at what's on the bed."

It was clear that Gunner wasn't used to taking direction – especially from me. But he had invited me into this mess. So he swallowed his machismo and set to work, starting with the closets.

I began with the "Dear John" note. It had been placed in the exact center of the white cotton bedspread and was written in a woman's cursive hand on linen stationery. I leaned over the foot of the bed for a closer look. I read the note without touching the paper:

> *George,*
>
> *I am leaving you forever. Our marriage has been broken for a long time and I can't fix it. Whatever we once had is over.*
>
> *My keys, cell phone and charge cards are here on the bed because I don't want anything from you and I don't want you to even TRY to find me. So please, don't bother to look.*
>
> *I have what I need. You take the rest. It's yours.*
>
> *Goodbye.*
>
> *Katherine*

Not very eloquent . . . but fairly direct.

I also looked at the cell phone, keys and charge cards. They were perfectly aligned across the bed, with the note in the middle. Either he had rearranged the items, or she too, was compulsively organized. I removed a small camera from my right front pants pocket and took a bunch of photos of the unusual display across the bed – both from a distance and close-up.

Messing with evidence or not, I knew I needed to look at the phone more closely, and to explore its contents. Fortunately, since "Be prepared" is not only the Boy Scout motto, but mine as well, I had brought with me some basic supplies.

Withdrawing a ziplock sandwich bag from my left front pocket, I turned it inside out. Wearing the inverted baggie like a mitten, I scooped the phone inside and carefully zipped the bag shut. The phone would remain safely uncontaminated in the bag. And while the cell remained protected inside the baggie, I could still operate it without worry of getting my own prints all over it. I would examine the contents of the phone later.

I couldn't immediately identify anything significant about the other items on the bed, or their placement. My photos would probably work fine for closer consideration, if necessary. Given that he hadn't seemed to disturb the room yet, I doubted that Whitson was going to move anything around without our permission at this point.

I started taking more pictures of everything I could think of. The master bath. The medicine cabinet and its contents. The toilet – inside and out.

I continued taking pics around the master suite. Then I moved to each other room in the apartment, in turn. I even got a shot of George asleep in the chair and one of Gunner sorting through Katherine's unmentionables drawer.

Connie stood quietly in a corner throughout the entire search process.

When I was done photographing, I checked with Gunner to see how he was doing.

"How are you coming with the panty raid?" I asked.

"If I ever see that picture at my cop shop, you are dead meat," Gunner said. He looked pretty serious.

"Don't worry. You know you can trust me."

Gunner gave me the raised eyebrow. I don't think he trusted me.

"Okay. I'll delete it as soon as I'm sure underwear isn't relevant to the case."

He still didn't look convinced.

"On a more serious note," I said, "I am truly interested in the results of your search – all of it, not just the undies," I added quickly.

"We'll have to confirm some things with Sleepy in there," Gunner tossed his head in Whitson's direction, "but I found some stuff I think might be probative."

"Probative?"

"Yeah. It means it's important stuff." Gunner looked offended.

"I know what it means," I said. "It just sounds weird coming out of your mouth."

Gunner gave me the eye roll. He does that a lot.

"Do you want to hear this or not?" Gunner asked.

I was stretching the limits of his patience.

"Please, proceed," I said, with a sweeping right-handed flourish in Gunner's direction.

"Here's what I've got."

He had made some notes and referenced them now.

"First of all, it looks like there are some of Katherine's clothes missing from the hanger bar in the master closet. There are still plenty of her clothes in there. The hangers in most sections of the closet are all a uniform one inch apart. But in this one section, it looks like some clothes are missing. The hangers aren't spaced the same."

I nodded my understanding.

"The medicine cabinet also seems to be short some stuff. But this is weird," Gunner said. "There is a nearly full prescription of diazepam, with Katherine's name on it, still in there."

"Ah, mother's little helper."

"Huh?" Gunner looked perplexed.

"It's a lyric from a Rolling Stones song."

Gunner still looked blank.

"Diazepam is generic Valium – mother's little helper?"

Still no recognition.

I took a moment to mourn the death of contemporary culture.

"Never mind. Please go on," I said.

"And like in the closet, there is definitely some of Katherine's stuff missing. But there is also some that is left behind. And there's no rhyme or reason to it."

"For instance . . ." I said.

"Well. Her toothbrush is gone; but her eyelash curler is still here. And there are contacts in a contact case, but no contact solution anywhere. It's as though random items were taken, and the rest left behind."

"Hmm," I offered.

"I can't find a wallet, or purse with anything in it. So she must have taken one with her. But all of the shoe compartments in her closet are full, except for one. And the empty one is in the 'business section.' You wouldn't believe how organized everything is."

"Sometimes organizing gives one a sense of control in an otherwise anarchic environment," I said.

"Now who's been reading the dictionary . . . anarchic environment. Geez!" Another eye roll.

I wondered if he could roll one eye at a time, or if it would always be both.

"I'll give you a list of other things I found to be unusual after we leave. I'll email it to you. If I'm stuck here with you in charge much longer I might have to shoot you." Gunner looked serious again.

Better wrap this up for now.

"Okay," I said. "I'm done with the photos and the note. Just one more thing before you go?"

"All right," Gunner allowed. "Shoot."

"Did you find out where they both work?" I asked.

Gunner left the room for a moment. When he returned, he had two slips of paper in his right hand. "Here's a pay-stub for each of them. Best I can do for right now. Maybe we can ask Hubby sometime when he's sober."

"Thanks, Gunner." Then, turning to Connie, who appeared a smidgen shocked at the multiple invasions of Whitson's privacy she had just witnessed, I said, "I will do everything in my power to get to the bottom of this matter. Please try not to be overly concerned. Your worries won't help George's situation at all. You've done your part. Let us do ours."

Connie looked reluctant to let go.

"All right," she said, finally.

"Now, you lovebirds run along. I'm going to finish up one or two things before I go. Gunner, I'll be looking for that email."

A brief goodbye and the Gundersons left me alone with the now-snoring Whitson.

As soon as they were gone, I retrieved the baggie-encased cell phone from my pocket. Sliding it open while it was still inside the plastic, I powered it up and searched the autodial list for George's cell number. I found it and pressed the call button. Almost immediately, the sound of classical music emanated from the vicinity of the liquor cabinet. The phone was lying next to a bottle of Glenlivet. I turned George's ringing phone off and put it in another pocket.

Maybe Whitson should get another chance to contribute to the investigation.

I approached the sleeping man. His head still rested on his chest. His hair needed washing. He smelled as though he hadn't showered recently. His hands on the chair arms were thin and bony, their skin a bluish-white.

I placed my hand on Whitson's shoulder.

"George." No response.

I shook his shoulder gently. "George, we need to talk."

Whitson slumped sideways under the light pressure of my hand, but didn't awaken. He was worthless for now.

I moved around Whitson's chair and hoisted his limp form over my shoulders in a fireman's carry, depositing him like a bag of potatoes on the sofa. He slept on. I found a cotton blanket and pillow in a guest room and situated Whitson properly on the couch. I looked at his face. His countenance as he slept hinted at his mental state: helpless, vulnerable, afraid and tormented.

I left him on the sofa.

Locating a pen and pad of paper in a drawer by the kitchen telephone, I wrote George a message: "Had to borrow your cell phone. I'll get it back as soon as possible. Beck."

I doubted he would even remember who "Beck" might be. But it mattered little.

With husband and wife phones in my possession, I departed Apartment 701 and headed for the elevator.

CHAPTER 7

Later Saturday evening.

Beth and I were seated on our red leather living room couch, sharing a bottle of Australian Cabernet, when our phone rang. The caller ID showed that it was Ottawa County calling. I pushed the button to receive the call.

"Hello?"

"Beck . . . it's Gunderson," the voice said.

I knew Gunner wasn't calling just to chat.

"What's up?" I asked.

"Can you come down to the cop shop right now? There's been a new development we need to talk about. I'd prefer face-to-face."

"No problem," I said. "I'll be there in five."

I turned to Beth. "Gunner's got something urgent. It probably won't take long. I'll be home as soon as we're done."

Beth had already retrieved a novel from the ancient wooden bass drum case that doubles as our coffee table and flipped the book open. "Take your time. I'll just hang out and relax a while."

As I was driving to the Law Enforcement Center, a journey of exactly eight blocks, I wondered what new development had occurred since this afternoon. And I hoped no one had been injured . . . or found dead!

Gunner was waiting for me when I walked through the main doors to the LEC.

"Thanks for coming," he said, and waved me through the door he was holding – the entrance to the investigators' office area.

He didn't sound panicked or particularly sad. Those were good things.

When we reached Gunner's office, he sat behind his metal desk. I took the only available side chair.

"So fill me in," I said.   "What are the 'new developments'?"

"About an hour ago," Gunner began, "Connie got a phone call."

Damn! I thought. I hoped someone hadn't upset her.

"Whitson?" I asked.

"No. It was a man's voice she didn't recognize. Caller ID was a No Name, too."

"Is Connie okay?"

"She's kinda shook up. I think the whole thing scared her."

"Tell me," I said.

"The man told Connie that she should butt out of the Whitsons' business, or she'd wish she'd never known the guy," Gunner said.

He looked at me with resolve. I could tell he was pissed. I waited for him to continue.

"After the call, I managed to get her calmed down a bit. Told her that it just meant that George was right to call us into this thing. And that she should try to not let it bother her." Gunner paused.

"So as soon as I could, I got a squad out there to watch the house. 'Course I didn't tell Connie that. She shouldn't have to worry any more than she already is.

Then I came straight down here and tried to trace the call. All I could get was that it came from a disposable cell phone and had bounced off a few towers in the Minneapolis downtown area.

But dammit . . . now I'm worried for Connie."

I could see the concern in his face.

"Geez, Gunner," I said. "I'm so sorry that Connie is taking the heat on this. What can I do to help?"

"I appreciate the offer," Gunner said. "I really do. But if I can't keep my own wife safe in my own freakin' County, I'm not much of a law officer. Connie's safe. And I will keep her that way. I just thought you should know about the call."

"Yeah. It makes it pretty clear that Katherine Whitson did not simply leave her husband of her own volition. Somebody took her, or did something to her," I said.

"But we don't know who," Gunner replied. "So I guess that's how you can help. Get to the bottom of this Whitson business as quick as you can."

"Absolutely! I've got my whole day tomorrow available to work on this thing. And I hate to ask you now, but I will need your emailed report to get the whole picture. Are you still able to get me that tomorrow?"

"Damn straight! In fact, it will be in on your computer when you get up. I can't sleep tonight anyway."

I rose to leave.

"Gunner," I said. "Objectively . . . you and I both know that the phone call was just a scare tactic, and that no one has any reason to screw with Connie for real."

He nodded.

"So you just keep her protected, to be extra sure. And I promise I'll get to the bottom of this mess."

"Thanks again," he said. "Look for my email in the morning."

"Got it. And Gunner?"

"Yeah?"

"You watch your own backside, too. Okay?"

"Right. Now I've got work to do."

I made my exit, leaving Gunner at his computer.

Now I was fully invested in the Whitson case. Whoever decided that they should mess with Connie had made a big mistake. There was no way I was going to stop now. Somebody needed to answer for the angst they had caused the Gundersons! And I was determined to make that happen.

CHAPTER 8

Sunday, October 18th, 7:00 a.m.

As promised, early Sunday morning, Gunner's crime scene summary arrived in my email "In Box." I was impressed with its length and detail, especially given the lack of Whitson's assistance, and the turmoil Gunner was going through as a result of last night's phone threat.

With a bagel masquerading as breakfast in one hand, and my computer in the other, I moved to our front porch on Jefferson Avenue. I now had Gunner's notes, the Whitsons' cell phone contents and my photos, all on my laptop.

As I opened the front door and stepped onto the porch I could feel the cool stillness of the October air on my face. In the distance, a flock of migrating Canadian Honkers echoed their namesake through the otherwise quiet river valley. A neighbor had mowed her lawn that morning. Grassy aromas from, perhaps, the last cutting of the season scented my screen porch. I paused for a moment, breathing in the serenity.

Today, my mission was clear. I needed to find out who had killed or kidnapped Katherine Whitson – and as expeditiously as possible. But I also had to be thorough. Not reckless. I wanted this case solved as badly as Gunner. But sloppiness in my attempt to resolve it was not going to help.

I made the cushioned rattan loveseat my workspace. Leaning back with my computer on my lap, I rested my feet on the glass-top coffee table.

I would read Gunner's email first.

Even at a quick glance, it was obvious that Gunner had been thorough. I first read the email in its entirety, trying to get a sense of the overall picture. He had observed the scene at the condo with the illuminating perspective possessed only by professional investigators.

After completing a first read-through, I sat for a minute with my eyes closed, absorbing Gunner's view of the scene. I pictured the impeccably-organized closet, with the single, less organized, clothing section, and only one pair of business shoes missing. Katherine's dresser drawers had appeared mostly filled with crisply folded garments – impossible to tell if any were absent.

There were no obvious fingerprints on the medicine cabinet mirror. While at the apartment, I had observed that opening the cabinet required a finger pressed against the glass to release the catch. Had someone wiped it down?

The recycling bins held two empty bottles of Glenlivet and two daily newspapers. Nothing else. In the dishwasher were two, pre-rinsed cereal bowls, two juice glasses, a few pieces of flatware and four low-ball glasses. The waste baskets throughout the apartment were entirely empty, except for their recently-replaced, white plastic liner bags.

Gunner had located the closet area in one of the spare bedrooms where the Whitsons stored their luggage. There were no large bags present, but a number of smaller ones were lined up precisely on shelves. Empty spaces on the shelving implied the absence of one or two sizeable suitcases. Gunner made a special note that both male and female toiletry kits were still present, and stocked with the usual personal items and travel accessories.

Who takes their suitcase and not their travel kit?

In the master bedroom, the bed was freshly made. No one had so much as sat on the spread, and the pillows were fluffed to symmetrical perfection. I had noticed that, too.

Gunner had already mentioned to me the odd assortment of toiletries and personal hygiene products either present or absent from the master bath – toothbrush, contact solution and some makeup gone; but Katherine's diazepam prescription, eyelash curler and contacts still remaining.

There were no computers anywhere in the condo. There were, however, several neat containers of software disks, encased in original jewel boxes or jackets, in a small desk in the third bedroom. Indentations in the carpeting and marks on the wall outlet near and under the desk indicated the earlier presence of a power strip, and possibly an external backup drive or other small peripheral device. There was no other trace of wires or computer components anywhere.

Nobody has *no* computers at all in the house. It's the twenty-first century, for god's sake. And Katherine works with computers. Her computer was obviously missing.

There was more. But most of the additional information pointed to the same conclusion. Katherine had been taken from the condo against her will. And whoever was responsible for Katherine's kidnapping had done a sloppy job of trying to cover up his or her crime.

Those were my conclusions. But I would consult with Gunner to get his take as well. Such matters were really more his forte.

I picked up my cell from the seat cushion beside me and called Gunner. He answered on the third ring.

"Gundersons."

"Gunner, it's Beck. How're you guys doing?"

"I think we're doing a little better today. Connie is still shook. But I managed to get my pants on straight. So what do you think about the case?" Gunner asked.

"Your report was very thorough," I said, sincerely. "And I've come to some tentative conclusions, but I was hoping for your professional input. What does your trained eye tell you?"

"Somebody took her from the condo and did a lousy job of covering up," Gunner said, then waited for my response.

"I had come to the same conclusion," I said. "Anything else? Is the husband still a suspect?"

"I think it's too soon to answer that question. The spouse is always the first place we look when there is a missing adult. My gut says he doesn't have the gonads to do anything violent. But he could maybe hire somebody. Hard to tell right now.

We should get some fingerprints, analyze the cell phones and talk to Whitson again. Maybe you can catch him at work and sober. Then we can see where that leads us."

I noticed the "*you* can catch him," but didn't say anything.

"I'm pretty sure we won't get any prints," I said. "I noticed that the bathroom mirror seemed to have been wiped down. No prints at all. Plus it seems likely that they were wearing gloves. Are any crooks stupid enough to kidnap someone barehanded these days?"

"You're probably right. But I'll see if I can get my hands on a print kit and make my own inspection today. Hope Whitson is in shape to let me in."

"I'd call ahead. Maybe tell him to leave a key with the guard."

"Good thought. Have you got other ideas on how to proceed?"

"I've got plenty of phone records and follow-up to do for the rest of today," I said. "But tomorrow, I'll be paying Mr. Whitson a visit at his office and trying to get the Minneapolis cops engaged.

Tell Connie I'm working on this thing in earnest.

Anything else I can do?"

"Yeah. There is. Whitson's called Connie a couple times already today wondering if we've got anything new. He sounds at least half in the bag when he calls. It's a real pain. Of course, I'll tell him to knock it off when we talk, but maybe you could reinforce that a bit."

I was planning to call Whitson as soon as I hung up with you anyway. I need to know if he has heard from Katherine, or from any kidnappers. I'll suggest he call me instead of Connie. No need for her to suffer further aggravation. She did her part when she handed this off to us – er – to me.

I'll keep you in the loop. We'll talk later."

"Thanks, Beck."

"My pleasure," I said, and disconnected the call.

I looked at Gunner's notes, and finding Whitson's home land line, punched up the number. The phone rang six times before Whitson picked up.

"Hello?" The voice sounded slurred and whiney.

"Hello. Whitson. This is Beck. We met yesterday at your condo with the Gundersons. Do you remember me?"

I was doubtful.

"Beck?" A pause. "Hey, you're the guy who took my cell phone. Who the hell do you think you are?" His voice was still slurred and whiney, but now tending more toward belligerent.

"That's me. Are you sober enough to talk?" I asked matter-of-factly.

"Sober? Of course, I'm sober. Who the hell are you again?"

This was a waste of time.

"Okay, Whitson. Listen good! Stop calling Connie Gunderson or I'll break your dialing finger. Got it?"

"Huh? . . . Okay."

I disconnected Mr. Whitson.

CHAPTER 9

Monday, October 19th, early a.m.

Monday morning arrived with a cold, steady rain drenching the turning trees and imparting a splashy black sheen to Jefferson Avenue. Beth and I were just heading out our front porch door, dressed in wet-weather jogging gear. I was still resisting the urge to abandon running shorts for long pants, but conceded a semi-water-proof wind-breaker to the October chill. Beth had pulled her hair back into a pony tail for the run. She wore purple, silky-looking running shorts over some sort of black hi-tech stretch tights. A black and purple Gortex jacket, black gloves and purple Puma running shoes completed her look.

Beth led the way along the concrete sidewalks past the nineteenth-century homes, keeping a steady eight-minute-mile pace. She ran a bit more slowly than I did when I ran alone; but her company was well worth the more leisurely jog.

At first, as our heart rates and breathing adjusted, and our bodies warmed despite the rain, we remained silent. I let Beth choose our speed, and lagged only a bit behind her on the narrow neighborhood sidewalks. Beth's liquid body movements as she ran were awe-inspiring. There was almost no sound as her Pumas floated over the wet concrete. Like her running stride, Beth's body, and all its proportions, seemed to me in perfect balance.

As we reached wider walkways, I pulled up alongside Beth on her streetward side, which I had learned was the mannerly position for a true gentleman out for a stroll with his lady-friend.   The history of this man-toward-the-street positioning was interesting.

Several hundred years ago, the gentleman walked nearer the buildings, so he would take the brunt of any wash water or garbage that might be flung from second-story windows. These days, given the lack of flying garbage, the greater danger to the damsel was the splash from a passing car. Hence, the gentleman stayed closer to the roadway than his lady companion.

"So what do you have planned for your day, my love?" I asked as we made the turn from Levee Road toward Baypoint Park.

"Although the rainy weather is truly lovely, I was thinking of, perhaps, some indoor activities today." Beth's breathing was steady as she spoke, with no hint of exertion. "I had considered running to a fabric warehouse to see if they have any new and inspiring options to spice up some of my clothing designs. And maybe a stop to look for some unique beads or baubles might be in order. Of course, if you would like to do something together, that would be much my preference."

"Actually, I need to make a run to the Cities to visit with this Whitson guy again. The longer his wife is missing, the less chance of locating her unharmed."

I wiped the dripping rain water from my brow with my left palm as we continued along the path near the river. "I thought I might catch him at his office. In addition to increasing the chances of finding him sober, I could possibly learn something from his co-workers or his work environment."

"Then it's settled," Beth said matter-of-factly. "You go your way and I'll go mine. I'll find the fabric while you solve the crime."

She smiled as if she had just said something tremendously clever. Seeing Beth's smile made me smile as well.

"A bit of a slant rhyme," I remarked. "But all-in-all, quite fine poetry, indeed."

Beth slapped me in the stomach with the back of her right hand. "If you've got the time, I've got the rhyme."

More of Beth's smile.

"Now, I can't argue with the artistic maturity of that one," I said, with only a hint of friendly sarcasm.

Beth increased her speed, leaving me behind for a moment. I soon caught up.

For the rest of the run we spoke of nothing in particular – the beautiful bluffs, the quiet river, late-migrating ducks paddling in the harbor. As we made the final turn for home, the rain began to let up. A small shaft of sun pierced the clouds and then was gone.

Back at 1011 Jefferson, the morning paper had arrived on our front step, protected by a clear plastic bag, sealed with a rubber band. I picked it up on our way in. Once inside the front screen porch, we sat for several peaceful minutes in wicker chairs. The outdoor scene viewed through the screen and the light rain reminded me of a Monet painting – slightly out of focus, yet eliciting the perfect impression.

As we stood on the porch, watching the rain, Beth broke the silence. "I s'pose we'll need to bring the Ficus inside for the winter soon."

"Of course." I said. "The Ficus."

We turned our faces toward one another and laughed. God, I love her laugh!

CHAPTER 10

At eight-thirty, it was still raining steadily as I drove the Pilot northwest along U.S. Highway 61 and then I-494 toward the southwestern Minneapolis suburb of Eden Prairie.

Gunner had already reported the utter failure of his fingerprint investigation. Other than those belonging to the Whitsons, the Gundersons and me, he had found no prints at all. Not even from a cleaning lady, a casual acquaintance, the Maytag Repairman. Nobody.

The absence of other prints was, in itself, a confirmation of foul play. Someone had wiped the place down. But that fact didn't help me rule out George Whitson as a suspect. He could have hired a thug to do away with Katherine, then eliminated any stray fingerprints himself. And he was certainly fastidious enough to have done a professional cleaning job.

The corporate headquarters of Equinox Advertising Specialties, Inc. was located in an office park development containing about half-a-dozen, 1980's-vintage, six-story, metal and glass commercial buildings. According to Gunner's information, this was Whitson's place of business.

I parked the Pilot on the middle level of a three-story parking ramp adjacent to the Equinox building in an area marked "Visitors." It wasn't raining on this level, owing to the third level parking slab above. Judging from the number of empty "Visitors" parking slots, Equinox didn't appear to be doing a lot of entertaining today.

Entering the building on the second floor, I took the steps down through the white, concrete stairwell to the doorway marked "Main Level." Leaning against the opener bar of the metal door, I entered the office building proper. Signs directed me to the Reception Area, just ahead down a carpeted hall lined with offices.

The receptionist's workstation was one of those metal-trimmed, teak jobs that looked sort of like a bunker. There was a wooden counter-top overhanging the workstation on three sides, including the side toward me.

I leaned on the counter.

"Could you direct me to George Whitson's office, please?" I asked the bored-looking, young female receptionist.

The phone rang and she said to me, "One moment, please."

It baffles me why someone calling on the telephone inevitably takes priority over a live person awaiting service.

After redirecting the call, the receptionist turned to me again. "I can connect you to Mr. Whitson's office if . . . excuse me. I have another call." She again answered the telephone.

I pulled my cell out of an inner pocket and dialed Whitson's work number, as provided by Gunner. Whitson's secretary answered.

"This is James Becker," I said. "Please tell Mr. Whitson I am on the line and it is urgent."

"And what is this regarding?" she asked, professionally screening Whitson's calls. The receptionist was giving someone on another line driving directions to the Equinox HQ.

THE MISSING ELEMENT

"Personal business. And please, it really is urgent."

"Very well," the secretary replied. "I will see if the Director is available." An instrumental rendition of the Beatles' "Penny Lane" filled my handset.

The receptionist turned back in my direction. "I have the Human Resources Department on the line for you sir," she said, holding a telephone receiver toward me.

"Would you please ask them to hold?" I asked politely. "I'm on another call."

The receptionist looked a bit flustered. I doubt that she had encountered this situation before.

"Well . . . ah . . . yes, of course. I will let them know," she finally managed.

"George Whitson," my phone announced in Whitson's voice, as "Penny Lane" suddenly disappeared.

"Mr. Whitson," I said. "I need to speak with you immediately. Shall I come up? Or will you be coming to meet me at Reception?"

The receptionist looked confused.

Whitson gave me directions to his office and told me to come up. I said, "Thank you. I'll be right there."

Then to the receptionist, I said, "Please tell Human Resources that I will be unavailable for the rest of the day; but if they wish to call again tomorrow, that would be lovely!"

"Yes sir," she said automatically. Her face wore a strange look as she reached for the button to connect to HR with my message.

Human Resources was on the second floor. But Whitson's office was on the sixth. I guess "Director" was as high as one could get in the HR Department at Equinox.

I located the heavy wooden door to the "Executive Offices," turned the brass knob, and let myself in. The waiting area was plush, even by corporate standards – overstuffed chairs and sofas, with glass and marble side tables. A professionally-dressed, middle-aged woman was standing at the far edge of the room, waiting for me as I arrived.

"Mr. Becker, I assume?"

Her greeting was warm and professional.

"The same," I said.

"I will be happy to escort you to Director Whitson's office. He is expecting you."

"Thank you," I said, as she turned to lead the way.

After a short walk down a stately hall, trimmed with dark oak base and crown molding, we arrived at Whitson's office. The woman knocked twice, then without waiting for a response, opened the door for me to enter. I thanked her again, and proceeded inside.

The man seated behind the desk was a sober version of the George Whitson I had met two days earlier – slim, pale, withdrawn. He rose, and stepping around the near side of his large, oak desk, he offered his hand. I took it firmly in mine, once again feeling it squish limply as I tried to get a grip.

"Mr. Becker, please have a seat," he offered, waving a thin arm toward one of his comfortably-upholstered side chairs.

"Beck, if you don't mind," I responded. "Nobody calls me Mr. Becker." Whitson nodded as he took a seat in his high-back leather chair.

Whitson spoke again.

"Beck. I'm afraid I need to apologize for my behavior the other day at my apartment. I've been quite distraught over Katherine's disappearance, and I haven't dealt with it very well."

He sounded sincerely apologetic. "I hope you won't judge my character on that unfortunate performance."

"Mr. Whitson, I understand that you are operating under difficult circumstances at this time. Your actions the other day mean little to me other than their delaying my search for your wife. So if we might get down to that issue . . . ?"

I could see Whitson's expression turn somber, and his face flush white, at the prospect of discussing Katherine's situation.

"Of course." He swallowed and tugged his suit coat. "How can I help?"

"Let's start at the beginning," I said. "When did you and Katherine meet?"

Whitson leaned back slightly and focused on the ceiling.

"We met a little over eight years ago at a social function put on by the Metropolitan Chamber of Commerce. It was a mixer at a downtown hotel – cocktails and hors d'oeuvres, that sort of thing. At the time, she was working as a computer person of some type at IBM in Rochester, and I was an accountant at the Winters firm in the IDS tower, downtown Minneapolis. We ended up at the same table and just sort of hit it off."

Whitson looked down from the ceiling and in my direction.

"And then . . . ?" I asked patiently.

"We dated for a while. Neither of us was a kid, you know. I was in my mid-thirties and she was about ten years my senior. So after a few months, we decided that we liked each other well enough and we should get married."

Whitson made it sound so romantic – almost like a business merger.

"We bought the apartment in the warehouse district just before the wedding and had the new furniture delivered while we honeymooned in San Diego. When we arrived back home, our accommodations at the apartment were all set."

I was thinking how glad I was that I was not part of the Whitson marriage. Their relationship seemed less like lovers, and more like roommates – at least to hear Whitson tell it.

"So how did you come to work here at Equinox?"

I needed to change the subject away from their personal lives. That avenue of questioning didn't appear productive. And Whitson was depressing me.

"Two summers ago, Equinox was having some business difficulties. Of course, this was true of many businesses at that time. Anyway, it hired the Winters firm as business consultants to get some ideas as to how Equinox might remain viable and economically competitive. When a business needs to downsize, it's not uncommon to hire a consultant who can be blamed for recommending all the necessary job cuts.

My part in the consulting job dealt with the Human Resources function. When I analyzed the HR Department, it was obvious that Equinox was operating on a 'staffing-based' model. They had been trying to manage existing personnel as a business asset – fostering a positive work environment, encouraging teamwork, bestowing lots of warm fuzzies on everybody.

In lean economic times, a financial model for HR makes much more sense. That is, you should run your HR Department just like your operating divisions. Expect productivity. Expect it to be lean and efficient. That's the recommendation I gave to Equinox at the time.

When the consulting job was done, Equinox approached me to come in-house as Director of HR, to implement my recommendations. Even though my former firm could have prevented me from taking this job, they chose to allow me to make the move. So here I am."

He spoke the last sentence with a two-armed flourish, indicating not only the expanse of his physical office, but the sweep of his authority over HR at Equinox.

"Can you think of anyone here at Equinox who might want to harm Katherine?" I asked.

"Oh, my god! Do you think someone here might have taken dear Katherine?" He sounded astonished that such a thing might be possible.

"I'm just trying to be thorough," I said. "Anyone here that harbors any ill will toward her at all?"

"No. Absolutely not! Why in the world would they? They hardly know her."

"How about someone who might want to hurt you by hurting Katherine?" I persisted.

"No one likes their boss," Whitson said. "But kidnapping? I can't believe it of anyone here. No. Not possible."

He was clearly flustered at the thought.

"Okay. You're probably right. But just to be on the safe side, could you provide me with names and contact information for all your reports? How many people report to you anyway, maybe half a dozen?" I figured he was far enough up the food chain to have only a few people he needed to manage directly.

"Good guess. There are exactly six, excluding Margaret, my secretary, of course. I'll have Margaret put that information together for you right now." He picked up his phone and pressed the intercom button.

While he spoke with Margaret, I took the opportunity for a quick glance around the office. There were a number of framed degrees and professional certifications. His desk held only one picture, and that was a closeup of Katherine. It was oriented for his viewing only – not a display piece. His desktop was clear of any sign of paperwork.

I took a second look all around. There was really no sign that any work at all was being accomplished in this office. No piles of papers. No reports showing on the computer screen – in fact, the screen was turned off, and it was presently . . . I looked at my watch . . . 10:30 a.m. No dictation equipment was in evidence.

Whitson hung up the phone. "All right," he said. "Margaret will have your information when you are ready to leave. She is very efficient."

"Okay. Thank you."

Time to try a new line of questioning. "Can you think of any reason why Katherine might leave you?"

Whitson looked irritated at the implication; but he didn't seem to have the gumption to object.

"None whatsoever," he stated emphatically.

"No recent quarrels? No declarations of dissatisfaction? No suspicion of infidelity?" I pressed on.

Whitson was still irritated and still lacked the *cojones* to say anything about it.

"No. None of those things. We were very satisfied with our relationship. We never even fought." Then . . . "This line of questioning is not going to help find Katherine. She did not leave voluntarily."

"In the face of her goodbye note to the contrary, why do you believe she was taken against her will?" I continued. Even though I had already concluded that Katherine had been kidnapped, George didn't know that. And sometimes suspects will divulge important details under pressure. So I wanted to keep him on edge.

"Because I know her!" And then he thought some more. "And even if she ever decided to leave me, she would never leave her job. She is absolutely devoted to her work. She loves it more than life itself! And she has been absent from work as well." Whitson folded his arms across his chest.

"You've checked recently with her employer and she still has not reported in?" I asked.

"Just this morning, about two hours ago."

I couldn't think of anything else to ask Whitson. This session had really been more of a character assessment in the first place. And Whitson's performance had done a pretty decent job in raising his character quotient from abysmal to somewhere in the vicinity of mediocre.

I concluded my interview, assuring Whitson that I would do everything possible to find his wife. I also advised that he stay around home when he was not working, just in case any kidnapper might call.

I also directed him to lay off the sauce. For his own good, and for Katherine's, I needed him to be sober and coherent.

As I turned to leave, I stopped. Reaching into my right inside sport coat pocket, I produced Whitson's cell phone. I turned halfway back toward Whitson and tossed it to him.

"Here's your phone. Make sure I can reach you when I need you."

Whitson fumbled the phone onto the carpet as I walked out the door.

While I was retracing my steps to the executive office suite exit doors, Margaret tracked me down with a business-size envelope in her hand.

"Mr. Becker. I believe this is the information you requested."

"Thank you very much for your assistance," I responded. "It has been a pleasure to make your acquaintance." I bowed, doffing my imaginary cap, and backed out the door.

Now to interview some of Whitson's reports.

I took the elevator to floor number two – Human Resources Department – and started looking for people matching the names on Margaret's list. A few employees looked at me sideways as I tried to appear as though I belonged there.

The first name I located was Jan Tyler, Employee Benefits Manager. She was in her office. I knocked gently on the open door. Jan looked up from her desk, "Yes?"

I gave her a big smile. "Hi. My name is Beck and I am an attorney doing some confidential work for the CEO concerning one George Whitson. May I come in for a moment?"

I pulled out my wallet and displayed my laminated lawyer's license from the Minnesota Supreme Court.

Jan examined my license closely. "Do you have some picture ID?" she asked. I withdrew another card from my wallet. Upon comparing my smile to my driver's license pic, Jan was apparently satisfied. She returned the documents to me and beckoned me inside her office.

"What can I help you with, Mr. Beck?"

"Just 'Beck,' please" I said.

"Okay."

"As I mentioned, this is strictly confidential. So please don't mention to anyone that I have come calling," I requested.

"Of course," said Jan, somewhat tentatively.

"George Whitson," I said. "Tell me about him."

Jan looked perplexed. "What do you want to know?"

"What kind of a boss is he?" I returned.

"You're sure this is confidential?" she asked.

I crossed my heart with my right forefinger.

"Okay. In all honesty, I think Director Whitson is probably a decent enough guy. But as a boss, he is extremely rigid. Everything needs to be his way."

"How so?" I probed.

"Everything needs to be accomplished, and reported to him, in a certain specific format. He's not at all flexible in that regard. It makes him very hard to work for."

That seemed consistent with Whitson's OCD personality. Both his condo and office had exhibited signs of an occupant compulsively obsessed with order for order's sake.

"And when he first came here a couple years ago, he completely reorganized the HR personnel into areas with which we were unfamiliar – so we needed to start our learning curves all over again. For example, I used to manage the staffing function – hiring, firing, interview and grievance protocols, that sort of thing. Now I'm trying to sort out the regulatory jungle of employee benefits. Qualified plans. Health insurance. Disability and maternity leaves. Vacation policies.

The laws, rules and regulations I have to deal with in these areas are myriad and conflicting. It's fortunate for me that the old head of Benefits is still here, working as the Manager of Health and Safety Compliance, so I can go to him for occasional help."

Jan's perspective was understandable in the context of a corporate reorganization. When a company has just undergone massive layoffs, the person who does the reallocating of personnel, in this case, George Whitson, was going to be the natural object of negative perceptions, possibly even fear, in the eyes of remaining employees.

"Any other complaints?" I prompted.

"Once you get used to his quirkiness, you can learn to live with him," she said. "He's not the worst boss I ever had."

"Do you think any employee here might dislike Whitson enough to do something criminal to harm him or his family?" I asked finally.

Jan looked genuinely shocked.

"Oh, my god, no! He can be very frustrating to work for; but someone harming him – that's a whole different thing. I don't know anyone here who might do something like that."

"Are you sure you can't think of anyone at all? Maybe someone who was fired when Mr. Whitson came on board?"

Jan thought harder.

"You know . . . ." She held up a finger as she thought. "Arthur Trample used to have Director Whitson's job. He got canned to make room for Director Whitson. Maybe he . . . ." Then she changed her mind. "No. I can't see even Trample stooping to criminal activity or threats. He was a dink. But not evil."

At least Jan had given me another name to think about. I concluded my interview with her, reminding her to keep it confidential.

I found two other names on Margaret's list of reports to interview that day. They both told me basically the same thing. George is a pain to work for. Nobody would hurt him physically – even Arthur Trample.

I had heard enough George Whitson info for the day, so I departed Human Resources and took the elevator down to the first floor. On my way past the receptionist's station, a point needed to be made.

Walking behind her desk, I noted the general number for Equinox and silently punched it into my phone. I did not hit the dial key.

I continued around to the front of the station while the receptionist was fielding a call. I stood and waited for her to finish.

"May I help you sir?" she asked politely.

I pushed the dial button on my cell as I held it by my hip. "Yes. I was just wondering . . ."

The receptionist's phone rang.

To me she said, "Could you hold one moment please?" It was more a direction than a request.

"Equinox Advertising Specialities. How may I direct your call?"

I put my phone to my mouth. "I just wanted to say, 'Have a nice day.'" I flipped the phone closed, waved a cheery goodbye, and headed back for the parking ramp.

Glancing behind me, I noted that the receptionist looked perplexed. I smiled to myself.

On the way out, I opened the metal door to the parking ramp stairwell and jogged up to Level Two.

The Pilot was visible as soon as I was two steps outside the building door . . . and I could see something was wrong. Both back tires were flat.

Most people would probably just go survey the damage, curse a bit, and then call the auto club. But in my experience, coincidences like getting two flat tires while investigating a possible crime, were not likely. Someone had intentionally flattened my tires. And that someone might have something else in mind as well.

Since I had already started off toward the Pilot, I continued in that direction, swinging my keys around my forefinger and whistling as I went. But I didn't stop at my vehicle. Instead, I kept going down the line of cars and around the large concrete pillar at the end of the row. Whoever it was that had punctured my tires might still be here. And he or she may not know exactly what I look like.

Maybe I could gain an advantage.

As I disappeared behind the pillar, I ducked low, then backtracked alongside the last car in my row. Slipping in front of the car, along the cable ramp supports, I maneuvered into a crouching posture between two vehicles. I'd roughed up my clothing a bit in this process. But at least my position was now hidden from most angles.

I could wait here and watch for further developments. But eventually, all the cars would be gone, and I'd be stuck out in the open. I needed to do something more proactive.

After about five minutes crouching behind the car, I had made a decision. I wormed my way back to the far side of the pillar. Still hidden by the concrete post, I stood upright. I took off my sport coat and stashed my shoulder holster in one pocket. Holding my .40 caliber Beretta short barrel under the sport coat, which I had draped over one arm, I lurched awkwardly toward the elevator.

If a stalker hadn't recognized me before, he wouldn't now. Without the sport coat, the happy whistle and my usual walking gait, I appeared to be a quite different person from the one who had emerged from the stairwell just a few minutes before.

Manufacturing an improvised disguise was a skill I had learned in my previous trade. It worked well for this situation, too.

Once I was safely back inside the building, I trotted down the stairs and placed a call for assistance. I had a friend who would occasionally help me out in similar situations. And if someone was, indeed, stalking me, this might be my first and best clue to Katherine's whereabouts. I didn't want to blow the chance by being impatient.

The friend I had called was Terry Red Feather – aka "Bull."

I don't remember when I first heard Terry called Bull. But the name fit his six foot four, 235-pound muscular frame, and his tendency toward stubbornness as well. So I had adopted the nickname. He seemed fine with it.

Bull is a full-blooded Mdewakanton Dakota Indian. Born on the Prairie River Reservation near Red Wing, he left his home and family at the age of sixteen to join the army. At the time, he was required to be at least eighteen to enlist. But documentation of his birth on the reservation was nonexistent. And he was big enough and strong enough. So the army was pleased to have his assistance.

After he left the Rez to "be all that he could be," Bull's family and friends heard nothing from him for more than twenty years. Based on Terry's behavior as a teen, they'd assumed he had been killed in a knife fight at some bar.

But one day about eight years ago, he had shown up at his parents' home on the Rez. By the time of his return, he had become the imposing figure whom I had come to know. Bull never told anyone where he had been for twenty years. And after a few altercations, folks quit asking.

Bull didn't live on the reservation. He owned a recently-built, log-style house on a Wisconsin bluff overlooking the Mississippi River Valley, together with forty acres of mostly wooded land to spare. A modern-day Native.

Based on Bull's knowledge, temperament and physical dimensions, I had some ideas about where he had been and what he had been doing. I would pursue them with Bull at the appropriate time. But that time had never yet presented itself. Maybe it would one day.

After speaking with Bull on the phone, I needed a place to kill some time. I consulted the building directory and located an employee cafeteria. I waited there, at a small café table, nursing a cup of coffee and an oatmeal raisin cookie, for the better part of two hours.

By the look of pedestrian traffic in the hall outside the cafeteria, some employees were starting to head for home. I hoped my assistance would arrive before any stalker decided to skedaddle.

Just then my cell vibrated and I answered the call. It was Bull.

"Beck," I said.

"Ready," the male voice replied. The line went dead.

I chuckled and shook my head. People have their idiosyncrasies – some people more than others.

I pocketed the cell, and with my jacket on and gun holstered, I made my way back to the second level of the parking ramp. This time I headed straight to the Pilot.

"What the hell?" I exclaimed histrionically at the flat tires. All four were airless.

As I walked around the Pilot, out of the corner of my eye, I saw him coming toward me from the back side of the ramp. Most of the visitors' cars were gone by now. So there was a lot of open concrete for him to cover before reaching me. As he got closer, I saw him raise his arm. I was pretty sure it held a gun.

Pretending to bend down for a closer look at the front tire, I used the Pilot as a shield. My action forced the man to either wait and keep his distance, or to keep coming and try for a nearer shot. From my crouching position, I couldn't see which option he had chosen.

When I next saw the man, he was lunging around the back of my truck and leveling a black 9 mm pistol at my chest.

His face held a look of supreme confidence . . . for a moment. Then the expression changed abruptly to surprise and confusion. Before he could get off a shot – or say a word – a large American Indian had lifted him from his feet and thrown him flat on his back on the concrete. The man's gun went skittering across the ramp floor, as a strong brown hand closed like an anaconda around his throat.

"I was wondering if you were going to make it in time, or if I was going to have to shoot him," I said to my Indian friend.

"Well . . . now you know," Bull said, his eyes on the attacker.

The squirming man on the concrete was maybe six feet tall, 190 pounds. Bull had tossed him one-handed, as though he were a rag doll.

The man was Caucasian with long, greasy brown hair and a bad complexion. He had the stringy look of someone who takes most of his nourishment from a liquor bottle.

He was choking for air and trying to scream at the same time. Both his hands pulled as hard as they could at Bull's arms, struggling to obtain release from Bull's viselike grip. His torso and legs thrashed violently – and ineffectively.

"Should we give him some air?" I asked Bull nonchalantly as I walked closer, looking the rapidly fading man in the eye.

"If you say so," Bull said.

Balancing on one knee and one foot beside the man's head, Bull loosened the throat grip slightly.

His windpipe made a hissing sound as the man sucked air into his lungs.

"What's your name?" I asked politely.

The man tried to spit at me, but Bull tightened his grip in time to abort the attempt.

"No name?" I said. "Okay. We'll call you 'Buffy.'

So Buffy, who hired you to shoot me?"

Buffy tried to say something; but it was indistinguishable.

"Loosen his air a bit please, Bull. I can't quite hear him."

Bull didn't say anything, but again loosened his grip.

Buffy tried to speak. "Jesus. I don't even know," he managed. "A guy paid me a lousy $500 bucks to scare you off."

"What guy?" I pressed, my hands casually tucked in my front pants pockets. "Scare me off from what?"

"I told you I don't know."

Bull placed Buffy's right hand flat on the rampway and knelt on it. Buffy winced and let out a squeal.

"Listen, Buffy. We're in no hurry. And you've got lots of fingers and toes and arms and legs and other stuff we can damage. But we would prefer you just answer my questions. Right Bull?"

I looked in Bull's direction.

He didn't move his steely gaze from Buffy.

"Um hmm. You say so."

"Geez," Buffy squeaked, his air flow still constricted. "I can't tell you what I don't know. This guy got my name from somebody – I don't know who – and gave me the five. Told me where you'd be and what your truck looked like. I was thinking I might just rough you up with a club, but you looked kinda big, so I was planning on shooting a leg.

Honest to god! That's all I know."

"Honest to god, Bull," I said, sarcastically. "He was only planning to shoot me in the leg. I guess I got his motivations all wrong."

"Hmm," said Bull.

"All right," I said to Bull. "Seems we mistook old Buffy's intentions, so we can maybe cut him some slack."

Bull shrugged.

"Okay, Buffy. Are you listening?" I said.

"Yeah," he wheezed.

"If it weren't for our charitable natures, you would be dead right now. And not peaceful dead – painful dead! Understood?"

Buffy tried to nod.

"Good. Now you go back to whoever hired you, or not. But if I ever see your ugly face again, we won't be so charitable next time."

I looked into Buffy's eyes to make sure he understood completely. The terror I saw there made it appear that he did.

"Okay, Bull. Please release the worm."

"You say so," he said, rising to his feet and lifting Buffy by the throat – holding him until he could stand on his own.

"You'll be donating the gun to us," Bull said. "Now git!"

He released his grip.

We watched as Buffy ran and stumbled down the ramp.

"You want I should follow him?" Bull asked.

"Naw. Waste of time. Strictly a first line flunky. We'd have to dig through eight different layers of crap bags before we could trace him to a real human being. He doesn't know anything."

"But we do," said Bull.

I nodded.

"Somebody wants me off this case."

CHAPTER 11

I thanked Bull for his able assistance and sent him on his way. I hung around the ramp until the tire repair truck arrived. Fortunately, Buffy had just cut the valve stems and I didn't need to buy all new tires. A relatively minor inconvenience, all things considered.

On the drive home, I had some things to think about. Who had hired Buffy to intimidate me? And did that person want to scare me away from the investigation of Katherine's disappearance? Or was there some other bees' nest I had inadvertently poked? And how had Buffy located my car at the Equinox lot? How did his employer know I drove a grey Pilot? And how could he guess I would be visiting Whitson's office this afternoon?

There were certainly a lot of questions. But of one thing I was certain. Now that I was pretty confident that Katherine had been taken from the condo against her will, we needed to convince the police to assist with the search. Time was of the essence.

I would need Gunner's help. I didn't know how much he could do himself. But I was sure he would tell me his boundaries. And at a minimum, he could direct me toward the right bureaucratic compass point.

By the time I finally got home to Jefferson Avenue, it was almost eight o'clock in the evening. I had called Beth earlier so she wouldn't worry, and because, well, it's the polite thing to do. The garage door opened obediently. I parked the Pilot, closed up the garage, and went inside through the back porch into the kitchen.

Slam!

"I'm finally here," I called.

"I'm in here," Beth answered from the living room.

As I cut through the dining room and foyer to the living room, I could see Beth reclining on the red leather couch, reading her novel. She looked up at me as I entered the room.

"You've looked better," she commented.

"Thanks," I replied.

"Seriously. What have you been up to today? Your jacket's all dirty and rumpled. Your pants look like you've been playing in a sand box. And your hands are pretty black."

I looked at my palms. They were covered with black rubber from my attempts to assist with the tire changing regimen.

"Sorry 'bout that. But you know what they say about dirty hands . . . ." I waited.

"Sorry. No clue."

"Okay. I thought maybe there was a clever saying in there somewhere. But I guess not."

Beth smiled, even though my joke wasn't funny. Suddenly, my day seemed brighter.

"I'm going upstairs to hit the shower and change clothes. Will you wait for me?" I asked.

"You know I will."

My day got brighter still.

"Okay. Back in a flash."

I jogged up the broad central staircase to the second floor, taking two steps at a time.

Before showering, I called Gunner's cell. I hoped we could get the cops working on the Missing Persons case yet today. No joy. I got his voicemail and left a message.

I gave him an update on my day's activities. I asked him to look into the background and current whereabouts of one Arthur Trample, former Director of Human Resources at Equinox Advertising Specialties. I also requested that he contact me as soon as possible about obtaining further police involvement in the investigation.

I'd done all I could. Might as well relax for now.

After my shower, I went to our bedroom and put on some clean, tan khakis and a burgundy golf shirt. Then I made my way barefoot back downstairs and into the kitchen, being careful not to disturb Beth's enjoyment of her novel.

The fridge held a couple nice cheeses and a bottle of California Merlot. I prepared a variety of cheese cubes, with individual toothpicks on a small plate, and uncorked the wine. Carrying cheese, wine and two oversized wine stems, I returned to the living room, setting the plate on the bass drum case.

Beth was now watching me, still reclining, holding her book, folded upside-down, on her firm mid-section. I poured some wine into each glass and set the bottle on the coffee table. Kneeling beside the red couch, I proffered one of the wine glasses to Beth.

"An offering for the princess." I bowed my head slightly as I spoke the words.

Beth sat up and placed her book on the library table behind the couch while I maintained my kneel/bow position. Accepting the wine stem in her right hand, she used her left as a royal blade, placing it regally on each of my shoulders in turn, karate-chop-style.

"I hereby knight thee, Sir Suck-up-a-lot," she said.

It was fortunate I had not yet sampled my wine, because my laughter would have caused me to spit it out.

"You really know how to kill a mood," I laughed.

"That was a mood? Sorry. I guess I haven't seen one in a while."

Beth smiled.

After that, I joined Beth on the red leather couch. We sampled cheese and enjoyed wine and conversation.

Eventually, I had to report the events of my day. Which I did. Beth listened intently to every word. When I had finished the story, I felt much lighter somehow, and totally refreshed. Maybe Beth has magical empathic powers. I hadn't thought of that before. I usually got distracted by her beauty, kindness, charisma and many other wonderful attributes before I got to questioning the issue of magical powers.

When the wine was drunk, and the cheese had been eaten, it was time to retire for the evening. I placed our dishes in the dishwasher, and the wine bottle in the recycling bin, while Beth waited at the foot of the steps. When I returned, she took my hand and led me upstairs.

CHAPTER 12

Tuesday, October 20th, 7:30 a.m.

Tuesday morning, as I enjoyed a bite of fried egg on wheat toast in our kitchen, I wondered how I had let myself get involved with helping George Whitson. Despite his decent performance during the office interview, I didn't like or trust the man. Apparently, his co-workers didn't either. The Gundersons' involvement with him had earned them an upsetting phone call. And on top of that, somebody was now seeking to do me bodily harm.

Oh yeah, and I had totaled my favorite chinos squirming around a parking ramp floor!

I looked at my face in the wall mirror across the room. Oh, god! Civilian life was turning me into a whiner!

Getting back to my principles, I knew why I had taken the case, and why I would see it through.

One important reason was Gunner. My friend had asked for a favor. It was my privilege to comply. I wasn't about to let him down – especially not in the eyes of his wife.

Another reason was Katherine Whitson. She appeared to be in serious trouble, and clearly, George wasn't competent to help her.

A nefarious caller had turned the Gundersons' life upside down. And that pissed me off.

The final reason was Buffy. I didn't like people messing with me. That confrontation was an unresolved issue that needed resolving. I wanted Buffy's boss – if for no other reason, to wreck his favorite pants.

As internal conflicts go, I had resolved this one fairly quickly, I thought. That was good. But thinking only gets a person so far; action is also required.

The first action for my day was a contact with the Minneapolis Police. Gunner had called me late last night and told me how Ottawa County would handle a Missing Persons report. He didn't know Minneapolis procedures. So I looked online.

Upon viewing the MPD website, I found it exceedingly confusing, and decided to call the universal "non-emergency" number. I picked up our land line and made the call.

"Minneapolis Police Information," a male voice said. "How may I help you?"

"My name is Attorney James Becker. My client, George Whitson, filed a Missing Persons report this past Friday, and I'm calling to check on the status."

"Which Precinct did he file the report with?" he asked.

"I'm not sure. He lives downtown." I gave the address for the Whitson condo.

"That would be the First Precinct. Please hold one moment."

The man's voice was replaced by a public service announcement of some sort relating to neighborhood safety organizations. In a moment, a female voice came on the line.

"First Precinct, Mitchell," she said.

I repeated my identification and the reason for my call.

"One moment. I'll check our records for Friday." There was a pause. "I see no Missing Persons report from Mr. Whitson. What is the missing person's name, please?"

"Katherine Whitson," I replied.

"Sorry. No Katherine Whitson listed as missing."

"I know that he did call to report her missing. In fact, I saw a record of his call to 911 on Friday morning. And I have confirmed that your precinct is the correct one for his report," I said, trying to keep the irritation I was feeling out of my voice.

"Is the missing person a minor, incompetent or incapacitated?" she asked.

"No."

"Is she a threat to herself or to others?"

"I'm pretty sure not. She may well be in danger *from* others, though," I replied, getting more irritated by the minute.

"Well, if none of those conditions is met, Department policy in Missing Persons cases is not to take a report. So if he answered those questions the same way you just did, we wouldn't have any paperwork." She recited all of this matter-of-factly.

I was irritated at the nonchalance with which Minneapolis PD had handled this situation.

"It now appears that she was most likely kidnapped," I said. "With whom may I speak about that?"

"Is there evidence of foul play?"

I could see where this was going.

"Yes. Ample evidence."

"Any note explaining her disappearance?"

"No," I lied. "What if there were?"

"Then it wouldn't be considered a kidnapping, and procedures would not allow us to take a report."

"Okay," I said. "No note. No explanation. Lots of blood. Whom do I talk to?"

"I will transfer you to an investigator," she said, "Please hold."

If Whitson had called asking for help with a "missing person," he had no chance of penetrating the myriad defenses inherent in this bureaucracy.

"Detective Blakeley," a man answered.

"My name is Attorney James Becker. I'm calling to report a probable kidnapping. Are you the guy I want to talk to?" I asked.

"That depends," he said.

It figured. He was going to see if this was, in reality, not a kidnapping, but a Missing Persons case.

"On what," I asked as politely as I could muster.

"Did the victim leave a note?" he continued.

"Look. I don't want to take this out on you. But I just answered all of these questions with someone in Missing Persons. There is a very high likelihood that Katherine Whitson has been kidnapped. Can I prove it?" I continued. "No. Isn't that what you guys do?"

"Did the victim leave a note?" Blakeley repeated, a bit of impatience showing in his voice.

"Yes, damn it!" I exclaimed. "But there is also plenty of evidence that it was not a voluntary note. If you would please come out to look at the scene, I believe your keen investigative observations would lead you to the same conclusion."

"What evidence is there of a kidnapping?" he continued. "Any blood at the scene? Any evidence of a struggle?"

"No," I said. "But Dr. Whitson departed without her car, key ring (including home, car and office keys), her cell phone, and her credit cards. She has not shown up for work – which, according to her husband and co-workers, is entirely uncharacteristic. I was assaulted by a man with a gun yesterday at her husband's place of business."

I took a breath.

"Did you file an assault report?" he asked.

"No. Damn it! This isn't about me. It's about the kidnapping of Katherine Whitson."

I was about ready to pull my hair out.

"But she left a note. Correct?"

This guy was determined to be difficult.

"No, actually," I lied. "I was mistaken about that part. Can I file a report and get some assistance from Minneapolis's finest in locating Dr. Whitson?"

"We'll see who is available and send an investigator around to see Mr. Whitson in the next couple days," Blakeley said.

"A woman has been kidnapped and you are going to wait a couple days to investigate. What the hell is this? Keystone cops?"

I knew I wasn't making friends with that crack. I just couldn't help it.

"The kidnapping is your opinion," he said. "But based on certain evidence conveyed to me a moment ago, she left a note. So it's not a priority item for this Department."

"Katherine Whitson is not an 'item' at all." I was fuming. "Connect me to your superior officer."

"I'm afraid that won't be possible," Blakeley said.

"Why not?" I asked, mad as hell.

"Because all I'm going to do is take the contact info for Mr. Whitson, and then I'm going to hang up."

There comes a time to admit defeat. I learned long ago that you cannot convince a particular person of any fact, regardless of your evidence, if that person refuses to be convinced. Possessing this knowledge had saved me a lot of wasted breath through the years.

I gave him the info and begged him to investigate.

Then he hung up.

This wasn't over. Katherine Whitson deserved better. I hung up the phone as well. Going back to the dining room computer, I looked up the address of the First Precinct and the name of its Commander on the MPD website.

Beth was in the kitchen reading the morning edition of the Metro newspaper when I walked in. "Hi, Babe." She looked up at me and smiled. The face that launched a thousand ships. I could feel myself melting, but resolved to steel my will against her feminine attractions.

"Hi, Doll," I said. "Listen. I've got a serious case of intractable institutional density to deal with at the Minneapolis Police Department. I need to go up there and see someone in person. I'm gonna head right out."

"Jousting at windmills, are we?" She smiled again. More melting of my innards. Then, with a shooing motion, she added, "Go for it! If not you, then who? I've got gobs of stuff to keep me busy."

"See ya as soon as possible," I said, grabbing the Pilot keys and striking out for the garage.

The First Precinct was located at 19 North Fourth Street in downtown Minneapolis. Fourth Street is a one-way headed south. I had to circle the block a couple times in search of a legal spot to park. But about an hour and fifteen minutes after leaving home, I had located a parking spot and was on my way up the steps into the Minneapolis First Police Precinct. It was 10:00 a.m. A male uniformed officer was seated at an elevated wood desk in the foyer – just like in all the old cop shows on TV.

I strode up to the desk and smiled.

"May I help you?" the officer said, returning the smile.

I have very frequently found that one smile gets you another. It's a good thing to remember.

I identified myself. Then I said, "I need to meet with Commander Reichert." I continued smiling.

"Do you have an appointment?" he asked, still friendly.

"No. Actually I don't," I admitted apologetically. "But it is a matter of utmost urgency. I fear the Press will be involved if it's not dealt with swiftly. And I had really hoped to help the Commander get in front of this thing."

I gave another smile. A good citizen trying to help the local police department.

"I'll call Inspector Reichert and see what I can do. Please have a seat," he said, motioning to one of the upholstered chairs lining the sides of the foyer. Red Wing could take a tip from Minneapolis on waiting room furniture – Red Wing's was molded plastic. I thanked the officer and took a chair.

After a bit of discussion on the phone, the desk officer hung up and told me, "The Inspector will be right down."

"Thank you," I said.

I hoped he didn't get in trouble for what I was about to do. He seemed like a nice guy.

About five minutes later, a small, slender woman in an olive business suit with black, medium-height pumps appeared out of the elevator. Seeing that I was the only customer in the waiting area, she approached me and I stood.

"I am Inspector Reichert," she said, extending her hand.

"Attorney James Becker," I replied as we exchanged a firm handshake.

"You have something to tell me?" she asked.

"I think a bit of privacy would be a good idea," I said.

"Very well. Please follow me."

She turned primly and headed toward a doorway at the left side of the foyer. It turned out to be a tiny conference room. She wasn't going to invite me to her office. No matter.

Once we were both seated at the small conference table, she asked again, "What do you wish to tell me?"

"My client's wife has been kidnapped," I began. "I have tried to make a formal report to your investigator, Detective Blakeley, but he refuses to take any action. I was hoping you could help."

I smiled.

She looked irritated.

The smiling thing doesn't always work.

"I understood that you wished to speak with me about keeping a police matter out of the Press." She didn't look happy at my deception. "How does this situation apply?"

"Well," I said. "If the Minneapolis Police Department refuses to properly and promptly investigate the kidnapping of my client's wife, my next stop will be the Editor's desk at the *Star Tribune*," I said. "They love a story where the police shirk their responsibilities to the great detriment of the helpless victim.

And I assure you, Inspector," I said, locking my eyes on hers, "that I would write that story myself, if necessary."

Now she looked even less happy.

"So what is it you want, exactly?" she said through clenched teeth.

"For the Department to investigate my client's kidnapping – nothing more, nothing less." I leaned back and rested my hands on the dark green linoleum table top.

After a moment of thought, she must have decided it was easier to give me what I wanted than to risk having to deal with a public fiasco, warranted or not.

"I will personally direct Detective Blakeley to proceed with the kidnapping investigation with due haste. Satisfied?"

I wasn't. Blakeley would probably still give the Katherine Whitson case short shrift. But it was the best I was going to get.

"Katherine Whitson," I said.

"I beg your pardon?" The Inspector looked confused.

"The case you are going to ask Detective Blakeley to work on is the kidnapping of Katherine Whitson."

"Of course," she said, standing.

I stood up as well. Never hurts to display good manners.

"Here is my business card." She accepted it reluctantly. "Please keep me informed."

"Good day," she said, making an inhospitable exit.

"Right back atcha," I called from my side of the conference table as she crossed the foyer.

CHAPTER 13

The entire fiasco with MPD had taken a big chunk out of my Tuesday. I didn't know if it had been worth the effort or not. In any case, it was now after noon, and with or without police assistance, I needed to move forward. The clock was ticking and Katherine's chances of a positive outcome to this abduction were lessening by the minute.

Gunner had been able to provide me with detailed background information on Katherine's education and employment. Seated at our granite kitchen table on Jefferson, I reviewed that info now.

To say that Katherine's educational background was impressive would be a serious understatement. She had earned her BA, *summa cum laude*, from Berkeley in mathematics and electrical engineering in 1976. Then proceeded to obtain Doctoral degrees – first from MIT in Electrical Engineering in 1978, then from Stanford in Mathematics three years later.

I had known some PhDs from MIT while at the Agency. They were, without exception, unbelievably intelligent.

Moving along to employment history, I noted that Katherine had worked at Control Data Corporation in St. Paul as a systems programmer and systems analyst until the company's demise in 1989. Then IBM hired her to work in Quality

Assurance and Testing at its Rochester, Minnesota facility, home to the manufacture of IBM's flagship supercomputers. In 2005, ComDyne Integrated, a new player in the world market for networking components, headquartered in the northwestern Minneapolis suburb of Maple Grove, hired Katherine away from IBM to head its own Quality Assurance and Testing Design Department – her present job.

I knew enough about the technology industry to recognize Katherine as one of its shining stars. She would have an IQ over 160 and a relentless drive for perfection. That explained some of the compulsive organization at the condo – arranging something as simple as an apartment layout might have been a form of relaxation for her. That her husband also appeared compulsively organized would be a plus.

I now knew what the documentation of Katherine's career could tell me. A visit to ComDyne was next. It was just before two o'clock Tuesday afternoon. I could probably still catch Katherine's co-workers at their jobs, if I hurried.

I tracked down Beth in her studio, explained the situation, kissed her goodbye and made a hasty exit.

As I headed back toward the metro area behind the wheel of the Pilot, I wondered if I should've asked Bull to join me. I didn't yet know the precise reason for the attack at Equinox yesterday. But since I hadn't told anyone of my planned visit to ComDyne, I felt reasonably safe acting alone today.

The ComDyne World Headquarters was a huge office complex on the edge of Maple Grove. Its campus must have covered twenty acres or more. The buildings were a more twenty-first century design than the Equinox offices. Less exposed metal. More obvious eco-efficiencies – insulated glass, solar panels on the building roofs, even a sizeable wind generator in the back corner of the lawn.

I parked near the rear of the huge, open parking lot, and hiked the hundred or so yards to the entrance to Building 100. The office building was a secure environment. In order to gain entrance, I needed to contact Katherine's department for permission to enter.

Rather than using the wall phone with its intricately-labeled button panel, I elected to try the old-fashioned approach and called Katherine's office number on my cell.

"Dr. Whitson's office," a male voice answered. "How may I assist you?"

"This is Attorney James Becker. I am Dr. Whitson's attorney and need to meet with her supervisor immediately. It is quite urgent, I'm afraid. I am at the front entrance to your building. Could you permit me access, please?"

"Would you mind holding one moment please?"

"Certainly. No problem."

As he placed me on hold, an electronic version of "Sitting on the Dock of the Bay" replaced his voice. Hearing sixties classics filtered through contemporary music generators grated on my sense of music as art. Yesterday, the Beatles. Today, Otis Redding. What next? "Smoke on the Water" on the autoharp?

"Mr. Becker. I can come down and escort you to Dr. Allister. He is in the conference room. Please wait where you are. I will be there momentarily."

"Thank you," I said, grateful that the music had ceased.

After about two minutes, a young man appeared at the glass door. He wore navy blue cotton chinos and a white cotton button-down oxford shirt, open at the collar. There was a pen in his shirt pocket and a cell phone in a leather holster on his belt. He opened the door and motioned me inside.

"Good day, Mr. Becker," he said. "I'm Dr. Whitson's intern, Sam. I will show you to Dr. Allister's office. He is expecting you there."

"Thank you." As we walked down the corridor toward the elevators, I asked, "Does Dr. Whitson have a secretary or administrative assistant?"

"I would be the closest person to that category," Sam said. "Dr. Whitson doesn't really require traditional secretarial or administrative assistance. She is quite self-sufficient in her position. I lend aid whenever there is some routine code to be written, or if time-consuming data collection is needed. Dr. Whitson is very efficient with her time."

We took the elevator up to the third floor of six. Apparently, the top floors were reserved for the business types, who valued the status a high-level view confers. Exiting the elevator, we proceeded straight ahead into an open office area where men and women, mostly under forty, worked in and around their cubicles. The workers, who I assumed to be programmers or software engineers of some type, appeared to wear whatever attire they chose. All looked comfortable.

Although workstations were divided into typical office cubicles by five-foot-high office dividers, there were several informal meetings taking place with participants leaning arms on the divider tops, or standing in aisles, to facilitate face to face conversation. Some groups were laughing. But none seemed to be wasting time. I wasn't sure how that was possible. But from all appearances, productivity did not suffer from either the casual dress code or the informal meeting arrangements. I found this all very interesting, though probably not relevant to my concerns.

I followed Sam along a winding path through the maze of cubicles to a glass-walled conference room in a back corner. A slender white man with salt-and-pepper hair was sitting at the wood laminate conference table, typing furiously on his laptop computer. When he saw me approach, he hit a key on the computer and the screen went dark. Unlike almost everyone else in the place, this man's attire was corporate formal. He wore a black power suit, white shirt, solid red tie and shiny black dress shoes.

He stood to greet me

"Mr. Becker, is it?" he asked, coming around the table and offering his hand. At the same time he subtly motioned at Sam to depart. Sam complied, silently disappearing into the maze of cubicles.

"Beck, please," I said, shaking his hand firmly. He had a strong handshake and looked me in the eye as we shook. "I hope I'm not disturbing you unduly. But there is a rather urgent situation involving your employee, Katherine Whitson. I am her husband's attorney and have been asked to inquire into her sudden disappearance."

"Oh, dear," Allister said. "When Katherine didn't show up for work Friday morning, I was concerned. She never misses work. And then when her husband called later that day looking for her . . . well, I didn't quite know what to think. Of course, I will help in any way I can."

"I appreciate your cooperation." I said. "Although originally, we were not quite certain whether Katherine had left her husband of her own volition, we are now convinced that she has been forcibly abducted."

"Oh my! How horrifying!" Allister seemed sincere.

"So I am pursuing any possible leads that might explain why someone would want to kidnap, or even possibly kill, Dr. Whitson."

"And you think there might be some connection at ComDyne?" Allister seemed dubious.

"Well. I am trying to be thorough. And she did spend most of her waking life in this office."

"Yes. I suppose that's true," Allister allowed. "Katherine works many hours. Still it seems unlikely that her work here would be connected. But please, ask your questions and I will do what I can."

He motioned me to a chair at the table and took one for himself.

"To start off with, it would help if I understood Katherine's job a bit better. Could you describe her position for me?"

"Yes. Certainly." There was a pause as Allister organized his thoughts. "To understand her position, you need to know something about our business here at ComDyne. We are a world leader in the manufacture of end-user computer networking components. We make smart switches, routers, connectors, hubs, control interfaces . . . . If it has to do with networking hardware, we probably make it."

"Okay," I said. "I don't know what all of those things are. But we can come back to them later if necessary. What is Katherine's role in your company?"

"I was just getting to that." Allister tried not to show arrogance and impatience; but it was seeping through, nevertheless. "Katherine heads up ComDyne's Quality Assurance and Testing Design Department."

I opened my mouth to ask what that entailed; but Allister raised a finger, and I waited.

"In layman's terms, Katherine is in charge of making sure ComDyne's products work reliably and according to their specifications. Of course, there are many employees who assist in this responsibility. But Katherine designs the methods by which the testing is conducted, and makes sure those methods ensure a quality product for our customers."

I raised my hand, like a school kid requesting the opportunity to speak.

"Yes?" Allister allowed.

"When you said Katherine is responsible for the methods of testing, what are we talking about here? Does she prescribe certain mechanical tools – like circuit testers or ammeters? Or does she compose software for the tests? Or what exactly does she do?"

Allister's impatience with my obvious technological stupidity was growing more pronounced.

"Mr. Becker . . ."

"Beck, please" I interrupted.

Allister took a breath.

"Mr. Becker," he continued, "suffice it to say that Katherine's responsibilities would encompass use of both hardware devices and complex software programs. She is quite adept at utilizing both to fulfill her job duties."

I could tell Allister's patience with my mere mortality was about to run out. I needed to get as much information as I could, as quickly as possible.

"Dr. Allister, could you explain your responsibilities and how they relate to Katherine's – in layman's terms, that is?" I tried to express 'humble' and 'sycophantic' at the same time. It was a stretch for me. It seemed to please Allister enough, though.

"I am the Systems Architect for all of ComDyne. There is only one Systems Architect. I alone bear complete responsibility for the ultimate design and technical implementation of every product we sell. I write the specifications for all hardware. I direct the creation of all software and firmware functionality. I personally select all component vendors to meet my high quality and performance requirements.

Without me, Mr. Becker, there would be no ComDyne."

An image of North Korean President, Kim Jong Il flashed through my mind. Allister was the poster child for megalomania.

"And Katherine's small part – what's the word – 'interfaced' with your responsibilities how?"

"Katherine is one of many at ComDyne who carry out their mundane secondary responsibilities. In Katherine's case, she reports all quality assurance issues to me for resolution."

"For instance . . . ?"

His patience was just about gone.

Allister took a breath before answering. "If her product testing revealed shoddy manufacture by one of our departments, or by a subcontractor, she would report her findings to me, and I would handle the problem. Is that simple enough?"

"One final question, if I may?" I tried to look as though I might kiss his ring.

"Very well. What is it?"

"How would you describe Katherine's abilities as an employee?"

"Average."

That was all he was going to say.

"Well, Mr. Allister . . ." I had dropped the "Dr." on purpose. I didn't like the man.

"It's Dr. Allister," he corrected.

"Yes. Well. Thank you for your time. I'll be sure to let the Whitsons know you wish them well."

He could tell I was getting cocky.

"Goodbye," he said as he returned to the laptop.

"And a lovely afternoon to you also." I smiled. He didn't look.

"SAM!" he called loudly.

Sam appeared immediately at the conference room door. "Please follow me, sir," he requested with a small bow.

"Thank you, Sam," I replied, and followed him out through the cubicles.

While we waited for the elevator, I asked Sam if Dr. Whitson took a laptop home from the office.

"Of course. She never goes anywhere without her computer. She told me that she might have a creative revelation at any time and she wanted to be ready when it happened."

"That makes sense," I responded. It was taking the elevator a while to arrive, so I took advantage of the opportunity. "How would you describe Dr. Whitson as a boss and company employee?"

Sam turned toward me.

"Oh, she is absolutely incredible! I graduated top of my class at Stanford in electrical engineering. Her thought processes are so far advanced beyond mine, it's actually scary. If she wanted, she could be the Systems Architect at nearly any company in the world. But she likes it here at ComDyne. She wants to stay in the Cities area, and most options for promotion would either be in Silicon Valley, or overseas."

We boarded the elevator and started down.

"Can you tell me, Sam . . . who is Dr. Whitson's second-in-command? Who is covering for her during her absence?"

"That would be Dr. Sustain – Julian Sustain. He is the Associate Director of Quality Assurance and Testing Design. He has been under a lot of stress with Dr. Whitson's absence. But he is doing as well as anyone could expect, under the circumstances."

The elevator doors opened and we walked toward the exit. I stopped just before we reached the doors.

"And your impressions of Dr. Allister?" I inquired.

"Oh. Of course, he is quite something as well," Sam managed, looking more at the floor than at me.

Quite something. Yes, indeed. Dr. Allister was certainly quite something.

CHAPTER 14

Tuesday, October 20th, 5:45 p.m.

I find driving to be a great time for reflection – provided, of course, that one is capable of competent driving and reflection simultaneously. Now that I was safely on the way home from ComDyne, having evaded any potential would-be attackers, I reflected on my day.

I now knew of three more persons in Katherine Whitson's inner circle. Her assistant, Sam. Her boss, Dr. Allister. And her able replacement, Dr. Sustain. They were all close enough to Katherine to have possible motives in her kidnapping. The most obvious one was Sustain's right of succession to Katherine's job. I wasn't sure what the others might be yet. But I would find out as quickly as I was able.

Besides the three new suspects, I had precious little to show for today's efforts. I'd taken a tongue-lashing from Minneapolis Police. I'd sucked up to a loathsome computer asshole. I knew a lot more about the law enforcement system, about ComDyne and about Katherine Whitson. Yet I couldn't identify any tangible progress toward finding her.

On the other hand, my attire was intact, and no one had tried to shoot me in the kneecaps. Could've been worse.

I slipped my cell out of an inner coat pocket and called home. A friendly voice would be nice.

Beth answered after three rings. "Hey, Magnum P.I., what's your e-t-a?"

"I'm just heading across the I-494 strip toward the airport. Depending on traffic, I should be home in about an hour. How about I whip us up some gourmet Tuscan cuisine for dinner?"

There was a pronounced gagging sound on the other end of the phone connection. So much for the friendly voice.

"Excuse me," Beth said presently. "I thought I heard you say you were going to cook. I experienced a sort of . . . ah . . . a visceral reaction. Were you wondering if I might make us some dinner?"

Beth was right, as she almost always is. I'm a lousy cook. I get distracted with other things and inevitably screw something up. I actually burned boiled eggs once. Seriously. I put the eggs into the boiling water. Then I took a phone call in the next room. By the time I remembered the eggs, the water was all gone and the egg shells were black on the bottom and smoking up the kitchen.

Anyway, Beth is the chef in our household – for painfully obvious reasons.

"If you would be so kind, I would be deeply in your debt," I replied with contrition. "Or I would also be delighted to have the pleasure of your company at a restaurant of your choosing."

"I'll throw something together on an appropriate timetable. See you soon. I love you."

Beth's words turned my insides to mush.

"Love you, too. Bye bye."

*   *   *

Dinner turned out to be fettuccine with portions of broiled walleye pike, all smothered in Alfredo sauce. A nice bottle of California Chardonnay complemented the meal – medium dry, rich and fruity, with just a touch of oak.

As we dined opposite one another at our black marble dinner table, we caught up on recent events.

"How was your day, my dear?" I inquired, following the line with a small forkful of Alfredo-drenched walleye.

"Really delightful. Lots of variety."

"Prithee, tell me more, m'lady."

Beth smiled politely at my feeble Renaissance repartee.

"Susan and I got in a workout at the 'Y' this morning." Susan was a neighbor on Jefferson Avenue. "Then we dawdled over coffee and scones at Lily's for more than an hour. It was so nice to catch up."

"That does sound fun," I said sincerely, sipping the Chardonnay.

"When I got home there was an email from my old work." She was referring to her top secret work for the CIA. "They had an encrypted file they wanted me to take a stab at. It's always fun having an opportunity to dust off the computer skills." Beth truly enjoyed her computer work.

"I bet. Were you successful?"

"In record time. They want me to come back to work in Washington."

"And what did you tell them?" I asked, nearing the end of my Chardonnay.

"I told them that if they could find me a better husband, I'd be right there." She smiled.

"So you're staying then." I said, taking a stab at some fettuccine.

Beth dipped a thumb and two fingers in her water glass and flicked a few drops at me across the table. I pretended to shield my face.

"Actually, I told them I had been thinking you were getting a bit long in the tooth and I would definitely consider a younger, more masculine spouse, if one became available."

She stuck out her tongue at me.

I stuck mine out back.

We are highly sophisticated folks at our house.

"Care for another splash of wine?" I asked. Beth's wine stem was still half full.

"No, thanks. Given your impish mood, I should probably keep my wits about me."

"Always a wise choice," I agreed, pouring the last of the Chardonnay into my glass. "By the way, if it would be okay to begin a new subject, you might be able to help me out with the mysterious disappearance of Katherine Whitson. Are you willing to give it a shot?"

"What's mine is yours. Fire away."

"Katherine's disappearance is almost certain to involve foul play," I began. "I haven't been able to track down any leads through her husband; though I was assaulted at his place of business. . . ."

Beth waited patiently.

"There's one guy who used to have Whitson's job and might have an axe to grind. But I would think if someone wanted to get at George by using Katherine, we would have seen a ransom note, or some claim of responsibility, by now. Anyway, Gunner is checking this guy out to see if he's a plausible suspect."

Beth sipped her wine.

"Today, I paid a visit to Katherine's workplace, ComDyne Integrated, in Maple Grove, and had a chat with her supervisor."

"Is that the same ComDyne that makes all the computer networking gear?" Beth asked.

"Yes, indeed. So you've heard of them?"

"They are one of the largest, if not the largest, network equipment manufacturers in the world. They certainly make more network routers than anyone else."

Beth never ceased to amaze me.

"That's the company. Katherine's job there was . . ." I glanced at a note from my pants pocket . . . "the head of Quality Assurance and Test Design. Does that mean anything to you?"

"Yes. She's probably incredibly brilliant. And she lives and breathes computer technology. You don't get that sort of a position at a company like ComDyne without earning a doctorate or two, maybe in math or double E. Then you've got to work your way zealously up through the ranks. You need to become more knowledgeable, more creative and more thorough than anyone else when it comes to your systems. In other words, you've got to be something of a computer god – or in this case, goddess."

"Wow!" I said. "That's impressive. How impressive do you need to be in order to be her boss, the Systems Architect for ComDyne?"

"At Katherine's level, whether she could be the Systems Architect for ComDyne would not be a question of how impressive, or intelligent, or hard-working she was. It would be determined either by seniority at the company, or by specific knowledge of ComDyne's particular hardware and software systems. In other words, she could have the Systems Architect job, unless there was another, very well-qualified genius already occupying the role – which I assume there is."

"He certainly thinks so. The guy's name is Allister and he's pretty confident he's god's gift to mankind – or maybe god is his gift to mankind – it could go either way." I continued. "So is there anything you could think of about Katherine's job at ComDyne that might place her person in peril?"

"Is money a motive for peril?" Beth asked, knowing the answer.

"Is that the refined version of 'does a bear shit in the woods?'" I asked.

"Um hmm," Beth said into her wine glass, then replaced it on the table. "ComDyne is a multibillion dollar business. Katherine's job is to make sure internal quality control is maintained. There are probably a thousand ways she could piss off someone badly enough to place her life in jeopardy."

"For instance?" I inquired.

This was great! My own personal computer expert – and an awesome cook and lover to boot.

Beth thought for a moment.

"Suppose that your company supplies a billion dollars per year worth of a particular part for ComDyne's smart switches. Katherine discovers that your company's product isn't meeting required specs. If ComDyne drops your company as a supplier, you go out of business. Is that enough motive for foul play?" Again, she knew the answer.

"Why yes, I believe it would be. And you say that there are potentially thousands of such scenarios that might create perils for someone in Katherine's position?"

"Yes," Beth stated. "Without a doubt."

"I wonder why Allister didn't mention any of this potential risk," I said it out-loud, but was really talking to myself.

"You're the guru on abnormal psychology," Beth reminded me. "I'm sure you can come up with a few theories." She was helping guide my thoughts in a direction they should have already gone.

There are no quick and dirty answers in psychology. I would need to let this issue course through my cerebral cortex a few times. Sleep is good for that. I'd be able to pursue this line of thought more effectively tomorrow.

"Doll," I said, looking across the marble at Beth, "you are one amazing chick."

"Should I get an 'Amazing Chick' T-shirt? Or should we keep it to ourselves."

"I like the T-shirt idea," I said. "But maybe yours should have an arrow pointing to one side and read: 'I'm with Stupid.'"

"We could do that." Beth smiled.

My insides turned to cream of wheat. I wanted a T-shirt for myself that said: "Can you believe she's with me?"

CHAPTER 15

Still Tuesday, October 20th.

Before I could retire for the evening, I had to make sure I was simultaneously pursuing as many leads as possible. Besides Arthur Trample, whom Gunner would be researching, and whom I considered a low-value target, there were four additional suspects that I knew of.

George Whitson was still among their ranks. But he wasn't going anywhere. And if he had done something to Katherine, it had probably been murder. Why . . . and how . . . would he kidnap her? Besides, George didn't strike me as enough of a mastermind to invite Gunner and me to investigate a crime that he, himself, had committed. I could put George aside for the time being.

There was Dr. Julian Sustain, Katherine's understudy at ComDyne. Someone should be checking him out. He would have the most to gain, from a professional standpoint, with Katherine gone. How cutthroat was the rarified air at very high levels of technology employment?

And Dr. Allister was certainly an unlikeable enough person. Plus his entirely narcissistic view of the world made him a strong candidate for psycho-social deviancy. No one could predict the level of behavior to which he might stoop if he felt that his ego was threatened.

And finally, there was Sam – last name presently unknown – Katherine's intern. What might he have to gain from her disappearance? He had seemed a very nice young man. But then, appearances can be deceiving.

I picked up the phone to call Bull.

"Watcha need?" he answered.

"It's Beck," I said.

"Got Caller ID."

"Right," I said. "I've got three guys I need to tail, and there's only one of me. Any chance you could help me out?"

"When and where?"

I gave Bull a description of Julian Sustain, which I had procured from his picture on a tech website. Apparently, he spoke at a lot of conferences. I also told Bull where Sustain lived and worked. And I explained why I needed him watched. Bull needed to know what level of danger he might be getting himself into. I asked if Bull could start tomorrow morning and we would see where it went from there.

He was on board.

I had two unmarked suspects left – Sam and Allister.

I chose Allister. I had liked Sam when we met, and Allister was a jerk. If I had to spin a bottle for surveillance choices, it was definitely going to wind up on Allister.

With Gunner tied up at work, and doing background work on Trample, surveillance on Sam would have to wait.

Field investigations would continue in earnest tomorrow. Now it was time for sleep.

CHAPTER 16

Wednesday, October 21st.

It was Wednesday morning around eight o'clock. Beth and I had completed our morning workouts and I was sitting on the red couch holding a large ceramic cup of steaming black coffee between both hands. It had been a brutally cold run – high winds and a temperature near twenty degrees Fahrenheit. It's pretty easy to dress properly for temperature; wind is another matter. The coffee was wonderful.

Beth had received another computer assignment from Washington and was cheerfully clicking away at her keyboard in the dining room. It is a verifiable fact that, in the working world, the better you perform at your job, the more work you get. That would seem a negative incentive to exemplary job performance to some. But to Beth, since she loved her work, the additional assignments were like getting an "atta boy" from corporate. From Beth's hummed rendition of George Harrison's "Here Comes the Sun," I surmised that she would be happily occupied on her project for at least a while.

Unfortunately, the clock was ticking on Katherine Whitson's absence. I knew the statistics. The longer she remained missing, the worse her chances of survival. I needed to work efficiently.

My job today was to put eyes on Allister. So as soon as I had finished my coffee, I showered, dressed and headed off to Maple Grove, and the ComDyne office complex.

Gunner had given me makes, models and license numbers for two vehicles owned by Allister – one was a gold Cadillac; the other, a black Lincoln. I circled the main lot until I spotted the Lincoln. It was parked in a choice spot near the main building entrance. The spot was clearly marked for "Dr. Allister," and was at least twice the width of typical parking slots.

Since I was in no hurry, I drove around the rest of the ComDyne parking lots, just to make sure that his Caddy wasn't also on campus. It wasn't. I returned to the main lot and parked near the rear, backing into my spot so I could make an expeditious exit if necessary.

At least it shouldn't be difficult keeping an eye on Allister's car.

I knew how tedious long-term surveillance could be. So I had brought some other work along with me. Maybe I could multi-task Katherine's case. Perhaps that would give me a chance for quicker resolution.

As I worked in my car, I would regularly peek at Allister's Lincoln, to make sure it didn't escape the lot without my notice.

Sliding my laptop from its case on the front passenger seat, I opened it on my lap. I had decided to revisit the downloaded phone records first. I had only given them a quick once-over before. I started with Katherine's detailed phone information.

As is true when examining most large data sets, no patterns or anomalies jumped out at me immediately. But the longer one looks, the more the mass of data becomes an intricately woven fabric. Designs repeat. And oddly-placed stitches stand out. After absorbing Katherine's phone data for the better part of an hour, I had found a few items of interest.

The only speed-dial numbers she had bothered to enter were: George's cell and work numbers; her home land line; and several numbers I recognized as ComDyne telephone extensions.

Two of the ComDyne numbers were for Sam and Allister. I had no idea to whom the others might belong. Maybe Sustain was among them?

I also noted that, every weekday, she would call George on his cell between noon and 1:00 p.m.

Sam called Katherine several times a week – usually on weekends or evenings. Sam had also called multiple times after her disappearance. Obviously, those calls went unanswered. Was he unaware of her kidnapping? Or just trying to make himself look innocent?

Even though Allister had made the short, speed-dial list, she hadn't telephoned him at all during the time period stored on the phone – which was roughly the past two months. He hadn't called her cell either. Apparently, they conducted their voice communications, if any, at the office. That seemed normal to me given Katherine's reported extreme competence and Allister's grating personality.

It was interesting, though, that Allister hadn't made an attempt to reach Katherine on her cell when she failed to show for work Friday. Maybe he had delegated that duty to Sam. That would be in character for Allister – too important to deal with missing employees himself. Or maybe the call from George on Friday had been all the notice he cared to have. He was a very busy and important man after all.

I would file this failure to call in my mind for future consideration.

There was one phone call from George early Friday morning. That was peculiar. Why would he call Katherine's cell when he knew it to be lying on their bed? Drunken desperation? Possibly. But early morning didn't seem a likely time for that.

Had Whitson been fibbing about coming home Thursday evening? Did he have something to hide? I would definitely have to confront Whitson about this call. Either he was lying about being home Thursday evening, or . . .

I couldn't complete the sentence. It made no sense. Why would he call her at a time when he knew she was already gone from the apartment and had left her phone behind – and he had already admitted as much to Gunner and me? He had to be lying about something.

Damn it! I hate being lied to.

And if he'd lied to me once, that called everything he had told me into question. I would, indeed, have another chat with George. I had to get to the bottom of this discrepancy, but carefully, and soon.

I flicked another glance through my windshield at the black Lincoln. Still there. I'd been looking out the window every few seconds. My pupils had established a rhythm.

Finding nothing further of interest in Katherine's cell records, I turned to the download from Whitson's phone.

His speed-dial list was as sparse as Katherine's. Home; Katherine's cell; work (only one number – presumably his secretary); and an entry labeled "BA."

His list of sent and received calls was longer than Katherine's. He'd called Katherine almost daily, but not at any consistent time. His incoming calls recorded the daily noontime visits with Katherine. And there were multiple call exchanges with "BA."

Maybe I had been focusing too much on Katherine's life and needed to home in a bit more closely on George. I added identifying "BA" to my mental to-do list for George's interrogation.

More complete telephone records might also reveal further important information. My next call was to Gunner's cell.

"I'm in a meeting," Gunner answered quietly.

"Then why the hell did you answer my call? That's what voicemail is for, Gunner. Sheesh! Call my cell when you get the chance." We both disconnected the call without a goodbye – at least I think it was both of us.

Ten minutes later Gunner's name appeared on my ringing cell phone.

"Geez, Gunner! I'm in a meeting. What the hell do you want?" I answered.

"Oh, cut the crap. You called me. What do you need?"

"So now that the coffee klatch is dispersed, you have time for me? The donuts all gone?"

"Spit it out or let me go." Gunner was in no mood for humor.

"All right. I need to get more complete phone records for the Whitsons. Can you get me a year's worth of everything on all of their cell phones, their home land line, and maybe, their office extensions?"

"The personal cells and home phone won't be a problem. But I am doubtful about the work info. The employers would have to consent – unless you can give me probable cause?" Gunner offered.

"That would be a 'No' to the probable cause," I conceded.

"Are you finding anything interesting in the on-phone data?" Gunner asked.

"Maybe. But only question marks so far," I responded.

"Isn't that the way of the world? More questions than answers." A brief pause. "Anything else I might find for you?"

"Yes, as a matter of fact, there is. Can you get me a name and address to go with this phone number?" I relayed BA's number to Gunner. "He may be what you cops call 'a person of interest,' so please don't let him catch on that you're looking."

"Gosh, it might be tough to be sneaky about it." His voice was a pretty decent impersonation of the Disney "Goofy" character. "But my assistant, Barney Fife, and I will do our best."

I ignored the remark.

"Anything new on Arthur Trample?"

"Nothing yet. Still waiting for some feelers to come back in."

"Okay. Thanks a million, Gunner. Shoot me an email with the Whitsons' telephone records, if that's okay?"

"Sure thing, Boss. Good luck and keep me posted. Connie is pressing for nonstop updates. I tell her it takes time. But that doesn't seem to console her much."

"In that case, I'll work as quick and sloppy as possible. Thanks again. Bye."

Still no movement from the Lincoln.

Back on my laptop, I took another look at the photos of the impeccably-organized Whitson home. The less-organized space in Katherine's closet. The cubby where the sole missing pair of business shoes should have been. I zoomed in on the medicine cabinet. Miscellaneous makeup and toiletries missing;

but Katherine's anxiety medication bottle and contact lenses still present.

I zoomed in further. There was another bottle of something I didn't recognize. On closer examination, it turned out to be a jumbo bottle of over-the-counter sleeping pills. I wondered if they belonged to Katherine or George.

I looked again at the pictures of the items on the bed. Katherine's phone had been turned off when I borrowed it. Why weren't there "missed call" notifications beeping at me when I'd fired it up? George and Sam had both called after Katherine's supposed disappearance. George must have turned it off at some point after the last call had arrived.

That sonofabitch was really pushing my buttons. And my list of questions for him was growing longer.

The photos of other rooms showed the lack of computer equipment and not much else of interest. Of course, the photos taken collectively, did seem to show the absence of a struggle. Had Katherine known her abductor? Had the abduction taken place elsewhere? Was the note truly in her handwriting? I had taken George's word for that one.

I wished I had a team from television's CSI to comb the apartment, looking for fibers, microbes, bodily fluids and such. "If wishes were horses," my father used to say, "beggars would ride." A metaphorical horse would be nice about now. Or maybe some assistance from Minneapolis PD!

I still had more of Gunner's report to revisit. I pulled that up on my screen.

Wow! George Whitson made close to $200,000 a year for shuffling paper. Maybe I should have been an accountant. I looked for Katherine's income information. Her salary was nearly double George's. That didn't surprise me; but it did explain how they could afford the nice digs.

The Whitsons kept their investments in separate accounts. George had some funds in his name and Katherine had a larger sum in hers. Only their checkbook and the condo were joint. This wasn't the way Beth and I handled our finances. But it was common enough. Nothing earthshattering.

Gunner had also come across a couple life insurance policies. Each of the Whitsons held a three million-dollar policy on the other's life – payable to the survivor. The insurance money would provide a motive for George to kill Katherine. But her substantial income was also a motive to keep her alive – unless she planned to leave him . . . .

As far as financial obligations went, neither of the Whitsons appeared to have any debt problems. They owned the condo free and clear. There was no evidence of gambling or other unusual cash flows in the check registers or bank statements. George used a fair amount of cash compared to Katherine. But it was not an extraordinary amount, given the sizeable funds available. All-in-all, there were no smoking guns to be found in the Whitsons' finances.

Gunner had also located copies of Wills for the Whitsons. Each left everything to the other, with various charities being the contingent beneficiaries upon the last spouse's death. The Wills also had provisions to allow the survivor to "disclaim," that is, to refuse to accept, some or all of his/her inheritance. I knew from my legal background that such provisions are designed to avoid paying more estate taxes than necessary upon the death of the last surviving spouse. Given that neither a surviving spouse, nor the charitable beneficiaries, would need to pay estate taxes anyway, these provisions appeared superfluous. But they certainly didn't hurt anything either.

I scanned through the remainder of Gunner's document report. Nothing leapt out at me. I closed my laptop and returned it to its case. Leaning back against the leather seat, I again reviewed my list of suspects.

George Whitson's apparent deception, Katherine's life insurance proceeds, and her Will leaving everything to George had moved him further up the list. As Ricky Ricardo would say, he definitely "had some 'splainin' to do."

BA was an unknown quantity, and therefore, had to be considered a possible evildoer.

Allister, Sustain, Trample and Sam were all still in play as well. I hoped we could weed some of them out soon.

And then there were the "thousand or so" people or companies who might want Katherine gone because of some aspect of her job. I also needed to try to get a better handle on this mega-group and whittle it down to a manageable number.

Maybe Bull and Gunner would come up with something definitive. One could hope.

I returned my undivided focus to the black Lincoln.

CHAPTER 17

Gunner, or Barney, or whoever retrieved telephone records for the Ottawa County Sheriff's Department, excelled in efficiency today. It was barely 1:00 p.m. when I received the cell call from Gunner that the email he had promised was ready. Still stuck in the ComDyne parking lot, I fired up the laptop again and downloaded the email, together with a large attachment containing very detailed information concerning the Whitsons' phone usage over the past year.

The identity and particulars for one Bruce Adams, aka BA, were in the message body. Apparently, Gunner hadn't been able to get the Whitsons' work telephone info, at least not yet.

Scanning the phone records for specifics I had been missing in my previous data, I found some additional information about the lengths of calls and the period of months over which they had been made that was most helpful.

Now I needed to speak with Whitson. Since my clone was unavailable, I would have to abandon surveillance of Allister. It couldn't be helped.

A surprise appearance at Whitson's office would have the best chance of success. But given the reception I had received in the parking ramp during my last visit to Equinox, I decided to ask Bull to join me.

Bull agreed to drop his tail on Sustain, but indicated that there was something he would need to discuss with me later. He had piqued my interest. But Bull had hung up before I could delve deeper.

We rendezvoused at a shopping center parking lot and rode together in the Pilot to Eden Prairie. I didn't want to miss out on a chance that my truck might bait the bad guys into action, as it had on the last occasion.

"Good to see you again," I said to Bull as he climbed into the front passenger seat of the Pilot.

"Uh huh," was his reply.

"Care to reveal your secrets about today's surveillance?" I asked as we pulled out of the lot and onto I-494 South.

"Nope." Bull was looking out his side window.

Bull was not one to make small talk. He was perfectly comfortable sitting quietly. Maybe it's an Indian thing? I don't know.

"Have anything tasty for breakfast?" I goaded.

Bull turned his head toward me, his long, black hair appearing to move in slow motion as his face arrived directly over his left shoulder. He raised his brows as his eyes pierced mine. He wasn't smiling. But he wasn't upset either. He was just letting me know to shut up unless I had something to say. I could live with that.

"Guess not," I answered for Bull, turning my attention back to the road ahead.

Bull resumed looking out his window. I wondered what he was looking at. For all I knew, he was making faces at vehicles as we passed them on the four-lane. That could be either very frightening, or very funny – depending on the faces.

As we eventually approached Equinox Headquarters, I pulled over and let Bull out. He would walk the last half-mile, to be certain we weren't observed together. It was his idea. "Stop here," he had said, then jumped out of the truck.

I watched for anyone acting in a suspicious manner as I rolled slowly through the ramp to the Visitors section of Level Two. Nothing unusual. I parked in nearly the same spot as before, then continued into the second floor building entrance. This time, since I knew where I was headed, I just kept going straight through the second floor doorway and down the hall to the elevators. I pushed the "Up" button and presently an empty car arrived. Boarding the elevator, I punched the button for the sixth floor.

As I entered the Executive Office Suite, I found the entryway unguarded. Apparently, most visitors call ahead. So I proceeded unimpeded to Whitson's office. I checked my watch – 3:00 p.m. Good time for a nice cordial chat. Without knocking, I opened Whitson's door and strode through.

Whitson was seated at his oak desk, but facing the matching credenza behind it. There was something on his computer screen that he clearly preferred I not see. Panicked at my abrupt entry, he fumbled for the monitor's power button and clicked it off. I waited. Then he rotated the chair toward me and stood.

"Becker! What the hell! Don't you knock?"

"I pay respect to those to whom it is due," I responded enigmatically.

Whitson tried to settle his nerves. He could see from my expression that I was not happy.

"What the hell does that mean?" he mustered, shifting his weight from one foot to the other, not sounding very intimidating.   In fact, his voice was nearly a whole register higher than at our previous meetings.

"It means," I said, "that you have been lying to me and I don't like it."

"What are you talking about?" Whitson stumbled into his chair and sat. "I have been completely honest and up-front . . . ."

I interrupted him.

"Bull shit!" I said, stepping closer and leaning forward, my knuckles on his desk.

Whitson's nose was about two feet from mine. He didn't like it.

"Where were you the night Katherine disappeared?" I continued.

"I've already told you" he said, fidgeting with his hands. "I got home around 7:30 that evening and was at work until then."

"In that case, I'm sure you can explain to me why you were calling Katherine's cell phone Friday morning from the home of one Bruce Adams, Hampton Greens Condominiums, Apartment 407, when you already knew damn well that her cell phone was unattended and lying on your bed?"

I leaned a bit closer. He scooted his chair backward defensively. He knew he was caught.

"How did you know I was at Bruce's Friday morning?" he asked sheepishly.

"You just told me," I said. "Now . . . can we have a discussion where you tell me the truth and no more BS, because your wife's life may very well depend upon it?"

"Yes." Whitson's appearance reflected guilt, contrition and a substantial fear that I was going to jump over the desk and smack him. "Of course."

"Okay then," I said. I closed the door and occupied one of Whitson's side chairs. "Tell me what you really know about Katherine's situation."

"Katherine really did disappear on Thursday night, sometime. I know because, when she didn't answer her cell early Friday morning, I went to the apartment and the bed had not been slept in. And there were no Friday breakfast dishes in the dishwasher."

"How do you know that she hadn't made the bed and eaten breakfast elsewhere, or not at all?" I pressed.

"Katherine and I have our routines. And we have divided the household responsibilities. I am very particular about how the bed is made. Katherine can never get it right. So I know it wasn't slept in, because she wouldn't have made the bed. And if she had made it, it wouldn't have been done right – and it was right."

That Whitson was OCD about how the bed was to be made was entirely believable.

"Go on," I said.

"And Katherine always has raisin bran and orange juice for breakfast and puts her dishes in the dishwasher. There was no bowl, no glass and no spoon in the dishwasher from Friday morning breakfast," Whitson continued.

"So the 7:30 time is made up?" I confirmed.

"Yes."

"But she did not sleep at the apartment Thursday night?"

"Yes. I mean, true."

I sensed that I was getting some candor from Whitson at this point. We would see how long it continued.

"So, tell me your actual whereabouts from the time you left work Thursday at . . . ?"

"7:00 p.m."

" . . . at 7:00 p.m., until you called the police Friday morning," I said.

"After work, I went right to Bruce's place. He can confirm that for you. We had dinner there and I . . . I . . . ah . . . spent the night. I left Bruce's right after Katherine failed to answer my call Friday morning and was home ten minutes later."

Whitson's drawn, tired face showed signs that he was telling me something he had held inside for a very long time. His hands no longer twitched. His shoulders sagged.

Again, I believed him. That he had been hiding this same-sex relationship from the world was, once more, very plausible.

"So you are Bruce's alibi and he is yours." I noted. "Isn't that a bit convenient for two lovers to be the only ones to vouch for one another during the commission of a felony against one of their spouses?"

Whitson looked panicky again. Then he had an idea.

"Listen! Bruce's building has security cameras and everyone needs to log in and out. The building security tapes should confirm what I am telling you." He appeared a bit relieved. "That should help. Right?"

I knew it was possible to circumvent any security system, having done so myself on many occasions. But it wasn't an easy thing to do without certain expertise and training, depending of course, upon the security system. Still, I would check the security tapes if I didn't get satisfaction from Whitson in today's conversation.

"Did you handle any of the items left on your bed?" I asked, switching topics.

"I picked up the note to read it," he said. "Then I put it back where it had been. Otherwise, I don't think I touched anything."

"Then how come I have irrefutable evidence that you turned off Katherine's phone Friday morning?"

I leaned forward in my chair, looking intimidating.

"Oh my gosh. I'm so sorry. I forgot. The phone was beeping, like when you have a missed message. I opened the phone, saw there were no messages from Katherine or any possible kidnapper, and then shut it off. I forgot I did that. I'm sorry, Mr. Becker. I really forgot. Honest."

This guy was too much of a wimp to be a violent felon. Again, I believed his tale about the phone. When you have experienced interrogation as much as I have – from both sides of the table – you develop a sense for when someone is lying, and when they are just clueless. Whitson was the latter.

"Okay. So tell me about Bruce. You met him about three months ago." I started the story for him.

"Yes. How did you know?" Whitson really was naive.

"Your phone records. Now, tell me about Bruce," I persisted.

"Bruce and I met at a gay bar on Hennepin Avenue, The Rainbow Bar-Fait. I go there often, but had not seen Bruce there before."

"Keep going," I said.

"Bruce was really cute. I was sitting at the bar and there was an empty stool beside me. Bruce came over and offered to buy me a drink. Things sort of went from there and I spent the night at his hotel."

"His hotel? Was he new in town?"

"Actually, yes. You are incredibly intuitive, Mr. Becker. I don't know how you know these things."

"Let me try a few more guesses," I offered. "After a few dates, Bruce, who is temporarily out of work while attending school of some sort, mentions that he doesn't have the money to stay in Minneapolis, and he will probably need to go back home soon. You kindly offer to put him up in an apartment at the Hampton Greens Condominiums, which offer he humbly accepts.

How am I doing so far?"

"He was studying cosmetology," Whitson replied, his mouth hanging a bit open.

"Anyway, you had plenty of cash and were looking for a long-term, same-sex relationship. Bruce seemed to provide hope of that developing. So you paid the rent, bought the groceries, paid for the utilities and cable TV. You even fronted Bruce some spending money from time to time, just to help him along with his education."

By this time, even Whitson could tell this was not a new story.

"What do you know about Bruce's background before two months ago?" I asked. "I mean, what do you really know about Bruce that hasn't come directly from Bruce himself?"

Whitson's jaw dropped even further. He was silent for a moment.

"I guess . . . really . . . nothing?" he managed.

"Okay. So are you still sure he was with you the whole time from Thursday evening until you left for home Friday?"

I watched Whitson's eyes for veracity.

"Yes. We were definitely together that whole time."

"You're positive?"

"Yes. And again, I'm sure the security footage will confirm as much."

Damn it! I believed him again. Oh well. It is what it is. If neither Bruce nor Whitson kidnapped Katherine, someone else did.

"Okay," I continued. "Where do you suppose Bruce is right now?"

"Probably in class."

"Hold that thought for a moment," I said as I produced my cell from a jacket pocket. I punched a speed-dial key and waited for an answer.

"Any news?" I asked. "Okay. Thanks." I closed my phone and put it away.

"Please call Bruce on his cell and let him know you are coming over to his place in half an hour."

Whitson looked reluctant.

"Do it!" I insisted.

Whitson reached for his cell phone and punched up BA's number.

A moment later Whitson said, "What the hell? Who is this? Who is this?" He looked at me in bewilderment.

"Let's take a walk," I said, gesturing toward the office door.

Whitson was too dazed to do anything but my bidding. We headed out of the Executive Offices, down the elevator to the second floor, and out the door to parking Level Two.

Standing behind my Pilot was a very large American Indian, and in his grip, a wriggling twenty-something year-old man with highly-coiffed blond hair.

Bull held a cell phone out toward Whitson.

"It's you," he said matter-of-factly.

Bull had found Bruce sneaking around my car and intervened before I would have need of further tire repair.

"Mr. Whitson," I asked. "Does this happen to be Bruce?"

Whitson could hardly speak. "Yes," he said finally.

The boy continued to squirm in vain. At one point, he tried to punch Bull in the face. Bull caught the swinging fist in his left hand and squeezed until Bruce stopped squirming.

"So, Bruce," I said, turning to the captive con-man. "You don't happen to know a guy named Buffy who tried to damage my kneecaps here yesterday, do you?"

Bruce remained silent.

Using only his right hand, Bull lifted Bruce by the shirt and shook him once, then put him back on the concrete.

"Okay. Yeah. Yeah. I didn't know his name; but I did send somebody over here to keep you away from George," Bruce admitted.

"Why?" I asked.

More silence.

Bull started to lift the boy again.

"Wait. Wait," he squealed.

Bull returned Bruce to terra firma.

"I was afraid you were going to find out I was a scam and that I was milking Georgy for all I could get. And by the way," Bruce asserted in his own defense, "it appears I was right to be concerned."

I laughed. "Apparently so."

"Mr. Whitson," I said, turning to George. "Would you care to press charges against Mr. Adams?"

Whitson lacked the energy to even decide the question. "Let him go for now," Whitson said. "I'll think about charges later." Whitson's head hung in utter embarrassment and fatigue.

"Well, Bruce," I said. "Mr. Whitson is willing to let you go for now. But I'm not so forgiving."

Bruce looked frightened.

"I had to fork out 450 bucks to get my tires fixed yesterday. And my friend needs to be reimbursed for his efforts. An even thousand should do it."

"Where am I going to get that kind of money?" Bruce whined.

"You blew $500 yesterday on a lame hit-man. I'm betting you're holding enough cash right now to satisfy your obligations. Shall I ask Mr. Bull to help you find it?"

"God, no!" Bruce dug through his wallet and then his pockets. "Here's your grand," he said. "Can I go now?"

"One more thing," I said. "When you depart here in about sixty seconds, you will clear out of Hampton Greens, leaving behind every single item that was bought with Mr. Whitson's money, but no trace of a mess. And if you do so, you may not have to deal with my friend and me again. Got it?"

"Okay. Okay." A recognition of defeat.

I nodded at Bull and he let go of Bruce's shirt. Bruce took a final wild swing at Bull, who grabbed Bruce's hitting arm and flung him skidding across the concrete.

"Ouch!" I said. "That road rash is a bitch. Make sure to clean all wounds thoroughly with warm soap and water."

Bruce scrambled to his feet and stumbled off down the ramp-way.

I turned to Whitson. I actually felt sorry for him.

"Did Katherine know about Bruce?"

"Yes. And the others before him." Whitson was on the verge of tears. "Please find her. You have to find her."

"We will certainly do our best," I promised. "Maybe you should knock off for the rest of the day. Catch a nap. You look exhausted."

"I'm sure you are correct. I will take your suggestion."

*   *   *

Back in the Pilot and on the way to his vehicle, Bull was, again, silent.

"Now, what is this issue we need to discuss about your surveillance?" I demanded. "Let's hear it."

"Saw Sustain and Sam together at lunch," he said, looking out his side window.

That was a development I had not anticipated; though it might not be unusual for co-workers to lunch together.

"What do you make of the meeting?"

"Don't know. But they was in the restaurant for an hour-and-a-half."

"Something else to think about," I said.

Bull continued staring out his window.

Just before we arrived at the lot where Bull's truck was parked, I asked him, "So . . . did you have any fun today?"

Bull turned toward me, as he had when we were heading for Equinox. But this time, after staring stonily at me for a moment, his face broke into a broad smile.

CHAPTER 18

There was still a little time before most of the employees would be heading home from their work day at ComDyne. If I were to have any hope of finding Katherine soon, I was going to have to back one horse against the others. My gut told me that Sam could be trusted.

But I needed to find out about his lunch with Sustain. The more I thought about it, the less routine it seemed for an intern to eat lunch with his high-powered superior. I needed to resolve the inconsistency.

I called Sam's extension on my cell.

"This is Sam," he answered.

"Sam," I said. "It's James Becker. Do you remember me?"

"Dr. Whitson's attorney. Have you found her?"

He sounded sincerely concerned.

"I'm afraid not. But Sam, I need to meet with you privately – as soon as possible. And it can't be at ComDyne. When and where can we meet?"

I held my breath, hoping he would agree to my request.

"Absolutely. There's a bar and grill called Dooley's two exits south of ComDyne off 494. I can meet you there in one hour . . . if that's okay?"

"Perfect. See you then. And Sam, please don't tell anyone that we're getting together."

"Got it."

So far so good. I would meet with Sam, and then go with whatever my gut told me was right. My instincts were usually good. I would need to trust them now if I had hopes of finding Katherine soon.

*   *   *

I found Dooley's right where Sam said it would be. Procuring a booth in a back corner, I waited for the intern.

Precisely at the appointed time, I saw Sam come through the door. I walked over to the entry, greeted Sam, and showed him to my booth.

I offered to buy Sam dinner. We could eat while we talked. But he graciously declined, professing to have dinner plans with a young lady later that evening. Instead, we ordered iced tea with lemon.

After the waitress left our table, I took a deep breath and dove in.

"Sam," I said. "I need someone I can trust to help me find Dr. Whitson – someone who knows the people at ComDyne. I think you might be that person."

Sam blushed. It is difficult to fake a blush.

"I would be honored to help Dr. Whitson any way I can," he said, finally.

"Great! But I have one question I need to ask you before you can help me."

"Go ahead," Sam said. "You name it."

"I understand that you had lunch with Dr. Sustain this afternoon. Is that right?"

"Yes."

"Do you lunch together often?"

"No," Sam said. "Never."

"How did you happen to end up eating together today then?"

I felt embarrassed even asking these questions. Sam seemed such a great kid.

"Dr. Allister asked us to both meet him at the restaurant."

"Dr. Allister? Was he there, too."

"You know, that was really weird," Sam said. "He told each of us separately to meet him at the restaurant. But then he didn't show.

Dr. Sustain was really mad. He had lots of work to do with Dr. Whitson out of the office. He said he couldn't afford to take a lunch break for no reason."

Allister! I should have stayed with his Lincoln in the first place. The arranged lunch between my other suspects was a diversion.

"I see. Did Dr. Allister later explain his absence?"

"Oh, no. And we wouldn't have expected him to either. You don't just question Dr. Allister."

I supposed that was true.

I had heard enough. I was convinced of Sam's loyalty to Katherine. And I was now focusing in on Allister.

"Thank you, Sam," I said. "I apologize for having to ask these questions. But it is all very important to ensure Dr. Whitson's safe recovery."

"I understand," Sam allowed. "How can I help?"

"As soon as I know, I'll be in touch," I said. "But maybe I should get your cell number, so we don't have to go through the ComDyne phone system."

That seemed good enough for Sam. And he happily provided me with his private number.

We finished our tea and went our separate ways.

CHAPTER 19

Thursday, October 22nd, 9:00 a.m.

It was already Thursday morning, the eighth day after Katherine's disappearance. I was becoming increasingly certain that this investigation was going to be more a recovery operation than a rescue.

To add to my frustration, I hadn't yet set foot in Becker Law Office this week. I knew I absolutely had to go in today – at least for a while. Even though my legal secretary, Karen, really makes the office tick, she would occasionally require my input, or at least my signature. Despite my intense desire to keep a full court press on the Katherine Whitson case, I couldn't renege on my client commitments.

So after making calls to Bull – to babysit Allister – and Gunner – to ask him to divert his research energies to Sustain – I couldn't ethically avoid doing legal work today. The Whitson investigation would have to survive for now on the strength of Gunner's and Bull's efforts.

Wearing my gun and my lawyer outfit, complete with London Fog topcoat, I climbed into the Pilot and headed to work. The weather was a little better this morning than yesterday, when Beth and I had battled the wind and cold on our run. But the northwesterly wind had blown a cold front through.

Temperatures today were unseasonably low, even for Minnesota in October. The high temp would only reach the upper teens this afternoon. I hoped that wherever Katherine was, if she was alive, she was at least staying warm.

Becker Law Office is located on the upper level of a two-story bank building. Because the bank was built into a hill, the second level is accessible directly from the upper level of the asphalt parking lot. I parked the Pilot and entered the building through the second floor entrance. My office was the first suite on the right.

I stepped through the heavy oak door into the waiting area. "Hi, Karen. How's tricks?"

"M-i-s-t-e-r B-e-c-k-e-r," Karen said, raising one eyebrow. "Long time no see. I was worried sick over you."

Sarcasm?

"Yeah, right," I said continuing into the main office area and unbuttoning my trench coat as I walked.

The main office area was divided into work spaces by oak-trimmed half-walls. I approached Karen's space and leaned both elbows on the oak top of the wall. I was looking down at her as she sat at her desk. Yet somehow, she appeared to have the upper hand. The fact that her arms lay folded across her chest indicated that I needed to offer an explanation, an apology, or more likely, both.

"Karen, I'm really sorry to have abandoned you for the first few days this week." She raised that eyebrow again. "Okay . . . for pretty much all week. But I have a good excuse."

"I can't wait to hear it." Karen had been practicing her sarcasm all right.

Somehow I sensed that I wouldn't be able to give my investigative pursuits the right spin to gain Karen's sympathy. So I tried a different approach.

"Karen. This is what happened.

I was visiting the Minnesota Zoo on Sunday afternoon," I began, shrugging off the trench coat, struggling with it a bit to buy some time. Finally, the coat was off.

"Anyway, I was standing outside the orangutan display. Have you been there?" I asked Karen. "It's pretty cool."

"Beck. Your excuse?" Karen can be very persistent.

"Well, I'm standing by the cement wall surrounding the orangutan habitat, and a couple kids next to me say how cool it is that the orangutans can climb trees like that, and they point at the monkeys climbing trees. And then they say how there's no way a human could ever swing like that on the ropes – you know, the ones that criss-cross between the plastic trees? And they point some more."

Karen watched me implacably. Arms still folded.

"So . . . you know how I am when somebody tells me I can't do something."

"And that's how you interpreted what the kids were discussing?" Karen commented doubtfully.

"Well, yeah. Wouldn't you?"

An eye roll from Karen.

"So I say to these kids, 'Watch this' and I vault the wall and drop to the dirt fifteen feet below – into the lion's den, if you will."

"Oh, for god's sake!" Karen exclaimed, trying to maintain her stern demeanor.

"Well . . . I land fine. So I run to the tallest tree and climb it. All the way to the top. And I yell to the two kids: 'Look who's at the top of this tree now, huh?'

They looked pretty amazed, Karen. I gotta tell ya."

I did a small victory dance for Karen to show how impressed they were.

"But then I remembered something about orangutans," I continued. I was on a roll. "The pack leader gets the highest spot in the tree. So the next thing I know, this big, bull orangutan is swinging through the ropes, heading right toward me, teeth bared and screeching hellishly."

Karen had started to choke on a laugh.

"Then it occurs to me that the fight for pack leadership is invariably a fight to the death. So I know I'm in trouble."

"Why," Karen asked. "A big guy like you can't handle a little red monkey?"

"Hey . . . they're really big. Anyway, that wasn't the problem. I remembered that orangutans are an endangered species; so I couldn't defend myself by killing this one. PETA would be all over my ass."

Karen was now openly enjoying my adventure.

"So what did you do?" she asked.

"As the rabid bull orangutan approaches, I use my pocket knife to sever one of the ropes on my tree. Using the now-free rope, I swing halfway across the habitat to another tree.

And just in time, too. The head simian is, pardon my pun, going ape-shit over my challenge to his authority. So while he is jumping up and down in the first tree and beating his chest, I cut the other end of my rope."

"And then what?"

"Well, the big-guy primate is determined to have my ass, so he is heading toward my new tree and raising a horrible ruckus. But just as he is swinging, hand over hand, along the last bit of rope near my new tree, I loop my freshly cut rope over another rope connected to the tree and I slide across the yard –

like on a zip line – this time landing on the dirt near the fifteen-foot high edge of the exhibit.

Whirling the free end of the heavy rope around my head like a lasso artist on steroids, I fling it up over the cement and around a lamp post. The end drops back down to me and I climb the thusly-looped rope to safety."

"Whew!" Karen said. "That was close."

Just like a kid enjoying a good fairy tale.

"But it isn't over yet," I said dramatically.

I crouched slightly, with my palms out, shoulder high, in a pose that screamed "Wait for it . . . ."

I know how to spin a yarn. Honestly! I could probably sell snake oil to P. T. Barnum.

Karen waited expectantly.

"The bull primate is still hot on my backside and he's climbing my rope, too. So I whip out my knife once more and slice the thick hemp right where it clings tightly to the post. Just when the goofy monkey is thinking I'm his banana, the rope severs and he falls back into the habitat – unharmed, except for his dignity, of course."

"Of course," Karen echoed.

"So do you have any work for me to catch up on?" I asked politely.

"Wait a minute. That was all on Sunday. How does that get you out of work for most of the week?"

You can't slip anything past Karen.

"Well, it doesn't. But although I escaped a mauling by the ape, I wasn't so lucky with zoo security. They promptly took me into custody. I was held in a snake exhibit, without bail, or even a phone call, until just this morning. Worse than Guantanamo Bay. No civil rights at the Minnesota Zoo.

So what can I do for you now that I'm here?"

"I had a list of things in mind," Karen said, with a smile. "But I'll be darned if I can remember them now. Just deal with the stuff on your desk and I'll be happy."

"Okay," I said hastily. "I'll be in my office." A step toward my door. "Please take messages." Another step. "And make sure I'm not disturbed." One more step. "Thanks. Bye bye." I waved as I slipped away into my office, closing the door swiftly behind me.

Karen was never angry with me in the first place. She just liked to hear me talk my way out of a tight spot. I would bet dollars to doughnuts that no client even had an inkling that I had been gone all week. She was that good!

Having made it to my office, I was now faced with the reality that "just dealing with what's on my desk" wasn't going to be a meager task. In fact, it looked like my office visit would be turning into an all-day affair.

Walking gingerly through the maze of piled paper, and around the huge mahogany desk, I took a seat in my infinitely-adjustable, swiveling, ultra-comfortable lawyer's chair. If I was going to be bored, I might as well be bored in comfort. With resignation, I moved the first stack of papers to front and center on the desk blotter and set to work.

CHAPTER 20

Thursday, October 22nd, 6:00 p.m.

Since Attorney Becker was still at the law office grinding through piles of paperwork, Thursday evening found Beth alone at home.

Sunsets come early in Minnesota in October, with the sun vanishing over the horizon around six fifteen and near total darkness engulfing the neighborhood on Jefferson Avenue by seven thirty. Beth was working on a government decryption project, attired in her typical cold weather casual loungewear – barefoot with black warm-up pants and a black sweatshirt.

At five minutes after eight, the door bell rang and Beth got up from her computer to answer it, pulling her hair back in a ponytail as she headed toward the entry.

The front entrance at 1011 Jefferson Avenue is an alcove formed by two similar doorways and the space between them. Each door is made of heavy, brown, quarter-sawn oak, framing a half-inch thick glass pane. Beth opened the inside door and stepped into the alcove to reach the light switch.

As soon as Beth had turned on the outside lights she could see the man standing on her screen porch. He was maybe six feet two, broad shouldered, and wore a navy pea coat with the collar turned up. At first his back was toward her. But as soon as the lights came on, he turned quickly to face Beth.

She saw immediately that the man had suffered some recent physical trauma. Small cubes of automobile safety glass littered his hair. A few glass pieces had embedded in his forehead and small trails of blood leaked slowly down the sides of his face. His glasses were missing one lens and appeared badly bent.

He came closer to the wood and glass entrance door, looking lost and bewildered.

"Could you help me, please," the man said in a calm tone through the closed door. "Believe it or not, a deer just ran into my windshield a bit down the street here." He gestured down Jefferson. "I'm not really hurt. But if I could use your phone to call the police and a tow truck, I would really appreciate it."

He smiled pathetically as he waited for Beth to consider the request.

A deer crossing Jefferson Avenue was not an unusual occurrence.

"Yours is the third house I've tried," he added. "No one else would answer their door."

"Just a moment," Beth said, holding up a finger. She spoke loudly so he could hear her clearly through the glass. "I'll be right back."

Beth stepped back through the alcove and punched some keys on her home security entrance box, deactivating the entrance door contact alarm. Then she took a few further steps into her living room, withdrawing a cordless phone from its cradle. Returning to the entryway with the phone in hand, Beth opened the door just far enough to hand the man the telephone.

"Here you go," she said, handing the phone through the slightly open door.

"Thank you so much," the man said, reaching toward the phone.

But instead of taking the phone from Beth's hand, he firmly grasped her arm. In rapid succession, he first pulled the heavy door violently closed against her elbow, and then shouldered his way forcefully inside her home, leaving the phone lying behind him on the porch floor.

Beth grimaced at the pain in her right arm, but had the presence of mind to take a swing at his nose with her left. She was in an awkward position and the man caught her arm easily with his other hand. Holding her by both forearms, he roughly pushed her backward and away from him . . . then let go. She sprawled unflatteringly onto the wood floor.

When Beth looked up from her half-seated position, propped against the foyer closet door and seated on the hardwood, she saw that the man had produced a black pistol from beneath the pea coat. She recognized the gun as a Sig Sauer 9mm.

"Thanks for inviting me in," the man taunted. The person on the porch with the desperate, polite demeanor had disappeared. In his place stood a wildly evil presence, his cold, hard eyes devoid of all empathy. Beth recognized the look of a dangerous psychopath when she saw one. This man clearly qualified.

Beth stayed down on the floor without moving, the Sig trained at her forehead from a distance just beyond her reach.

"Is your husband home?" The intruder looked around for a brief moment. "No. Of course not. Otherwise, he wouldn't have let you answer the door on a dark, cold evening."

Even the man's voice was eery – a blend of Peter Lorre and Vincent Price.

Although Beth was shaken, her government training had already kicked into high gear. The Beckers had prepared several responses to intruder scenarios. She would employ one of them now.

"You're here for that damn money! Aren't you?" she said, looking at the floor, shaking her head from side-to-side with disgust. "I told my sonofabitch husband we shouldn't keep the cursed stuff in our home, for god's sake. But did he listen?"

The voice didn't sound like Beth's; but she knew she had to sell her character if the scene were to play out effectively.

Nothing attracts a bad person's attention like the opportunity for easy money. Even criminals bent primarily on killing are willing to let themselves be distracted long enough to pick up some dough.

"How much of it is left?" the man asked. A pause. Then "Tell me, bitch!"

The man was smart enough to play along. Good.

"Damn it!" Beth swore again.

Then looking the man in the face: "All of it – half a mil. Shit!" More head shaking.

Beth could see the wheels turning behind the man's facial expression. He had come here for one certain purpose and was now rethinking his plan. The man glanced at the security system keypad. The little green light next to the "System Off" label was illuminated.

"Okay. Up!" he commanded Beth.

She got slowly to her knees and then stood, making sure to exaggerate the pain in her right elbow as she did so.

The man backed away slightly as she rose, still keeping the gun just out of her reach.

Beth guessed he outweighed her by about eighty pounds. And judging by his exposed neck muscles, he was pretty strong as well. Of course, there was also the Sig to be considered. For Beth to attempt a frontal assault right now would be a bad idea.

"Take me to the money," he ordered, waving the pistol at Beth.

Beth continued to mutter curses and insults at her "sonofabitch" husband as she led the man through the dining room and kitchen toward the back stairs leading to the basement.

"Where are we headed, bitch?" he inquired.

Beth stopped and turned toward the man.

"Look, asshole! You want my money. I get that. But I swear to god, if you call me 'bitch' one more time, you'll never see a dime – and I don't give a shit if you shoot me dead right here."

He would most likely put up with the comment. He still needed her to get to the money. If he moved closer, maybe she could get the gun. In any case, if she was going to die tonight, she might as well maintain some dignity.

Beth and the man locked eyes.

"Let's go," he said finally.

Beth continued through the kitchen and down the back stairs to the basement.

The basement on Jefferson Avenue was partly finished – a carpeted and comfortably-furnished family room opened up to the right at the base of the stairs. Beth turned left into the unfinished laundry room. The walls in here were painted-white limestone, more than a hundred years old; the floor, a loose piece of thin red carpet thrown over poured concrete.

Beth stopped. Turning to the man she said, "It's under this corner of the carpet." She indicated an area with her hand. "Buried in a big fucking safe. You want me to show you?"

"Move over there," he said, waving Beth a few feet to one side. Then he moved to the area she had indicated and lifted a corner of the free carpeting. As he raised the carpet further, he could see what appeared to be a rectangular floor drain – a slatted metal grate. Letting the carpeting rest against his right arm, and still pointing the Sig at Beth, the man inserted his fingers into the grate and lifted it out of its seat in the concrete. It was fairly heavy; but not so heavy that he needed both hands. Using the grate as an anchor, he secured the folded carpeting back far enough to expose the hole where the grate had been.

With one eye on Beth, he glanced into the hole. It looked like some kind of safe all right. But unusual. The door faced upward, into the opening left by the floor drain. There was no dial or keypad. A lever handle was its most recognizable component. The entire safe setup appeared formidable. It was embedded in god knows how much concrete. And the door was made of thick metal. He was going to need Beth's help to get inside.

"Okay b . . . ma'am," he managed. "We're going to switch places and you're going to open this safe."

"I suppose I am," Beth said with resignation. "But first I want your word that, once you have the money, you're not going to kill me."

She knew any such assurances were worthless. But it was all part of the role. If she knew she was going to die anyway, why would she open the safe?

"You have my word," he said, crossing himself. "Swear to god."

A mention of taking God's name in vain came to mind; but Beth discarded it in favor of sticking to her plan.

"Okay," she said. "I guess I'll just have to trust you."

She and the man circled the room, him keeping a safe distance from her with the gun, until she had reached the safe.

"I need to get something out of my pocket," Beth said when she arrived at the safe. "It's a sort of computer key."

"Okay. Reach in there with two fingers and pull it out – nice and slow."

"I don't know if I can reach it with two fingers; but I'll try," Beth said.

Fortunately, the "key" was in her left warm-up pants pocket, so she didn't need to maneuver with her throbbing right arm. As the man watched closely, she stretched the side of the pocket until she could reach what she needed. Pinching the small device between thumb and forefinger, she slowly withdrew it from the pocket.

"What's that?" the man asked.

Beth held it toward him. Displayed between her left thumb and forefinger was a computer jump drive – a data storage device about two inches long and the width of a flat carpenter's pencil.

"It's a jump drive," Beth said. When the man showed no signs of recognition, Beth continued. "You know, a thumb-drive, a flash drive, a pen-drive, a USB storage device?"

She gave up.

"This little item holds a password to let me into the safe," Beth said finally. "I'm going to stick it in the tiny slot on the top of the safe and it will let me open it."

In reality, any USB plug would work the same. There was no password for the safe.

"Show me," he said.

Beth knelt by the concrete hole containing the safe and, being careful to avoid any sudden movements, inserted the jump drive into the USB port on the safe door.

A dark-red glass panel illuminated adjacent to the horizontal door handle. Numbers began flashing rapidly across the display. After about ten seconds, the flashing stopped and a ten-digit number appeared in glowing red.

"Okay, you move away from there. I'll take it from here. I don't want you reaching into there and pulling out a gun or something."

Beth protested – not too much, but convincingly enough.

"I wouldn't do that if I were you. You should really let me continue."

"Back over here!" he ordered.

"Have it your way," Beth said, standing and rotating back to her former position in the laundry room.

The man knelt down by the safe. With the gun still pointed at Beth, he twisted the safe lever a quarter-turn clockwise. Something clicked and he was confident the safe was now open.

"Good job, dipshit," Beth announced. "You just screwed us up for another two minutes."

"What? What are you talking about? It's open."

He glanced down at the safe and saw the numerals in the display counting down from 120. He pulled up hard on the handle. The door didn't budge.

"What the fuck!"

"Gee, whiz kid," Beth said. "Guess you should have let me finish. You've just locked both of us out. We have to wait for the timer to get to zero before we can try again."

He jerked on the lever some more.

"Oh, yeah. That's gonna work," Beth said, crossing her arms and rolling her eyes.

"All right you . . . ," he started, then thought better. "Get back over here and do it right this time."

He waved his gun and he and Beth did another circle routine.

Beth stooped down by the safe, watching as the display gradually counted down to zero. It seemed to take an eternity. She was sure it felt longer to the man with the gun. This detour was taking longer than he had anticipated.

When the time came, Beth removed, then reinserted, the jump drive and the flashing numbers appeared again. When the numbers stopped flashing, Beth asked, "Okay if I continue?" Then more quietly, "Shithead!"

"What'd you say?"

"I said, 'Okay if I continue?'" Beth replied.

"All right. But I don't want to see that safe door open without me expecting it. You tell me what's goin' on every step. Got it?"

"Yeah, yeah, yeah." Beth continued. "Before touching the lever, I need to take this key out and put it back in again. Okay?" She looked up at her assailant for his permission.

"Do it," he said, sounding impatient and looking around the room for possible intruders.

Beth removed the jump drive and then reinserted it into the USB slot. Again the flashing red numbers filled the display. After another ten seconds they came to rest on a new ten digit number.

"Okay," Beth said, still stooping over the safe. "There is one more step and then we can use the handle and the safe will open."

"Tell me," the man commanded.

Beth indicated two small green dots on opposite edges of the safe door. "These are pressure switches. You need to press both simultaneously – that means at the same time," Beth said condescendingly.

"I know what it means. Hurry it up!"

"Okay," Beth went on. "So you need to apply pressure to both green dots simultaneously and hold the pressure for five seconds. A counter will display to show how long to hold them. When the counter reaches zero, the safe can be opened with the handle.

Shall I go ahead?"

"No, thanks," he said, waving Beth back to the opposite corner of the room. She complied.

In order to press both green dots, the man needed two hands. That meant that the gun wouldn't be pointed her way for at least a few seconds. And there was another surprise Beth was pretty sure the bad guy hadn't anticipated.

*   *   *

Just before eight o'clock in the evening, the Red Wing Police Department received a silent alarm signal from 1011 Jefferson Avenue, the residence of James and Elizabeth Becker. Although there are many security system false alarms, this one seemed unlikely to be inadvertent.

The homeowner had entered a special code to temporarily suspend the system for two minutes, and then to set off the silent alarm if he or she didn't enter the clearing code. The second code had not been entered. It was highly likely that there was an intruder at the Becker home.

* * *

Our home security was a bit more elaborate than most. In addition to calling the police, the security system had sent a text message to my phone, alerting me to the intrusion. I raced out of the office and through the bank doors on my way to the Pilot, and sped off for home, tires squealing. As I drove, I switched the cell phone security report to the microphones we had had wired in at various locations around the house. From what I could hear on my cell, Beth had just called somebody an "asshole" in our kitchen.

There was a man's voice, too. It sounded familiar; but I couldn't quite place it. I needed to hear more words.

They were headed for the basement safe. Beth had said he wanted money. Good. She had a plan. And at least so far, it was working.

As I arrived just up the street from my home, I could see that two groups of cop cars had blocked off three blocks of Jefferson Avenue, with my home being on the center block. There were no signs of sirens or flashing lights. Great! They had set up a perfect perimeter.

I pulled up to one of the cop car clusters and dropped my window. "I'm James Becker," I said, "and that's my house you're eyeballing. Who's in charge here."

One of the officers stepped forward. "Until the SWAT team arrives, I'm in charge," he said. "I'm Officer Green."

The name did not inspire confidence. And neither did the lack of experience his voice and carriage betrayed.

"Okay, Officer," I said firmly. "Here's the deal. That's my house and my wife inside. There is at least one male intruder, probably armed. We don't need to spook him with a bunch of cops. So make sure to keep your people out of sight."

He started to interrupt me; but I stopped him with a hard glare and my open hand, held palm out.

"I'm going in there to help my wife," I said. "And you're staying out of it unless there's shooting in the house. Got it?"

"Listen, Mr. Becker," he started. "I am in charge here."

I cut him off again. This time I got out of the truck and stood face-to-face with Officer Green in the dimly lit street.

"I'm not asking," I said. "Now don't go getting my wife and me killed, or so help me, I will come back from the grave and haunt you for life."

With that, I slipped past him and jogged toward our back yard, where my presence would be less visible from inside the house.

Just as I was sneaking through the thick spruce trees marking our easterly lot boundary, I heard the explosion. Abandoning all attempts at stealth, I sprinted for the back door.

* * *

"Don't try anything while I'm holding these buttons. I can lift my gun hand in about half a second if I need to."

"Okay," Beth agreed. She was suddenly compliant.

Still holding the gun in his right hand, the man stooped over the safe and, after glancing up at Beth to make sure she wasn't trying to escape, he depressed the two pressure dots with his thumbs. For a second, nothing happened. Then the display showed a "5" and began its countdown.

The man looked up at Beth and smiled. "4." She was smiling back.

Beth hit the deck, covering her head with her hands. Before the man could react, as the counter reached "3," there was a loud explosion. The blast force went straight up, launching the heavy top of the safe upward into the man's chest and breaking both of his thumbs. Unfortunately, instead of landing where Beth could get it, the gun flew behind the washer.

At the moment, Beth's odds were looking more favorable. It was time to act.

The bomb had staggered the man and he was leaning back against the dryer, trying to shake the fog from his head. Beth dashed across the room and struck a painfully accurate bare foot upward into his groin. He groaned and doubled over.

She followed immediately with a knee to his nose, standing him up again. As he struggled to get his bearings, using all the leverage she could garner, Beth drove her left fist into his solar plexus, landing him wheezing on the floor, sunny-side up.

Stepping across the dazed intruder's torso, Beth grabbed his left forearm and wrenched him over onto his stomach. Forcing the arm behind him, and using her left knee and both arms for leverage, she pinned it high on his back, making sure to grab the broken thumb for extra effect.

Despite the explosion and the beating, he was starting to come around.

"Get the fuck off me, bitch!" he managed, while struggling to get free.

"Damn it. I told you not to call me that," Beth shouted into his left ear.

She applied more pressure to his left arm, elbow and thumb. There was a loud pop as his shoulder left its socket. The man groaned and lay still.

At that moment Beth noticed me standing in the laundry room doorway with my Beretta drawn, but held at my side.

"Sorry I couldn't make it here any sooner," I said with a smile. "Looks like you might have permanently damaged the guy."

Beth was clearly enjoying the leverage she now held over her assailant.

"Oh hey, Babe," she said taking a breath. "I didn't see you come in."

She was perspiring heavily and smiling brightly. In short, she looked divine.

*   *   *

I spoke with Officer Green for a few minutes while his team cuffed the intruder and stuffed him into a squad. I had recognized the man and I wanted to make sure the police knew the kind of criminal they were dealing with.

And Officer Green had a question, too. "What the hell was that explosion?"

I had to come up with a quick explanation to avoid discovery of the C4 used in the safe detonation.

"You know how the plumbing in these old houses is – not exactly state-of-the-art. Sometimes we have sewer gas build-up in the basement. Guess he was lighting a cigarette and set it off. Pretty good timing, huh?"

I doubt that Green believed my story; but he had his bust. No need to create more paperwork.

After the police took the man away, Beth and I sat for a while on our front screen porch. Actually, I sat. Beth reclined with her head on my lap on the settee, a cloth-wrapped bag of ice chilling her right elbow. She needed to cool down a bit from her recent physical encounter.

"Do you know that asshole called me a bitch?" she said, looking up at me. Then turning her head toward the street: "Pissed me off!"

"Me, too, Doll. You want me to petition for him to be drawn and quartered?" I asked with a smile.

"You're so romantic," she said sweetly, her head still on my lap.

We rested silently on the porch until Beth's adrenaline had waned and she began to feel the October cold.

"How about we head in and get ready for bed?" I asked, as soon as I perceived her chill.

"It's only 9:30," she said.

"Well. We both could use a warm shower," I replied. "And we could read books or watch TV . . ." I looked down and she turned her face toward mine. " . . . or something."

"Are you offering a massage?" She had intentionally misconstrued my proposal. "Sounds heavenly." Then a pause.

"You know you are going to have to tell me that crazy asshole's story someday soon. I know he was here for you. He's not my type."

"Someday," I said.

"Someday soon," she clarified.

"Someday soon."

We untangled ourselves from the position on the settee.

"You go up first," I said. "I'm going to shut off lights and lock up."

As I walked through the house locking doors and straightening up a few items that had been displaced by the evening's activities, I thought about the animal that had, until only a few minutes earlier, held my wife captive. His name was Snark, and it suited him well.

In the late nineties, Snark was importing heroin to the U.S. from Afghanistan, through an intermediary in France. I had infiltrated his operation in Europe and we were about to shut them down completely when some local New York cops stumbled onto a drug transaction in Yonkers. Shots were fired and Snark killed a cop.

After I had testified as the prosecution's star witness against him, Snark had been sentenced to life without parole. I understood he had checked into one of New York State's finer resort communities at Sing Sing. I hadn't expected to see him again.

Even though the Agency had advised me of his prison-break during a medical visit two years ago, I figured he would be too busy running from the law to bother with me.

Guess I was wrong.

It was a very good thing that Beth and I had a few contingency plans in place. And a good thing that Beth was so incredibly brave as to carry one of them out this evening.

Re-setting our home security system, I turned off the last of the first floor lights and headed upstairs. It had been quite a night.

CHAPTER 21

Friday, October 23rd.

As Friday dawned, I lay awake in bed, frustrated that it had now been nine days since Katherine Whitson's kidnapping. My suspect pool had narrowed. But I still had no idea where I might find Katherine.

There had been no ransom demand – at least none that George Whitson had told me about. And according to Gunner, there had been no banking or credit activities traceable to Katherine either. She had completely vanished and I didn't like the feel of the whole situation. I was pretty sure she was in very deep trouble. In the unlikely event that Katherine was still alive, she might not stay in that condition for much longer.

With Bull still tailing Allister, and Gunner finding nothing suspicious in the backgrounds of either Trample or Sustain, I decided to have another chat with Katherine's husband – this time, at the condo. George Whitson still knew something that could be helpful – even if he wasn't aware of it. I hoped to shake that bit of knowledge loose today.

After my usual morning routine, I said "Good bye" to my lovely wife, and once again, headed the Pilot north on Highway 61 toward Minneapolis. As I drove, I called Whitson's office.

After talking my way through his secretary, I got Whitson on the phone.

"George, you need to get over to your condo right away," I said. "There are some new developments and you need to be a part of this."

There hadn't actually been any new developments yet. But I hoped there would be some once I got Whitson alone in the condo.

He agreed to meet me there.

I parked in the pay lot on the block adjacent to the condo building and looked around me.

The parking lot was on the very edge of the densely-developed Minneapolis downtown. Open blocks like this one were once the sites of manufacturing or milling businesses that had succumbed to modern technology or foreign competition – their buildings having been razed years ago.

As things stood now, the lots served as a buffer between downtown and the Mississippi River, a few blocks distant. Within the year, several of the empty blocks would be occupied by the Target Field development – the new home of the Minnesota Twins baseball franchise.

I looked across the poorly-paved parking lots, and the sea of cars blanketing them almost completely, and wondered if mass transit could possibly replace all the lost parking spaces. Certainly that would be desirable; but was it possible?

I got out of the Pilot and walked to Whitson's building. He had given me a "Visitor's Pass" to get me through security, and a key to enter the condo. I took the elevator to the 7th floor.

Approaching Whitson's condo, I ignored the brass knocker and rapped my knuckles solidly on the door, three times. I waited a moment and then knocked again.

Whitson wasn't home yet. So I let myself in.

The space was the same sterile, impossibly organized apartment I had visited this past weekend. A place for everything and everything in its place. Was there a place here for people? A marriage? I wondered.

I heard a key in the door, and presently, Whitson appeared from the entry hall. He saw me and gave a start.

"Geez, Becker! You scared the crap out of me. I didn't expect you to beat me home."

"Who would?" I said.

Whitson looked confused. Then, "What are the new developments you mentioned on the phone?"

"We're just developing them now," I said. "Take off your coat and let's get to it."

Whitson still looked confused. But he took off his hat, coat and gloves and put each in its designated place in the entry closet.

When he had closed the closet door, I said, "Let's start with your bedroom."

I headed off in that direction. Whitson followed like a puppy.

Upon entering the master bedroom, I proceeded first to the closet space I knew to be Katherine's and slid open the door. The less-organized section of her clothes rod was obvious next to the meticulously-spaced portions.

"What did Katherine have hanging in this area?" I asked, stepping directly in front of the suspicious spot and gesturing toward it.

"I try not to look in Katherine's closet more often than necessary," Whitson said, coming closer. "She doesn't arrange her things as I would. It bothers me."

Whitson looked carefully at each section of Katherine's closet. "I think the missing items would have all been dresses or suits," he said finally.

"And the shoes?" I asked, indicating the single open slot.

"Judging from the other shoes around them, it looks like those would have been work flats of some sort," Whitson judged.

"Okay," I said. "Notice anything else unusual about Katherine's closet?"

Whitson looked at each section carefully again. He was nothing if not thorough.

"I'm sorry," he said after a moment. "I don't see anything else amiss."

"Very well. Let's move to the master bath," I said, leading the way. Once inside the large tiled room, I again asked Whitson if anything looked unusual.

He turned slowly in place, taking in the entire room – the tan marble double sinks; the glass shower; the jacuzzi tub; the white porcelain toilet.

"Katherine's towel has not been used," he offered. A moment later: "And there are no splashes on the mirror. When Katherine washes her face before bed, she always splashes soapy water on the mirrors."

"Good," I said encouragingly.

This tour really wasn't going anywhere so far. But the mental processes of recollection are complicated, and one never knew when something important might come to the fore.

Three mirrored doors fronted the medicine cabinet. I opened all three completely. Turning to Whitson, I said, "Now look carefully in here and tell me what's missing, please."

Whitson was being helpful. I wanted to politely reinforce that behavior.

Whitson stepped closer to the section of cabinet nearest him.

"Her contact cleaning solution bottle is gone. It was quite large. And her tooth brush is missing. My tweezers are gone, too. She wouldn't take those . . . Why would she?"

Whitson had turned to me.

"Keep looking," I said. "Every little bit can help."

He returned his eyes to the medicine chest.

"Her multiple vitamin bottle is gone. But her prescription is still here. Oh my god! She could have seizures if she goes off that medicine too rapidly. Oh dear!"

I needed him to refocus. Knowing that Katherine might have a seizure probably wasn't going to help us find her any sooner.

"Whose bottle is that?" I asked, pointing to the rather large plastic container of over-the-counter sleeping pills.

He looked toward where I was pointing. "Those are mine. They're sleep aids. I don't use them often – but every once in awhile, I take one to help me get to sleep."

Whitson kept looking, but try as he might, he couldn't come up with other missing items in the medicine cabinet.

Now . . . back to the foot of the bed.

I produced the baggie containing Katherine's cell phone and carefully emptied the phone back into its previous location on the bedspread.

"It was a little farther to the right," Whitson said.

"Okay, George. I don't want to touch it again. So let's pretend it's close enough," I said.

How could either of them live with his obsessive-compulsive organization?

"Did you move any of the items on the bed?" I asked.

"Well . . . I checked the cell and turned it off. Then I put it back exactly where it was before," Whitson said.

I had no doubts about the "exactly" part.

"So your prints will be on the phone," I said.

Whitson looked dismayed.

"Anything else?"

"No. I read the note by leaning over the end of the bed like this."

He demonstrated. Holding his hands behind his back, he bent at the waist, just as I had done when I first read the note.

"Please read the note to me out-loud," I asked.

Still bent over the bed, he turned his head to look at me. "Why?" he asked. "You've already read it."

"Sometimes hearing the words will trigger different feelings, impressions, understanding, in different parts of your brain. Please read the note," I asked again politely.

He read the note aloud.

George,

I am leaving you forever. Our marriage has been broken for a long time and I can't fix it. Whatever we once had is over.

My keys, cell phone and charge cards are here on the bed because I don't want anything from you and I don't want you to even TRY to find me. So please don't bother to look.

His voice was starting to crack.

I have what I need. You take the rest. It's yours.

Goodbye.

Katherine

Whitson had tears in his eyes. I gave him a moment after he had finished.

"George," I said. "Does anything in the note sound unusual to you? Can you detect any hidden message or clue that Katherine may have left us in the note itself?"

"The whole damn note is the most absurd thing I've ever heard!" he sobbed. "Katherine would never leave me – not voluntarily. We're soul mates."

He wanted to say more. So I waited.

"You probably don't believe me, because I lied about my relationship with Bruce. I understand that. But Katherine and I are a perfectly matched couple. Her extreme genius makes her socially awkward. And her intellect intimidates most people. I am one of the few who can admire her extraordinary intelligence and not be intimidated by it.

For my part, Katherine sees past my obsessive tendencies to the person I really am. She tolerates the sexual flings because she knows I'm gay. But she also knows that she is my only true love." Whitson was openly sobbing now.

The relationship he described was unusual, to be sure – but it fit what I knew about the Whitsons so far.

I gave him some more time.

"George. You need to be strong right now," I said comfortingly. "For Katherine."

I gave him another moment. Then I asked again, "Might any part of this note be a clue of some sort?"

I didn't know if Whitson would recognize a clue if I he tripped over one; but he was all I had right now.

There was a long silence. Whitson looked at the note, then back at me.

"Think about what the words sounded like," I reminded. "Anything at all?"

"'I have what I need. You take the rest. It's yours,'" he said finally. "That line doesn't make sense. How can I take the apartment? I would need her signature. Or how could I take anything else of hers? It's all in her name. What could she be referring to?" He looked at me again.

"Good question," I said, mulling the phrases over in my head. "You take the rest," I whispered to myself several times. George made a good point. This was a strange series of statements under the circumstances. But I couldn't come up with anything useful from it.

Whitson and I spent another hour going through rooms and closets, finding missing suitcases, and no missing toiletry kit. Finally, Whitson just couldn't do it anymore. I could hear it in his voice. He was emotionally and physically spent.

"Why don't you go lie down for a while," I suggested. "I'll let myself out."

"Okay," he said quietly. A moment later. "Please remember to lock the door. I'll try to get some rest."

Whitson disappeared into the guest room. I started toward the kitchen.

"Rest," I thought to myself. "Rest. You take the rest." I had an idea. It was a long shot. But easy to check out.

Walking back into the Whitson master suite, I made a B-line for the medicine cabinet. I opened the third glass door and removed the bottle of Whitson's sleeping pills. I drew a deep breath and held it. Then I emptied the bottle's contents into my hand. At first just pills. And then . . . YES! I couldn't believe it. Lying in my hand among the low-dose downers was a small, black jump drive.

CHAPTER 22

Friday, October 23rd, 4:00 p.m.

I was waiting on the red leather couch on Jefferson Avenue late Friday afternoon when Beth arrived home.

She poked her head around the corner of the kitchen so she could see the living room. "Oh. It's you again." She smiled and withdrew behind the door frame. "I didn't expect to see you home so early."

"Thought I'd be unpredictable and maybe catch you red-handed in some illicit activity," I said, feigning anxiety.

"You caught me," she confessed. "I've got six bags of illicit groceries." Beth stepped around the corner and entered the living room. "Now that I'm busted, I assume you'll want to secure all that evidence in the appropriate storage locations." She took a seat on the couch and picked up the newspaper.

"Damn. Looks like I'm the one who's busted." I stood up and took care of grocery stowage.

Once I had put everything away, I re-joined Beth on the red couch. She had finished reading the local paper – it's only eight pages, including Classifieds. "So what brings you home so early? I figured you'd be visiting with Mr. Whitson, or ruining some chinos, for a while longer," Beth said.

I sat forward on the edge of the couch facing Beth. I did my best impersonation of an excited person. "I found a clue," I said proudly, chest out.

"Really." Beth mimicked my excitement. "Is it a good one? Like a smoking gun or something?"

"Better." I tried to make my eyes twinkle. Not so sure I succeeded.

"Wow! Must be hot stuff," Beth played along. Then she said in quick succession, "Can I see? Can I see?" She sat forward, rubbing her hands together as though awaiting goodies.

"Of course. Drum roll please."

Beth did her best drum roll with both hands on one leg. It was unimpressive; but it would do.

"Ta da!" I said, producing the jump drive from my shirt pocket as if by magic. I displayed the prize to Beth, holding it vertically between my right thumb and forefinger.

"Hey," she said. "That's pretty good. Do we know what's on it?"

"Nope. But I bet you can help me find out."

I tried for another twinkle.

"I bet I can," she said, snatching the drive from my fingers. Before I could object, she was on her feet and heading into the dining room toward the computer.

"Hey. Wait for me," I said feebly.

Beth sat down at the computer and removed the protective end-cap from the jump drive.

"Wait a minute," I said. "Aren't you worried it will be carrying a virus or will self-destruct if we do this wrong?"

"You know the answer to that," Beth said, as if speaking to a child.

Of course. If Katherine had left this jump drive as a clue, she would want it to be read – not have it destroy her would-be rescuers' computer.   There was no way it would be booby-trapped.

Beth popped it into an open USB port. In a few seconds the screen displayed a message that it had recognized an "external storage device."

"Okay," Beth said. "Let's see what you've got baby?"

She clicked on an icon that should open the jump drive. A message appeared asking for a password.   Apparently, although Katherine wanted the information to be found, she didn't want to have it found by total hacks.

"I've got a couple programs I can use to open it up," Beth said immediately. "You get outta here and let me do my thing."

I recognized marching orders when I heard them. Fortunately, Twins vs. the Yankees post-season baseball was just starting on Channel 61. I returned to the red leather couch and turned on the game.

It took exactly one and a third innings for Beth to resolve the password problem.

"Hey, Mr. Becker," she called. "I got it."

I went back to the computer and looked over her shoulder. I could see that the jump drive, which had been designated as "Drive K:," was open, and a single filename appeared in the drive. That name was "AS-246C-01.TXT."

"Only one file?" I asked.

"Maybe. There could be others that are hidden. But let's make a copy of everything on the jump drive before we go further, shall we?"

"Excellent idea, Watson," I said in a lame British accent.

Beth looked over her shoulder at me.

"You are Watson," she stated clearly. "I am The Master."

"The what?"

"The Master is the nickname developed by fans of Sherlock Holmes to refer to the great sleuth himself, of course." She shook her head in disbelief.

"I don't get out much," I offered by way of excuse.

The entire jump drive contents had now been duplicated in a folder on our computer's hard drive.

"Okay. Let's have a look," Beth said with anticipation. She moved the mouse arrow over the filename and clicked it once to open the file.

What appeared on the screen was a word processing document that held, not sentences and paragraphs, but multiple lines of computer gobbledygook. Beth may have been able to make something more of it. I would ask to find out.

"So what do you make of that?" I asked confidently.

"It looks like a test results printout. By the title at the top, I would guess the item tested to be something known as AS-246C-01." Beth continued. "The date and time stamp in the first line, I assume, indicate that this particular test was run last week at 15:12 on Thursday."

"Exactly what I was thinking," I agreed.

I could see Beth's eyes roll through the back of her beautiful head.

"There are fifty-three pages of printout here. Let me skim it for a moment," Beth said, staring intently at the lines of text rolling by on the display.

This time I elected silence. Who was it that said, "It is better to remain silent and be thought a fool, than to open one's mouth and remove all doubt?" Wise person, whoever it was.

It didn't take Beth long to finish skimming. "It looks like the item passed all tests but one," she said presently. "On page forty-seven, there was a failure. Look." She pointed at the line.

I read where she was pointing. It said:

Security Outlet Check: CRITICAL FAILURE   Functionality: UNKNOWN

Location: {0ce4991b-e6b3-4b16-b23c-5e0d9250e5d9-20n9}

"Ah. So that's the problem," I said, clearly without a clue.

Beth turned her chair around and looked up at me. "We need someone familiar with an AS-246C-01, whatever it is, in order to explain what this failure code means."

"Okay," I said. "Where do we find someone?"

"Beats me. I've never heard of an AS-246C-01," Beth confessed. "Seems likely that it has to do with ComDyne, though."

"No sweat," I said. Never daunted. "Let's Google it!"

We did. Nothing even close.

"Okay. That's it for my computer arsenal." I know my limits. "We'll approach the situation with fresh minds and clear heads tomorrow."

"Probably wise," Beth conceded. "We'll figure it out. Let's just let it settle for a while."

"Right."

CHAPTER 23

Saturday, October 24th, 7:15 a.m.

As it turned out, we were both so excited about the discovery of the jump drive that we talked about it in bed that night. We had even mapped out a plan of action for the morning. So on Saturday, we were both up early, preparing our operational logistics.

Beth was going to work up something in writing, describing the nature of the data we had found on Katherine's drive, to be relayed to any experts with whom we would need to consult.

My first assignment was to contact Sam, Katherine's intern, to obtain his assistance. I called his cell number. Sam answered his phone on the second ring.

"Sam," I began. "It's Beck. We need to talk."

"Of course. Is there any news about Dr. Whitson? Is she okay?" he asked.

"Sam, I'm sorry. But I don't have anything concrete yet on Dr. Whitson's situation or whereabouts." I could feel the let-down in Sam's emotions through the phone lines. "But we do have some new leads, and I was hoping you might be able to help us out."

"Anything!" Sam responded without hesitation. "But what can I do? I've already told you what little I know."

"What I am about to tell you has to be kept completely confidential, Sam. You cannot even discuss this with your co-workers, or your superiors, at ComDyne. Can you live with that?" I asked.

Sam hesitated for a moment. He was not the rule-breaking type. Then he said, "If there is any chance it might help Dr. Whitson, absolutely."

"Okay," I began. "Dr. Whitson has left us a clue to her whereabouts. But we need help deciphering it. Does this sequence of letters and numbers meaning anything to you: AS-246C-01?"

"Sure." Sam said immediately.

Was it possible that this was going to be easy after all?

"That's a part number for a chipset in ComDyne's newest network router," he explained.

Okay. Maybe not so easy.

"What, exactly, does that mean?" I asked. "I'm not that computer savvy."

"I'm sorry," Sam apologized, though there was no need. I was the one who lacked knowledge in this sphere. "The number refers to a component of one of our new network devices. Each device has multiple components. The number refers to a specific one of them."

"Okay. I get that now. Here's another question for you. Dr. Whitson left us a text file that appears to contain the test results from a rigorous examination of the AS-246C-01. The file comprises about fifty pages. Each page contains multiple lines, with each line apparently naming an item or function that has been tested and the results of the test. Do you know what I'm talking about?" I asked.

"Yes," Sam replied confidently. "That would be a typical output for many of the test programs we run here at ComDyne."

"Okay. Good," I responded. I wished I understood this damn computer jargon better so my questions would sound more intelligent. "On this particular set of test results, all tested items appear to have passed their tests, with one exception." I read the failure message to him. "Does that message mean anything to you?"

"In all of our prior tests, the AS-246C-01 has tested out perfectly. So there are only two possibilities that I can think of to explain the failure message.

First of all, it is possible that the particular piece of equipment that resulted in that test report was improperly manufactured. That happens all the time, of course. No manufacturing process is flawless and there will always be a certain percentage of duds, if you will."

I liked Sam's ability to make this comprehensible to mere mortals.

"Please go on," I said.

"The second possibility is that Dr. Whitson had refined the test methods, and the newly-improved test revealed a flaw in the AS-246C-01 that previous tests had missed. In this case, the entire chipset would be faulty and every single AS-246C-01 chipset would need to be junked and replaced.

This second scenario seems unlikely, since this particular chipset is made by one of our most reliable suppliers in South Korea. For the chipset to have made it through the supplier's quality assurance procedures, and then have the entire batch be bad, would be exceedingly rare. In fact, I've never seen it happen."

"Understood," I said. "Would you mind holding for just a moment while I give this some thought?"

"No problem."

Although Sam seemed to think the report probably reflected an isolated failure in a particular sample of the chipset, the circumstances surrounding discovery of the report said otherwise. Why would Katherine hide a routine failure report in her medicine cabinet? Why would she disappear shortly after having printed the report? In my mind, there was no doubt that the test results in my possession indicated a widespread, and likely very expensive, chipset design problem. But what was the best way to get at the issue?

I got back on the phone with Sam.

"Can you give me any more specifics about which part of the chipset has failed, at least according to the test results I just read to you, and what the effect of that failure would be?" I inquired.

"I wouldn't be able to help you with that information. You are talking about a potential problem embedded inside a microchip itself. If I had Dr. Whitson's test program, I could certainly run it on other samples. But as far as telling you more details about the type of failure identified, that's above my head." He paused. "Sorry."

"No need for apologies," I replied quickly. "You have already been a tremendous help." I thought for a moment. "Sam. Who would be able to give me more details about the failure?"

"Well, Dr. Whitson, might be able to. Though it is possible that even she may not know the exact details of the failure without seeing the ASIC design code."

"ASIC design code?" I asked.

"Application-Specific Integrated Circuits, or ASICs, are computer chips, or chipsets, that are hardwired to perform specific functions. The people who write the programs that direct the design, and ultimately the manufacture, of these ASICs, are Systems Architects like Dr. Allister."

"Can you give me an example – extremely simplified, please?" I asked.

"In our business, we work with networking devices. But none of them are simple. How about an analogy?" Sam offered.

"I love analogies," I replied.

"Okay," Sam continued. "Suppose you want to automate a machine to fill cola bottles and screw the tops on."

"All right. A soda bottling machine."

"The machine is controlled by a computer, whether complex or simple, a computer nevertheless. Someone has to decide what steps the cola bottle filling machine needs to go through to accomplish its task.

The soda company's design requirements might read something like this:

- Acquire bottle from bin.

- Insert bottle in filling chamber.

- Insert soda contents into bottle.

- Remove bottle from chamber.

- Move filled bottle to capping station.

- Apply cap.

Those requirements are then given to the ASIC designer, the Systems Architect, who writes a software program to design the specific computer chip that will direct the bottling machines to carry out the bottle capping process. This program is the ASIC design program.

Once the ASIC design program is ready, the designer forwards it to a computer chip manufacturer. The manufacturer's computers use the ASIC design program to control the machines that build the customer's chipset. There is no human intervention or assistance required. All the instructions for building that soda bottling computer are included in the ASIC design program, and implemented by the manufacturer's computer and its related chip manufacturing equipment.

The result of the manufacturing process is a computer chip, or chipset, that is designed specifically to control the customer's bottling machine. The chip manufacturer sends the chip to the bottler, who installs it in its bottling machine computers. Now the machines know how to bottle soda."

"That's amazing," I said. "Do I understand you to say that the chip itself is uniquely designed and built to run bottle-capping machines, and bottle-capping machines only?"

"That is correct."

"How do humans control the chip manufacturing process? I mean, those chips have super-tiny circuits, right?"

"Actually, once the ASIC design code is written, the machines totally control the process. The manufacturer may not even know the exact chipset design it is producing, because the computers run everything. Humans are not physically capable of operating chip manufacturing equipment without the aid of computers. The tolerances are simply too small."

"Hold on a second," I stopped him. "You mean the people making these computer chips might not even know what the chips are designed to do?"

"That is also correct."

"Doesn't that seem a little Orwellian to you? Or maybe a reference to *The Terminator* is more apt."

"Not to me, it doesn't," Sam replied matter-of-factly. "It's just the way it is."

"So we are building tools that are smarter, or at least more capable, than their designers or operators. And if the tools, the ASIC design programs or the manufacturing computers, malfunction in some subtle way, humans may not even notice?"

"True. In fact, you may recall when the first Intel Pentium Processor hit the market in the 90s, it had a design flaw that caused it to do certain mathematical calculations incorrectly."

"That's right. I thought it was weird that a high-tech computer chip was bad at math," I said.

"And imagine all of the Intel programmers, engineers, mathematicians and other mass quantities of human brainpower who put their stamps of approval on that chip before it was offered for sale. Chip production is even more complex today. You just can't expect humans to find the flaws without knowing exactly where to look," Sam said.

"Doesn't that scare the shit out of you?" I asked in amazement.

"No," Sam said. "It's the way of the computer world."

"So if I handed this test result report, and one of these failed chips, to an independent testing lab, they might not be able to do anything with it at all?"

I was still in shock.

"It's possible," Sam said. "But the computer industry is filled with super-geniuses like Dr. Whitson, and I can't rule out that one of them might be able to figure something more out."

It didn't sound encouraging.

"Okay, Sam. Just a couple more things and I can let you go for now."

Sam waited silently.

"Let's suppose that what Dr. Whitson discovered was not one bad chip, but an entire manufacturer's run of bad chips. What would she do with that information?"

"She would probably report it to Dr. Allister," Sam said.

Naturally.

"Do you know whether Dr. Whitson and Dr. Allister met on her last day of work?"

"Let me think." Sam paused for a few moments. "Yes. They were meeting for maybe two hours or more on Thursday afternoon. Actually, it was probably the meeting that caused Dr. Whitson's headache. It can be stressful to spend extended time with Dr. Allister," Sam offered candidly.

"Another question that just came to mind," I said. "If the entire batch of chips were bad, and not just a few rejects, how many chips would that be in the case of the AS-246C-01?"

I wanted to get a handle on possible motive.

"We are building an initial production run of one point five million routers using that chipset. The production is expected to be completed by November 15, and advance marketing has already begun. Does that help?" Sam asked.

"Yes, indeed," I said gratefully. "Last question. And this is asking a big favor. But it's not a favor for me; it's a favor that might save Dr. Whitson's life."

"Anything," Sam said bravely.

"I need two of the routers that contain the AS-246C-01 chipset, and copies of any test programs you can find relating to that chipset. Can you do that?"

He paused. "If I give you what you ask for, will you guarantee that you will use it only to help find Dr. Whitson and that nothing secret will get out to ComDyne's competitors?"

It was a more than reasonable request.

"Absolutely," I said.

"When and where can I get you the stuff?" he asked.

"I'll get back to you soon," I said.

Thanking Sam profusely, I concluded the call.

Now I was hoping that Beth had had some success with her assignment. If so, perhaps we could combine our results and make some serious progress toward finding Katherine Whitson.

CHAPTER 24

While I had been on my phone with Sam, Beth was making calls on her cell phone as well. She was just disconnecting a call as I approached her. She was seated in the secretarial task chair at the dining room computer, her back to me, deep in thought, and she hadn't noticed my presence.

I took a minute to appreciate the silky drape of fine blonde hair on her neck, the refined posture, the strong yet feminine line of her shoulders. That I could also see a portion of her tan, faux-suede jeans as they perfectly outlined her posterior beneath the chair's back support, was a bonus.

"How goes the Silicon Valley branch of our partnership?" I asked.

Beth rotated the chair to face me, her slim, athletic legs slanting elegantly to one side as she turned. "Oh. Hey, Babe," she said. "I've made some nice progress. And you?"

"Spectacularly successful!" I said with a smile.

Beth smiled back.

"So what have you got?" I asked, pulling a chair out from the dining table and sitting on it backwards, facing Beth.

"I've got a computer hardware and software genius that will help us analyze the jump drive and the test results, and anything else we can give her. Do we have anything else?" she asked expectantly.

"Why, yes, we do."

It was starting to sound like a game show. And behind door number three where Carol Merrill is now standing . . . .

"I know what an AS-246C-01 is." I paused for effect, and also to allow me time to look at my notes. "It is a chipset to be used in a new line of ComDyne routers."

I was pleased with myself at getting all the computer lingo in the right places.

"That makes sense," Beth said. "Well done."

"But wait . . . there's more," I said. Now I was sounding like an infomercial, offering not one, but two widgets, and a lifetime supply of widget refills, for three easy payments.

"Sam, Katherine's intern, is going to get me two of the computer thingys . . . ah . . . routers, and copies of all of Katherine's test programs. Do you think your genius geek might be interested?"

"I'm sure she will. But you might not want to use the word geek in front of her, or in front of your computer goddess wife, either."

"Good point," I offered. "Duly noted. So tell me more about the computer genius. How did you come upon her?"

"Actually, Washington gave me her name, address, home, work and cell numbers and email address. I wonder sometimes if there is any such thing as privacy anymore – the government seems to know everything."

I nodded.

"Anyway, her name is Rosa Mendez. She has doctorates in more subjects than you can count, and is everyone's consultant for high-level computer security," Beth continued.

"That sounds perfect, given that our chip failure notice is related to something called 'Security Outlet Check.' But if she is the fighter pilot of computer technology that you describe her as, her schedule must be horrific. How soon is she available?"

"Her schedule is terribly full. You're right about that," Beth replied. "But Washington has somehow arranged to have her . . . what did they say? . . . at our disposal." Beth smiled broadly.

I got up and gave her a big kiss. "You are most certainly the queen goddess of living things."

"I know," she said matter-of-factly. "But I am too modest to say so myself."

"Of course'" I said with a wink.

The pieces were starting to fall into place.

"Do we let Gunner in on this info?" asked Beth.

"I don't think that would be a good idea," I said. "I've basically asked a very nice kid to violate his employment contract and commit grand theft to help out Katherine. Now's not the right time to fill Gunner in on the details."

"You do know some things after all," Beth said. "I knew there had to be a reason I keep you around."

With a few phone calls and some very cooperative consultants, we were able to arrange a meeting with Dr. Rosa Mendez, D.Sc. and Sam at the University of Minnesota Center for the Development of Technological Leadership for that afternoon.

Beth and I had never had an opportunity to work together on a matter where each could display his/her former life expertise. We were excited for the chance.

*   *   *

We arrived at the Tech Leadership Center a few minutes before our scheduled 2:oo p.m. meeting time. Dr. Mendez was already in the conference room, just off the waiting area. She greeted us warmly.

Dr. Mendez was Latina, approximately 45 years of age, with dark but slightly greying hair, and an open face. She appeared to be a likeable person on first blush.

"We are so grateful that you have made yourself available to help us out, Dr. Mendez," Beth began.

"Please call me Rosa," Dr. Mendez requested. She spoke with a very slight Hispanic accent – perhaps Mexican? I couldn't be sure because the accent was so faint.

"Certainly, Rosa. I am Elizabeth Becker and this is my husband, James," she said, indicating my presence with her hand. "Please call us Beth and Beck." Beth shielded her mouth from my view with her hand. "Nobody calls him James," she whispered to Rosa, as if it were some big secret.

"Got it," Rosa said. "The Beth and Beck duo."

Just then the waiting room door opened and Sam appeared. He was carrying a small banker's box, about the size of a case of bottled beer, by both of its handles, and backing into the room as a result.

"Hello, Sam," I said, before he got the chance to turn around, causing him to jump just a bit.

Turning to our threesome, he said, "Hello, Mr. Becker." He looked at the two women.

"Sam, this is my wife, Beth and our friend and computer consultant, Rosa. Beth and Rosa, this is Sam." I wanted to keep any details of Sam's connection to this matter as close to the vest as possible.

Beth and Rosa greeted Sam without handshakes, owing to the box he was holding.

"Shall we get started?" Rosa asked, motioning for us all to follow her into the conference room.

"No time like the present," I said.

Upon entering, I could see that this was a conference room the likes of which I had never seen before. Computer equipment occupied more space than the tables and chairs. And most of the equipment was such exotic looking stuff that I wouldn't dare to venture a guess as to its application.

We all took chairs at the table. Sam set his box down on the carpeting at his feet. He looked uncomfortable. In my mind, that was a sign of intelligence for someone in his situation.

"Beth has given me a rough idea of what we are looking for. Dr. Whitson appears to have located a fault with a certain chipset and my assignment is to attempt to identify the nature, scope and functionality of the fault. Beth has also provided me with Dr. Whitson's jump drive. Now," turning to the young intern, she said kindly, "what have you brought us in your box, Sam?"

Sam placed the contents of the box on the table, one item at a time, explaining what each was as he did so.

"These papers are sample test results from our previous testing of the AS-246C-01," he said, placing a two-inch thick stack of paper on the table. "They all show the chipset to be functioning properly as a router component. However," he cautioned, "none of these previous reports mentions the 'Security Outlet Check' referenced in Dr. Whitson's last report. There is neither a 'Pass' nor a 'Failure' listed for any such item in any previous test result. The portion of the test program that generated this error message must have been a recent refinement."

Sam continued by producing a portable hard drive and placing it next to the papers.

"This drive contains all of Dr. Whitson's test programs and procedures relating to the AS-246C-01 chipset. I looked everywhere I could think of. Unfortunately, I couldn't find any test program more recent or comprehensive than the ones that generated the paper reports."

Last, he produced two, identical silver boxes with LED lights, on/off switch and computer connection ports.

"These are samples of the very latest version of ComDyne's network router for business and commercial use." He looked at each of us in turn. "I must receive these routers back, and absolutely no information about them can be disclosed, except as necessary to locate Dr. Whitson."

"I have already promised you as much, and I am confident that Beth and Rosa will also agree?" I said, looking at the two ladies.

Beth and Rosa both assured Sam his company's secrets were safe in our hands. We each further vouched for the other two.

"That's it," Sam said. "That's all I've got."

"Thank you, Sam." It was Rosa. "If I have all of your permission, I need to open up one of these routers to see the chipset."

We all nodded our assent. Then we sat quietly watching the adept hands of Dr. Mendez as she meticulously dissected one of the routers on the table in front of us.

When the router lay in pieces on the table, Rosa asked Sam, "Do you know which elements comprise the AS-246C-01 chipset?" Sam indicated the soldered components on the green motherboard that were, in essence, the AS-246C-01. He had pointed to two black squares, each less than one half inch on a side.

"Thank you, Sam," Rosa said. Then she paused. "Your hard drive doesn't happen to include any ASIC code, does it?"

"No," said Sam. "I'm afraid I don't have access to that."

"Thank you, Sam. We shall proceed with the information and tools at hand." Then she turned to Beth and me. "This is going to take a while – at least several hours – for me to make even preliminary findings. May we adjourn this meeting and I will contact Beth when I have something to report?"

"That would be terrific," Beth said immediately. "Please get back to me as soon as you are able. And thank you again for all you are doing." Then turning to Sam, "and for your help as well. Without your information, we would have nothing further to go on."

Sam blushed, but didn't say anything.

The three of us, minus Dr. Mendez, left the Tech Leadership Center together. At the outside entrance to the building, I thanked Sam again and assured him he had done a very brave – and very important – thing to help Dr. Whitson.

Sam turned to me. "Oh, my god!" he exclaimed. "That was really Rosa Mendez? Oh, my god!" He was nearly hyperventilating. "I forgot to ask for her autograph."

CHAPTER 25

Even before our meeting with Rosa Mendez, I had come to the conclusion that Dr. Allister was at the top of my suspect list in Dr. Whitson's disappearance. She had found a problem in a chipset for which he was responsible. It was a multimillion, and maybe multibillion, dollar problem. She had had a stressful meeting with Dr. Allister just before she disappeared. Allister hadn't told anyone about the problem with the chipset. Production of the new-generation router was proceeding as normal, at least as far as Sam knew. And finally, when I had spoken with Allister, he hadn't mentioned anything about Katherine's discovery of the chipset defect or her meeting with him.

Maybe all of that didn't add up to a conviction in a court of law; but in my world, it was plenty to focus our investigative actions.

I called Bull to check on developments in his surveillance of Dr. Allister. He said Allister was at home. Nothing interesting had happened.

I relayed to Bull the new evidence casting even greater suspicion regarding Dr. Allister's involvement with the kidnapping. I told Bull that Allister was very likely our guy, and that his surveillance of the man was of critical import.

"Okay," Bull had replied.

Bull would continue watching Allister for the remainder of the day today. I would relieve him on tail duty at 9:00 p.m.

*   *   *

I was glad that we had Beth and Dr. Mendez working on the technical angles. But sometimes technology is no substitute for boredom and dogged persistence. That was my department – and Bull's.

At 4:30 p.m., I called Bull's cell to see what was up with Allister.

Bull answered, "Yeah?"

"Bull. It's Beck," I said.

"I got caller ID I told you," he replied.

"Oh yeah. Sorry again."

A person could be offended by Bull's abrupt manner. But he didn't mean anything by it – most of the time. He was just being Bull.

"Anything doing with Allister?" I asked.

"Nobody in or out of his triple garage all day. Somebody's in the house though. Can't say if it's Allister. Main activity is upstairs. Lights, TV and such."

"Okay," I said, disappointed. "Keep me posted."

"He takes a crap, I give you a call," Bull said.

What a comic!

Trying to make myself useful while Rosa and Bull worked, I decided to call Detective Blakeley to see if he had any progress to report.

"First Precinct, Blakeley," he answered.

The MPD must not have upgraded their phones to caller ID yet, or I'm sure he wouldn't have answered.

"Detective, this is Attorney James Becker," I said.

"Oh, god," I heard Blakeley say through a covered mouth piece. Then much more clearly, "What can I do for you, Mr. Becker?"

"I was just calling to check on the status of the Katherine Whitson kidnapping case . . ."

"Alleged kidnapping," he interrupted.

"What are you, the evening news?" I snapped. "Cut the crap and tell me what you have done to solve the disappearance of Dr. Whitson."

"Mr. Becker. I can give you every assurance that we have assigned all available manpower to the task of finding Dr. Whitson."

That was bullshit and we both knew it.

"So what did you think of the Whitsons' apartment? Anything unusual?" I baited.

"Nothing worthy of mention," he waffled.

"You haven't been there have you." It was a statement, not a question.

"Not personally. No."

"But another investigator?" I pressed.

"Not actually."

"A patrol officer?" The next step down was meter maid.

"All right. We've got tons of cases and we haven't been able to make any headway on this one yet. But we're doin' our best," Blakeley lied. "Can't ignore black folks dyin' in the streets just to find a rich white woman. Now how would that look?"

"Like police work," I said. "Like part of your job," and I hung up the phone.

CHAPTER 26

About six o'clock Saturday evening our land line rang on Jefferson Avenue. It was Rosa Mendez for Beth.

Beth took the call and immediately lit-up her own computer. I'm not sure exactly how they did it; but within about two minutes, our home computer was flashing all sorts of computer gobbledygook at the speed of light. Things were happening even without Beth touching the keyboard or mouse.

"I've given her control of our computer so she can show me her results more quickly," Beth said without taking her eyes off the monitor.

As the computer screen continued its unintelligible display of text and images, Beth and Rosa were speaking a foreign language – and it wasn't Spanish.

After a while longer, I gave up and went into the living room. Flopping onto the red leather couch, I reclined with feet and head resting on throw pillows at either end. The leather felt cool and comfortable. I closed my eyes, trying not to focus on the telephone conversation in the dining room.

The next thing I knew, Beth was touching my shoulder. I had dozed off.

I have often found it important to be able to sleep under adverse circumstances. But I hadn't intended to do so this time. I was just overtired and had passed out.

"Hey, Sleeping Beauty." Beth shook my shoulder. "Don't you need to meet Bull somewhere at nine?" she asked.

"I squinted at my watch – eight o'clock. Right. Yeah." I said, trying to shake off the grog. "I've gotta wash my face."

Rolling off the couch onto the floor and gradually managing to stand erect, I made my way to the first floor rest room.

A minute later I exited the rest room wide awake – pretty much.

"Was Rosa helpful?" I asked Beth, remembering the phone call and the flashing computer images as I had been falling asleep.

"Quite; but not completely. It's kind of complicated," Beth said. "I'll try to have it translated into English when you return home . . . which will be?"

"Sorry. Probably not until after ten tomorrow." Tomorrow was Sunday already. Where had the week gone? "I'll have my cell."

I was running late. I was already wearing my jeans and Reeboks. So I grabbed my leather bomber jacket, stocking cap, gloves, and my guns – the Beretta as my primary weapon, and a smaller pistol for backup – and headed straight to the Pilot. I rendezvoused with Bull at nine fifteen near Allister's house in the ritzy Minneapolis suburb of Edina. I parked down the block and walked to Bull's vehicle.

Opening the passenger front door on the red Jeep Cherokee, I handed him a large steaming cup of Hawaiian Blue Mountain Coffee. A peace offering of sorts for being a bit late. Then I climbed in with my own cup.

Bull took a sip of the coffee through the hole in the plastic lid.

"You're late," he said, undeniably.

"True," I admitted. "But I did bring coffee as a peace offering. I thought you Indians appreciated that kind of stuff."

Bull snorted. "Pale Face!" he said. Then he laughed again and had another sip.

"Okay," I said. "Help me out here. I try to be culturally sensitive and bring you a gift – very expensive coffee, by the way – and in return, you insult me. Am I missing something?"

Bull laughed again. "Some day we gonna talk some Dakota Indian philosophy. Then maybe you get it, maybe you don't," he said, enigmatically.

That's Bull: a riddle, inside in a mystery, wrapped in an enigma.

"I shall look forward to the Indian Philosophy discussion, perhaps over a couple beers?" I offered.

"Of course," he replied, staring straight ahead. "It is our way." A hint of a smile twitched at the corner of his mouth.

"So anything new with Allister?" I asked.

"Boringest sonofabitch in the state," Bull replied. "Hasn't budged an inch from that house. 'Course I've only been here since midnight."

"Midnight! How the hell did you stay awake staring at that house since midnight?" I asked in wonder. "I thought you'd take a break and go home when he went to bed."

"Ah, Grasshopper," Bull said impersonating a Shaolin monk. Or maybe David Carradine. I wasn't sure which. "You have so much to learn and only eternity remains in which to learn it."

Bull was still looking straight ahead, but his smile was now very evident.

"I thought the Grasshopper thing was a Buddhist trademark," I objected.

Bull turned his face toward me.

"Hey, we Indians got grasshoppers. Nobody can patent grasshoppers. Ain't no fucking intellectual property. We can have grasshoppers."

He sounded incensed. But then, it's hard to tell with Bull.

"As long as we're talking Indian heritage," I said. "I still can't understand why you, a Dakota Indian, don't drive a Dodge Dakota instead of a Cherokee."

I had asked Bull this question before. I assumed it would irritate him.

"Lousy suspension on the Dodge."

That's all he said.

Just as we were finishing our coffee and I was about to send Bull packing, one of the garage doors at the Allister house started to go up. It was easy to see with the darkness outside and the bright garage light inside.

"Two trucks or one," I asked Bull.

"One oughtta do. It's dark. We keep our distance. I drive the best-selling SUV on the road. We blend in."

He just had to get in another Jeep Cherokee dig.

"Okay. Follow that hideously-designed Cadillac," I directed with a wave of my hand. Tally ho!

It's really not too difficult to follow a car if the driver is not expecting a tail, as long as they don't drive some place very remote.

Traffic was about perfect as we followed Allister onto Crosstown Highway 62 going east. Bull kept at least two or three cars between us and Allister. And the Caddy's taillights were pretty distinctive, if not attractive. He stayed on the Crosstown east through the I-35W commons area and past Fort Snelling.

To say that Fort Snelling is not one of Bull's favorite spots would be an understatement. One of the saddest chapters in Dakota Indian history was the U.S. – Dakota War of 1862. The largest mass execution ever carried out in the U.S. occurred when government-supported officials hanged thirty-eight Dakota men in Mankato. Many more Dakota Indians, including old folks, women and children, were imprisoned here at Fort Snelling, where hundreds of them died in the harsh winter conditions. It wasn't something that a Dakota Indian could, or should, easily forget.

We continued to follow Allister south and east onto State Highway 55. Crossing the Minnesota River on the mile-long stretch of buttressed concrete known as the Mendota Bridge, Allister was quickly approaching the boundaries of the metropolitan area. Traffic was still fairly constant, though somewhat more sparse. When Highway 55 joined, and then split from, U.S. Highway 52, the Cadillac took the southerly route down 52.

This length of highway was bordered mostly by flat fields of recently harvested corn and soy beans. The aromas of natural pig fertilizer occasionally filled the Cherokee.

"Liquid gold," I said. "That's what farmers call manure."

"Stinks," Bull replied.

He had a point.

About ten minutes after crossing the Minnesota River, Allister's car made a right turn onto Ottawa County Road 46 heading west. Now we were going from a well-traveled four-lane, to a two-lane road with many fewer vehicles. Bull had to drop back to avoid detection.

About three miles along County 46, Allister illuminated his right signal and turned off the road on the north side. Bull had no choice but to maintain his speed until he was fairly close to Allister. Fortunately, Allister left the roadway before we actually had to pass him.

We continued west on County 46, beyond the dirt road onto which Allister's Caddy had vanished. After a couple miles, Bull slowed his Cherokee and made a U-turn at a farm driveway. Turning off our lights, we returned to the dirt road to follow Allister's trail.

"Well, well," Bull commented, as we looked for a place to ditch the Jeep. "Looks like Mr. Allister has a little hidey hole out here some place."

"Doctor Allister," I corrected.

"Oh that's right. Genius man. We see soon enough."

Bull found a small patch of trees and weeds that would work well to conceal the Jeep. We parked and got out.

First, we listened to see if we could hear any sounds from the direction in which Whitson had disappeared. We could hear traffic on Highway 52 a few miles east; and the occasional vehicle went by on County 46. There were no obvious sounds from ahead, down the dirt road.

There was no way to tell how far Allister had driven down this path. But whatever the distance, we would have to go it on foot. Being ever-prepared, we were both wearing shoes and clothing appropriate for physical exertion. So we set off at a seven-minute-mile trot. Every minute or so, we stopped briefly to listen. Then we were off again.

After about five minutes, we could see the reflection of the nearly full moon off the roof of the parked Caddy, a hundred yards or so ahead. Allister's car was parked adjacent to a tall tower, resembling a concrete smokestack.

I remembered having seen several of these structures on drives through this part of Ottawa County. Someone had once told me that they were part of a now-abandoned, World War II artillery facility. It appeared that this one had been converted into a "hidey hole."

Crouching low in the tall, dry grass, well off the dirt roadway, we surreptitiously approached the car and structure. As we got closer, we could see two more vehicles. They were mostly hidden behind the concrete tower and completely out of sight from County 46. We didn't have a good view. But they appeared to be American-made sedans. Maybe rentals?

We could also make out a sliver of light, outlining a metal doorway in the tower, near the front of Allister's car. It appeared that all occupants of the vehicles were inside the structure. Just maybe Katherine Whitson was in there, too.

I motioned for Bull to circle the tower to check for lookouts, booby traps, alarms and other pitfalls – potentially including, actual pits. Bull was exceedingly skilled in such things.

I stayed put, listening. I could faintly hear the sound of male voices coming from the structure. But I couldn't make out any of the words. Even cupping my ears with my hands didn't help, though sometimes that trick is more effective than you might imagine.

Presently, Bull appeared silently behind me. He just about scared me to death. But I wasn't letting on. He probably knew it anyway.

"All clear," he reported, speaking in a whisper. "Just got to deal with whoever, and whatever, is inside that bunker."

Describing the tower as a bunker was an apt military analogy. It had many of the same characteristics. In essence, a bunker is nothing more than a fortified structure, often built of concrete. Usually there are no windows larger than a gun slit. And we saw no windows at all in this place. A "bunker" it would be from now on.

"If Katherine is in there," I said, also whispering "we'd have a tough time guaranteeing her safety, given that we don't know who we're up against, how many, what weapons they have, or what the floor plan of that bunker is," telling Bull what he already knew.

"What have you got to work with?" I asked.

".357 Magnum and a back-up nine," Bull whispered. "You?"

".40 caliber Beretta and a .25 caliber on my ankle."

"Recon and report?" he said.

"I reckon so," I replied. "Rules of engagement: Defensive confrontation only, unless we know we can keep Katherine safe."

"Check."

Bull disappeared to take a position where he and I, collectively, would have a view around the entire bunker. And we waited . . . .

I checked my watch. It had been nearly an hour since Bull and I separated. Even with my leather jacket, cap and gloves, it was cold standing still for so long and I could see my breath.

Then the door opened and Whitson stepped out of the bunker into the shaft of light. He was speaking loudly and slowly to someone inside, as if they were deaf, or understood English poorly.

"You two need to keep her locked in the back room for just a couple more days," Allister said.

"We kill her and go now."

A mandarin accent – I recognized it from a visit to Beijing during my former life. The kidnappers were tired of baby-sitting Katherine.

"No. Not yet. I still need to make sure there is absolutely no evidence that she left behind at ComDyne. I've deleted her test files and reports. But I can't always get into some places I need to go to look for other problems," Allister explained. "And if anyone does find her stuff, and I go down, we are all going down. Understand?"

"Better kill her now than later. But you boss. Two more days only?" the man with the accent asked.

"Yes. Two more days." Allister got into his car and lowered the window. "I will call you. Do not kill her until I call. Understand?"

"Yes."

Allister raised his window, backed up the Caddy and drove away, leaving a cloud of dust to settle in the tall grass.

The Chinese man stepped out of the bunker and moved a few steps to his right. I could have shot him easily. But what about Katherine's safety? Looking almost straight in my direction, he unzipped his fly and urinated. When he finished, he zipped up and went back in the bunker, closing the metal door behind him.

I decided to call Bull's cell phone. There was absolutely no way he would have forgotten to mute the ringtone. It rang twice.

"What?" came Bull's voice in a deep whisper.

"I'm calling Gunner. We're on his turf in Ottawa County now. I'll withdraw out of earshot of the Bunker and get him on the cell. I'll call again when I'm back at my position."

"Out," Bull said. Never one to mince words.

I did as I had said I would. Having retraced my tracks more than two hundred yards back from the bunker, I called Gunner's cell.

He answered. He was whispering. Probably in bed with a sleeping wife.

"Becker. It's nearly midnight and I've got a five a.m. shift tomorrow. What couldn't wait until then?"

"We've found Katherine Whitson," I said nonchalantly.

I could hear Gunner sit up in bed. He was speaking in a loud and excited tone now.

"Great! Is she okay?"

"Probably still alive. But I can't say anything else for sure," I said.

"Alive is good," Gunner said. "Can you get her out? Do you need help?"

"That's the great part," I said. "They're holding her in Ottawa County."

"No shit!" His voice went up a register. "I'm getting a pen and paper. Then you gotta give me everything."

After Gunner had retrieved his writing gear, I gave him the whole situation report. He was really pumped.

"If you can get the BCA to marshal its forces and get up here in time to surround the place before dawn, I think I have an idea."

I told Gunner my plan.

"See you soon," he said.

I returned to my Recon position and called Bull again. Bull picked up, but didn't say anything.

"Honey, I'm home," I said.

The line clicked off. Bull was a real professional. No unnecessary talking while on Recon.

CHAPTER 27

Sometime between three and three-thirty a.m., I got the call from Gunner. "We are at the staging area along County 46," he whispered.

"You can talk normally," I whispered back. "I'm the one within earshot of the bad guys."

"Right . . . Oh, shut up!" Gunner said. "You gonna come guide us in?"

"Sure. Be there in five minutes."

I again called Bull to let him know the status before leaving my post.

Once I reached the dirt road, it was a pretty quick run out to the grassy area where Gunner and the BCA SWAT team were waiting. All the lights were out on the vehicles and everyone stood quietly.

Gunner was whispering to the person I assumed to be the commander of the SWAT team. I approached them slowly with my hands in the air, just to make sure I wasn't inadvertently mistaken for a bad guy and shot. It's always smart to be cautious around people with guns.

"It's okay," Gunner said to the Statie. "He's with me."

I lowered my hands and joined the twosome. We went over the plan just to make sure everyone understood it the same way. Poor communication gets more people killed than bad taxi drivers. Once I was sure we were all rowing in the same direction, I reminded them of Bull's presence and location and described his apparel.

"Remember," I said to the Statie. "Indian good. Chinaman bad."

He gave me a nasty glare.

The troops got themselves assembled and everyone followed me slowly down the dirt drive. Where one man can run quietly, twenty-five booted policemen sound like a herd of elephants. We had to take our time and get it right. It was likely the bad guys were sleeping and wouldn't hear us anyway. But we couldn't take chances with Katherine's life.

When we took to the tall grass, I pointed out Bull's approximate location and the orientation of the bunker's single doorway. The SWAT team deployed quietly and in the locations we had previously discussed.

Bull knew we were coming, so I didn't worry about him shooting the good guys. He had probably heard us whispering back at the highway – listening to the ground or some other tricky Indian shit. I needed to get him to teach me that Indian Philosophy someday soon.

By 4:30 on Sunday morning, all of the law enforcement folks were in place. Gunner and Mr. SWAT stayed with me. I didn't have any idea where Bull would be. But whatever position he had selected, it would be exactly the right one. Bull was very good at jungle warfare.

In case a change of plans was necessary, every team member had on a headset for communication – except Bull, of course.

Now we waited – two dozen guerillas, armed to the teeth, lurking in the weeds and scrub brush surrounding the bunker.

Sooner or later, one or both of the Chinese men would come out to take a pee. When he did, a sniper was supposed to take him down with a shoulder shot, and another SWAT officer would shoot a flash-bang into the bunker from close range. That should stun the remaining captor(s) long enough for five more SWAT members to storm the bunker and capture any other hostiles. With Katherine in "the back room," the danger to her should be minimal.

That was the theory anyway.

Just after seven o'clock, the metal door handle rotated, and the door started to creak open. We were well hidden and not likely to be discovered prematurely.

The door swung wide. I heard a male voice speaking in English. That was not a good sign. He had to be speaking to Katherine. A second later, Katherine appeared from the doorway, with one of her captors holding her arm. In his free hand, he held a pistol.

She appeared healthy enough. At least she was walking okay.

Shit! He was going to stand beside her as she went to the bathroom. A shoulder shot was no good with Katherine in close proximity to the armed man. We could still take him out fairly safely with a head shot. But that would eliminate one witness against Allister as well – maybe the only one who spoke English and could testify as to discussions with him.

As she squatted in the tall grass, the man stood behind her with the gun. He was looking around as if he suspected something. But there was no way he would detect our presence. Maybe it wasn't suspicion.

I got an empty feeling in my gut. He was acting instinctively, making sure no one could see him. He intended to execute Katherine right here. He wasn't going to wait the forty-eight hours Allister had demanded.

"Shit. He's going to shoot her right now," I said to the SWAT commander. "Tell your sniper to take the head shot."

Everything seemed to move in slow motion now. The Chinese man raised his pistol until it pointed at the back of Katherine's head.

The SWAT commander was relaying the head-shot order to the sniper. But I knew it would be too late. I didn't dare try a head shot with my Beretta from this range. Shit! Shit! Shit!

And then, still in slow motion, right before my eyes, the Chinese man fell violently backward, as if mown down by a scythe. Suddenly, I was back to seeing things at full speed.

Katherine pulled up her undergarments and ran.

"Shoot the flash-bang and take the building" the commander ordered.

A second later, the explosion went off inside the bunker and five men in black uniforms with black flak jackets, black helmets and black AR-15s raced inside the door. A moment later, someone inside yelled, "Clear."

Katherine was still running through the grass. Gunner went after her. He would catch up to her in a few seconds. I was curious about the downed captor.

I cautiously approached the place where the man had formerly stood. When I got closer, I could hear a grunting sound, coupled with a wheezing hiss, as if someone were gasping for air. As my view cleared the weed tops, I saw Bull with his legs locked around the Chinese man's abdomen from the back – squeezing the breath out of him. The gun had fallen free and Bull held the grunting man's arms in a "Full Nelson."

"He be passing out soon," Bull offered, his own breathing slow and steady.

"Okay, but don't kill him," I said. "We may need information or testimony from this guy."

Bull was right. A few moments later, the man went limp. Bull loosened his leg grip slightly, but waited to completely release it until some SWAT members arrived to take the man into custody.

As Bull got up and dusted himself off, the SWAT team loaded its captives into the back of a caged minivan for transport to the Ottawa County Jail. There they would be printed, photographed and booked for kidnapping, at least – probably all the things their mamas had told them never to get their names in the newspaper for.

When Gunner had caught up with Katherine, she found his Ottawa County Sheriff's Deputy uniform comforting, and practically collapsed into him. I saw her draped in his arms and went over to assist.

"Can we get an EMT over here?" I yelled over my shoulder as I headed toward Gunner and Katherine.

The EMTs and I arrived simultaneously. They immediately laid her down on a stretcher and took her vitals and all the other EMT stuff. Gunner and I watched. After a few minutes, they pronounced her malnourished, but in condition to travel.

Picking her up on the stretcher, the EMTs carried her to an ambulance and started off down the drive. They would take her to Hennepin County Medical Center (HCMC) in downtown Minneapolis, where she might be kept for observation. But more likely, she would be treated and released to her husband. Someone would have already called and told him to meet her at the hospital.

Looking around as all the activity wound down, I saw Bull standing at the periphery of the action and walked over to him.

"Great job, my friend," I congratulated him. "If you hadn't intervened, he would have shot her right then and there."

"Yeah," Bull said. "S'pose so."

"So you're a bona fide hero," I said.

"Again," he said.

"True. Again," I agreed.

We set off walking back to the Cherokee. No one had offered us a ride. But we didn't mind. We had accomplished a lot already today, and we hadn't even had breakfast yet.

CHAPTER 28

Sunday, October 25th.

When I arrived at home on Jefferson Avenue a few minutes before eight Sunday morning, Beth was at the dining room computer.

"Home is the sailor. Home from the sea. And the hunter home from the hill," she said as I entered through the sliding glass entrance from the back screen porch.

"Not Robert Louis Stevenson. Not right now, Beth. He's way too perky."

"Okay. Guess someone's grouchy." Beth smiled. "I'll try for more conventional. How was your night?"

"More productive than one could possibly imagine."

My voice sounded tired. It was hard to work up enthusiasm after being awake all night, hunkered down in a Minnesota version of the African veldt.

"We found Katherine Whitson and she is alive."

Beth rose from the task chair and practically ran to meet me in the kitchen. "That's terrific!" she exclaimed giving me a huge hug. "Awesome! Is she going to be okay?" she asked over my shoulder.

"I think that physically, she will fully recover. Mentally? Who knows?"

"Let me get you a cup of coffee. Then we can relax for a bit on the couch and you can tell me all about it," Beth offered.

"Could we make it a Diet Mountain Dew instead of coffee, please?" I requested. "It doesn't really feel like morning to me yet."

"Your wish is my command. You know that I'm not happy 'til you're not happy!" Beth smiled as if she was funny.

Too much perky again. "Oh, dear God," I said. "I've arrived in an alternate reality and I'm married to Don Rickles."

Beth got the pop, as we native Minnesotans call soda, and I sank comfortably into the red leather of the living room sofa. It felt like heaven. I could just stay here forever.

But there was still work to be done, and a rigid deadline applied – two days from last night. By that time, Allister would have found out that we had liberated Katherine and were holding his cohorts in custody. Once he had that information, there was no telling what he might do, or how well he would be able to cover his tracks.

Beth arrived with the Diet Dew and perched on the edge of the leather couch next to me. I thanked her and took a large swallow from the one liter, largemouth plastic bottle. It would be empty in a couple minutes.

"So wake up and fill me in," Beth said. "I want every detail."

"I'll give you the important stuff," I said. "But then we need to get right back to work. Allister wasn't at the site when we busted it. We still need to find out what he is involved in that prompted him to kidnap Katherine in the first place. He should go down for more than just kidnapping."

Beth nodded her understanding.

She leaned back on the couch, her eyes fixed on me, while I gave her the abbreviated version of last night's action.

"I bet a certain detective at the Minneapolis PD is going to feel excluded when he hears what he missed out on in the 'Missing Persons' case." Beth laughed. "And how great is it that Gunner gets to be a hero for his wife! That's just icing on the cake."

Then she moved closer to me and put her arm around my tired shoulders. "And of course, you are truly Katherine's savior. Without your hard work, dedication and creativity, no one would ever have thought to follow Allister to Ottawa County in the first place."

"Aw, shucks, 'tweren't nothin' ma'am."

It was corny, I know. But one could cut me some slack given my mentally and physically fatigued state. Beth did. She leaned over and gave me a big smooch on the cheek.

"You tell me when you're ready to continue our pursuit of Allister. And I will do what I can," she said. "Right now, maybe you can rest for a minute? I need to let Rosa know that Katherine is safe."

"Good idea," I said. "But please tell her not to let anyone else, including Sam, in on our secret. I can't have it get back to Allister."

"Got it," Beth said cheerily, and made for the computer.

Way too perky!

I sat on the couch until my first liter of Diet Dew was gone. Then I went to the kitchen to retrieve another, returning to the couch with the fresh supply of ambrosia.

By the time I had finished the second bottle of Dew, I was ready to go – in more ways than one. Since I had to make a rest room stop anyway, I might as well squeeze in a shower and shave and make myself presentable.

After the shower, I put on fresh clothes. Casual would be okay for my assignments today. I donned fresh blue jeans, brand new Reeboks, and a white, long-sleeve cotton broadcloth shirt – open at the neck.

I looked in the mirror. A fairly trim and muscular guy for forty-something, I thought. But then, I'm pretty sure every guy sees himself the same way in the mirror. Still, the fact that my shirts were "athletic fit" said something.

I ran my fingers back through the mirror-man's thick shock of salt and pepper hair in lieu of combing. Pretty respectable. After the shower, I felt like a new man and was ready for the rest of the day. The caffeine in the Diet Dew may have started to kick in as well. It sure didn't hurt.

I trotted down the central stairs to find Beth still at the dining room computer, deep in thought.

"Ta da!" I exclaimed, extending both arms and one leg in the classic "ta da" position.

Beth rotated her task chair so she could view the finished product.

"Lookin' good," she said. After a moment of considered appreciation, Beth asked, "Are you done being crabby?"

"What? Me?"

"Okay. Good," Beth said. "Do you have the energy to listen to what Rosa discovered before we strike out after Allister?"

"Absolutely." I was fully caffeinated and ready for anything. "What have you got?" I asked, pulling up a black-lacquered chair from the dining set.

"Actually, quite a bit," Beth answered. "Let me try to boil this down to non-computer-goddess level."

I smiled. Beth smiled back. Usually works. And Beth's smile was my favorite.

"Please proceed," I said. "I will try to be an attentive student. Or should I get the dunce cap out before we begin?"

Beth ignored the crack.

"First of all, I'll tell you what Rosa did. Then I'll give you her conclusions."

"Okay."

"Rosa started by loading all of Katherine's test programs onto Rosa's own system. Then she plugged the suspect router into another computer and into an internet connection. Using her own computer, she was able to determine that the router allowed her to connect to the internet as expected."

I interrupted Beth. "In other words, the router works for its intended purpose?"

"Yes. Very good. You get a star from the teacher."

"Woo hoo," I said.

"If I may continue?" Beth inquired.

"Please proceed," I said, sweeping my arm in a "right this way" gesture. This caffeine was working great.

"Rosa ran several of her more detailed diagnostic programs on the router and it passed all tests. Nothing unusual." Beth checked to make sure my attention hadn't wandered.

"Then she fully dismantled the other router – the one that she had open on the table when we were at the U. And she has some device that allows her to diagnose just the part of the router that we are interested in – the AS-246C-01 chipset. She attached that chipset to her testing device and then ran Dr. Whitson's test routines. As Sam had predicted, the chipset passed all of those tests."

I was starting to have trouble focusing on all this computer . . . stuff. "Can I get a bit more of a Reader's Digest version?" I begged.

"Of course. I just wanted you to understand how thorough Rosa was in her testing procedures. I'll skip ahead to the good parts."

Beth turned to her computer. A window with what looked like computer code filled the display.

"Since Rosa didn't have access to the program that Dr. Whitson had written to identify the security error we found earlier, she wrote some testing programs herself. Trust me," Beth emphasized, "that is no small task."

I nodded my appreciation of the difficulties.

"When she ran her new diagnostic tests on the chipset, one of them identified the same issue raised by the test results on the jump drive." Beth looked at me apologetically. "I'm sorry, but I need to explain a bit about chips for you to understand the rest."

"Okay," I said. I was determined to learn what I needed to know, regardless of my attention deficits.

"These chips are basically micro-miniaturized versions of electrical circuits. I know you understand those."

I nodded.

"The 'wiring' is incredibly tiny. Millions, or possibly billions, of wires on a tiny chip. A 'chipset' is two or more chips working together to perform a specific function. Each chip has wires running all over the place – some useful to the desired function of the chip, and some superfluous.

Mass production of identical chipsets that can be used for multiple purposes is cost-efficient. So that's what chip manufacturers do. They build chips that will execute all sorts of functions, and then close off the parts that aren't relevant to the client's needs. It's much cheaper and easier than building a completely custom chip from scratch for each application.

Still with me here?"

"Sure. When they build cars, every car has plugins for lots of optional equipment. If you don't buy the options, the wires just hang there, unused. This is the same idea." I looked to Beth for confirmation.

"Precisely," Beth said, pleased that I was following so far.

"Anyway," she continued, "the manufacturing instructions are in the form of a computer program written in ASIC code."

I frowned.

"Don't worry about the terminology here. You'll get it in a minute."

Beth continued.

"So the ASIC code tells the chip maker which 'options' to activate on the chip for its intended use. The code gives instructions for the unused functionality of the chip to be physically closed off, leaving only the necessary parts active. Those unused parts of the chip are left vacant and disconnected – like the 'dangling wires' you referenced earlier."

I was certainly understanding more than I had thought I would. "Please keep going," I said. "This is interesting."

"Now comes the part where I get to tell you what both Katherine and Rosa found," Beth said. "On the AS-246C-01 chipset, there was a gate left open to part of one of the chips that is not useful or necessary for the chipset's use in a router. The gate – and by the way, that's the term computer goddesses actually use for this type of opening – leads to a rather substantial area of the chip. In other words, there is quite a bit of potential processing power available in this 'dangling wire.' It could be used for thousands of purposes. Or it might just hang there, doing nothing."

"So what does that mean to us?" I asked. "Could Rosa figure out what our 'dangling wire' is used for?"

"No. She would need to see a copy of the ASIC code for that. You'll remember, perhaps, that Rosa asked Sam if he had access to any of the ASIC code during our meeting at her office?"

I raised one eyebrow and made a face that demonstrated my non-recollection of the term.

"Anyway, that is as much as Rosa can do with the chipsets from Sam," Beth concluded.

"Did she happen to check both routers to make sure they both had the same open gate?" I asked.

"Of course," Beth said, looking like I had just asked a dumb question. I always had heard there were no dumb questions. So much for that axiom. "And both chipsets possessed the exact same open gate at precisely the same location on the aberrant chip."

"So it's a flaw in the whole batch, and not just a bad apple," I said.

"Yes."

"But we don't know what the flaw does, or might do. And possibilities are endless?"

"Yes," Beth said calmly.

I was hoping for Rosa to discover something more concrete and more devious than an unused connection that appears to be available for use. I looked up at Beth. She was smiling. I couldn't help smiling back. That darn trick works almost every time.

"Aren't you going to ask me something?" Beth inquired, still smiling.

I thought for a moment.

"So, how do we figure out what the open connection on the chip is connected to?" I tried.

"Good question."

"And you have the answer?" I asked hopefully.

"Not by myself," she said. "But I bet our recently-liberated computer genius does. Or at least that she can figure it out."

Great idea, I thought. I smiled broadly.

"But we may need a copy of that ASIC code."

Instant frown. Where were we going to get that if Sam couldn't get it for us?

"I bet Katherine can tell us where it's located on the ComDyne servers," Beth said with another smile.

"I was just thinking the same thing," I lied badly.

"Uh huh." Beth verbalized her skepticism.

"So then . . . I'm off to HCMC to check on Katherine's condition. I hope you're coming along to interpret computerese," I said.

"Wouldn't miss it."

I stood up.

With Beth still seated, I bent over and gave her a gentle kiss on the lips. "You are my goddess," I said after the kiss had ended.

"True." She smiled.

I smiled back.

CHAPTER 29

On the way to HCMC, with Beth driving the Pilot – we thought it might be safer for her to drive, given my sleep-deprived state – I phoned Gunner on his cell.

"I thought you would be taking a nap," he answered.

"I had hoped to wake you from yours," I replied. But Gunner wasn't going to let my sarcasm irritate him today.

"How may I serve you?" he said, uncharacteristically. "I owe you big time."

"We'll check the status of our markers later. I'm still at the table," I said. "Is there any way you can get a warrant to search for some computer software at ComDyne? I don't have the details yet. But I hope to fairly soon. And the whole thing is extremely time-sensitive."

"I'm not a good bet for that one." Gunner sounded disappointed. "I hate to say it, but MPD's probably your best shot."

I really didn't want to take the MPD route. I had pretty much burned my bridges with those folks.

"Any way I can get the FBI involved?" I tried.

"No state lines crossed in the kidnap. Do you have any other theory that might give them jurisdiction?" Gunner asked.

I thought for a moment.

"Commerce clause," I said cryptically.

"I beg your pardon?"

"If I can show that there is a crime involving interstate commerce, that will invoke federal jurisdiction," I said. I'd learned that one in law school; but I'd never had need of that particular bit of constitutional law in my practice. I was actually shocked that I'd remembered it.

"That's true" said Gunner. "But you've gotta come up with another crime, because an all-Minnesota kidnap won't do it."

"That's okay. I've got something in mind. Thanks, Gunner. You've been a big help . . . really." I was atypically sincere.

"You're welcome, for what it's worth. Good luck!"

"And Gunner . . . please remind the BCA to stay away from Allister until I can wrap up this other angle," I said.

"Already done. And will do again."

"Great! We'll talk soon. I'll have my people call your people. We'll do lunch." I terminated the call.

"Beth," I said. "I need to make another call. I think it's time for some additional high-powered law enforcement assistance."

"You have to push the little buttons to make it dial," she said, still paying attention to the fairly thick Sunday afternoon traffic.

Wise ass.

There was only one person at the FBI in whom I had complete confidence. He and I had worked together on a field operation a number of years ago. And he had helped me just recently when a ghost from my past tried to abduct one of my daughters.

Scrolling through the speed dial list, I stopped on the private cell number of Daniel Trew. Trew had a big office in Washington and was no longer a field agent. But he would put me in touch with someone I could trust.

I pushed the "connect" button on the phone.

"Executive Assistant Director Trew."

"Dan, this is the guy you helped out with some Mongolians last year," I said. "Do you recognize my voice?"

"Hold on a second please," he told me.

He covered the mouthpiece and there were muffled sounds of music and conversation in the background. A minute later, the background noises had faded.

"Sorry about that. We're hosting a barbecue at our house and I needed to get away."

"No problem, Dan. Sorry for the interruption. But I have what might be an important issue to address in Minneapolis, and I need a reference."

"So your name these days is James Becker according to my caller ID. Do I call you Jim?" he chuckled.

"Beck," I said. "It's a nickname I've had a long time."

"Beck. Very manly. I like it," Trew said. "Of course, I will do what I can to assist. What sort of matter is it?"

"It appears to be a cyber-crime of some sort. I expect to have more details in a few hours. But I need to have someone from the FBI on board ASAP. Things are going to move pretty quickly."

Trew was silent for a moment.

"The person you want is Renee Dupont, in the Minneapolis Field Office. It's on Washington Avenue downtown, I think."

"Would you mind greasing the skids for me, Dan?" I asked. "It'll really help if Agent Dupont and I can get off on the right foot."

"You wouldn't have any problems working with Renee anyway. She's topnotch. Very professional and field savvy. But of course, I'll make some calls. And I can make sure the Field Office SAC clears the assignment."

SAC is Special Agent in Charge.

"Then I'll talk to Renee myself," Dan continued. "How do you want to make contact with her?"

"Please give her the cell number I am calling you on right now and tell her she is needed ASAP at the hospital room of Katherine Whitson at HCMC – she'll know where that is. Does that work for you?" I asked Dan.

"Consider it done. Hey. It was good to talk to you . . . ah . . . Beck. Good luck!"

"Thanks for everything, Dan," I said. "Be good."

"Always." He hung up.

We still had nearly an hour of travel time from Red Wing before we would be at HCMC. Maybe we'd get lucky and Special Agent Dupont would be able to catch us there. One could hope.

I had one more call to make – to Bull. I hated to wake him if he was sleeping. But the need was urgent. And he was the only person I could think of who would be up for the job.

Bull's cell phone rang twice.

"Yeah."

He didn't sound like I had awakened him; but it's hard to tell for sure from a "Yeah."

"Sorry if I disturbed you," I said. "But you did such a great job this morning, that I would really appreciate your services again today."

"Sure."

I explained my needs and Bull was overjoyed to help out. "Okay," he had said.

CHAPTER 30

Beth located a parking spot in the Medical Center ramp and we were able to procure a room number for Katherine Whitson. When we exited the elevator on floor six, I noticed that the round, white, institutional clock on the wall read 2:35. A lot had happened in the last twelve hours. If things went well, the next twenty-four promised to be equally significant.

We located Room 622 and peeked through the window slot in the wooden door. Katherine was sitting up in bed talking with George, who was perched precisely on the edge of her mattress. I could see, even from the hall, that the bedspread was devoid of any wrinkles, form-fitting to Katherine's legs and torso.

I knocked, then opened the door enough for Whitson to see me.

"May I come in?" I asked. "And I've brought my wife along."

Katherine didn't recognize me from earlier that morning. That wasn't surprising.

George stood and politely said, "Yes. Please come in. Would you like a chair?"

It was a private room and there was a fair amount of sitting space, considering this was a hospital. I guessed the Whitsons could afford a few extra amenities.

"Thank you," I said, stepping into the room and approaching the Whitsons.

"Dr. Whitson," I said to Katherine, "my name is Beck, and this is my wife Beth."

"Hello, Dr. Whitson," Beth said.

Katherine looked up at George, but didn't say anything.

"Katherine," he said, "the Beckers are the people responsible for your rescue."

Katherine appeared frail and tired as she greeted us. No wonder. God only knows what hell she had been through for the past ten days.

"Thank you," was all she said.

Whitson approached me and shook my hand as firmly as he was able. I can't thank you enough for bringing my Katherine back to me. Bless you.

And you, too, Mrs. Becker." He shook Beth's hand. "I understand that you also worked tirelessly to help save my wife. Thank you so much. I don't know how I can ever repay you."

"You're welcome, of course," Beth said. "No repayment of any kind is necessary."

Whitson returned to his wife's bedside and perched, once more, beside her, smoothing the bedspread before and after he sat. I decided it might be less intimidating if we sat as well. Motioning Beth toward an orange vinyl and wood armchair, I chose one for myself and sat down.

I looked at Whitson.

"Is it okay if I ask Katherine a few questions? I will be as brief as possible. But we need to move quickly to apprehend every person responsible for her abduction."

He looked to Katherine. "Sweety. Do you feel up to helping the Beckers catch the rest of the people who kidnapped you?"

Katherine slid herself a bit higher up the inclined bed.

"Could you please sit me up further, George?" she asked.

He found the appropriate control and raised the head of the bed until she said, "That's perfect. Thank you."

She looked at me. "Beck, is it?"

"Yes."

"I apologize for my current appearance. I'm afraid you've not caught me at my best." She smiled. Beth and I smiled back.

"Of course," I said. I waited because I sensed she wanted to say more.

"Have they arrested that pompous bastard, Allister, yet?" she asked quietly.

The contrast between her weakened voice and bold words struck me as remarkable. And I was pleased to see that she hadn't suffered any ill effects from the sudden withdrawal of her anxiety meds.

"I'm afraid not," I said. "It is in relation to catching Dr. Allister that I believe you may be able to help us."

Again, I waited patiently for Katherine to respond.

"I am completely at your disposal," she said. "Including sticking a needle in the self-absorbed asshole's arm if necessary."

Katherine's speech again reflected an inner strength of will that her external appearance belied.

"I may be a bit physically weakened as a result of my captivity," she said matter-of-factly. "But my faculties remain entirely intact. What can I do to help?"

I could see she was marshaling all of her physical assets just to conduct the conversation. So I began with a bit of conjecture, to see if I could move this discussion along quickly. I didn't want Katherine's fatigue to get the best of her.

"Beth and I surmise that Dr. Allister has intentionally designed some nefarious functionality into the AS-246C-01 chipset for ComDyne's new router. We also suspect that you discovered the design anomaly and brought it to his attention, thinking that, perhaps, the manufacturer might be the culprit in the faulty design.

How am I doing so far?" I asked.

Katherine nodded. "Keep going," she managed. "You are apparently quite adept at what you do."

"Believe me," I said. "It was a team effort. And don't underestimate the value of your own contributions. Your handwritten note and jump drive clues provided our compass."

Katherine smiled. I smiled back.

"When you brought the chip failure to Dr. Allister's attention, he first tried to pass it off as an isolated defect. But you had already tested multiple chipsets. So you refuted his assertion. Then he undoubtedly tried to convince you that it was probably a manufacturing problem, the single open gate was of little significance, and he would deal with it."

"Do you read palms?" Katherine asked with a feeble chuckle that turned into a cough. She regained her composure quickly. George gave her a sip of water from the glass on the bed stand before she could even ask.

Without speaking, she motioned with a rotating movement of her hand for me to continue.

"Your meeting lasted nearly two hours. So you must have had quite an involved discussion – more likely an argument – about the significance of the chipset problem. But Dr. Allister proved intractable and you ultimately relented.

By this time you probably suspected that Dr. Allister was involved in something criminal.   Furthermore, Allister's temperament and supercilious attitude had given you a headache. You decided that you would leave work early – around five o'clock – and deal with Allister the next day. But not before you took at least some precautions for the safety of your discovery. You didn't really believe that Allister would try to harm you physically. But just to be safe, you stored your test results as the sole file on a jump drive, which you then hid in George's bottle of sleeping pills."

Katherine was shaking her head. Maybe I had gotten something wrong.

"Am I headed astray?" I asked.

Katherine laughed softly. "Not at all. I'm just amazed. Please, go on."

"You had probably taken some Tylenol for your headache and lain down for a rest. You knew George would be bothered by the wrinkled bed clothes in your own bedroom; so you chose a guest room instead. After only a few minutes, Dr. Allister was at your door; you saw him through the peep hole. Still not suspecting that he would do anything nearly as dramatic as kidnapping, you reluctantly opened the door to let him in.

At this point, one or two Chinese men forced their way through the door and into your condo. You knew that a physical confrontation, given your stature and the forces allied against you, was not realistic.

It was Allister's idea that you leave a note. Unfortunately for him, he was foolish enough to let you choose the words.

After looking it over, he considered it harmless enough. He then demanded your key ring, cell phone and credit cards, which he arrayed very neatly across the bed – just as he assumed you would have done it.

Being careful not to disturb anything in the apartment, the goons – I guess there had to be two, since Allister wouldn't stoop to manual labor – located your luggage, clothing and some toiletries. They hastily packed some of your things into the suitcases to support the conclusion that you had left voluntarily.

They weren't very thorough though. I suspect you noticed as well. They left your contact lenses and prescription medication behind, among other blunders. They also wiped down the bathroom mirrors and other hard surfaces to make sure they had left no fingerprints.

Then they probably drugged you with chloroform or some other knockout drug. The next thing you knew, you were inside a cement cell in that bizarre tower.

How did I do?" I asked.

Katherine applauded briefly in approval. "Actually, I took ibuprofen," she said.

"It was a fifty-fifty shot based on the contents of your medicine cabinet," I conceded.

"If you know all of this, what do you still need my help for?" Katherine asked.

"First off, knowing is different from proving," I pointed out. "I might spin a good yarn based on circumstantial evidence. But I have precious little in the way of proof to support any of it."

"So you need my testimony? Of course. It will be my pleasure," Katherine offered.

"Yes. That will likely be needed. But there is also the matter of the defective chipset. I still don't know what functionality that chip anomaly has. And maybe my background makes me a bit paranoid; but it strikes me that the possibilities for cyber-terrorism, or at least cyber-theft, are very real. I would very much like to know to where that chip's open gate leads."

"You and I both," Katherine agreed.

"Do you have any ideas?" I asked.

"The extent of my testing had only reached the point of identifying the open gate. I planned to review the functionality issue on Friday. Obviously, I didn't get the chance."

"Can you help us with that issue now?" I inquired hopefully. I thought I knew what she was going to say.

"I need the ASIC code to do that. If you can get me the original ASIC code – not the dummy copy that Allister has already substituted onto every computer to which he has access – I am confident I can tell you the functionality of that logic loop."

"Do you have any idea of where we could get that original code?" I crossed my fingers.

"Your best chance would be on the offsite storage drives. You would need to find a backup copy of the code that predated the day I was attacked," she said. "I know where they are stored. But I'm afraid security is very tight. They can't be hacked into, because they're air-gapped."

"I beg your pardon?" My computer ignorance was showing again.

Beth stepped in. "That means the storage drives that hold the original ASIC code cannot be accessed from any computer system outside the storage facility itself. There is literally an 'air gap' between the storage system and outside connections, like the internet."

"Very good, Beth," Katherine complimented.

There was a light knock at the door. I got up and went to see who it was. Allister might still try something to do away with Katherine if he found out she had been freed. Best to be safe.

In the hallway, just outside the door, stood a short woman with dark brown hair, wearing a navy jacket over a white shirt. I could recognize FBI when I saw it.

I opened the door a few inches and put my face in the opening. "Yes?" I offered politely.

She already had out her badge and ID. She held them up to my face.

"I'm Special Agent Renee Dupont, FBI. I'm s'posed to speak with a Mr. Becker."

"Beck," I said, as I opened the door for Agent Dupont and offered her my hand. "Please come in and let me introduce you."

After we had exchanged all the niceties, I summarized our situation.

Agent Dupont looked at me. "You want a search warrant for the archived computer code," she said.

She had caught on quickly.

"Do we have enough for probable cause?" I asked.

"I think there should be plenty with Dr. Whitson's and your Affidavits. I can get a stenographer to type up the papers for signing yet tonight. And I should be able to get the warrant first thing in the morning. I'd rather not disturb a federal judge on a Sunday unless I have to."

"Unless Allister decides to make contact with his Chinese buddies before then, tomorrow morning should be fine," I said. "But I have a couple other related requests we might discuss in the hall?"

We were done with Katherine Whitson for the time being. And it was a good thing, too. She was tired and fading fast into the Land of Nod. We said our goodbyes and Beth, Agent Dupont and I quietly left the room and walked down the hall to an empty family waiting area.

After all three of us were inside, I turned to Agent Dupont.

"I have a couple concerns. First and foremost is Katherine's safety. We don't yet know who all is tangled up in this mess. Those Chinese guys didn't come to Allister's rescue on a moment's notice without some serious crime connection."

Agent Dupont considered my request. "I'll post an agent at Dr. Whitson's door until she is released. Then a two-man detail will stay with her wherever she goes. Does that help?"

"Very much so. Thank you.

I have one other concern. If Dr. Allister gets access to those archived disks before we do, they will be erased and we may never be able to convict him on an espionage charge. It would be a shame if we missed that opportunity."

"I will also get a team to keep an eye on Allister. If he goes anywhere near the building with the back-up records, we'll pick him up."

"Perfect." I said. "Thank you very much.

I should expect your call sometime tonight to sign that Affidavit then?"

"You'll be the first to hear when it's ready," she said.

"Very good. Until then," I doffed my imaginary cap toward the Agent. Then Beth and I left her in the waiting room, writing up her notes.

"You're still doing the fake cap thing?" Beth cracked. "Sheesh!"

"Time to retire the invisible Stetson?" I asked.

"Years ago."

CHAPTER 31

Since it appeared that we were going to be spending time in the metro area tonight and again early tomorrow, Beth and I decided to save some driving and checked into the Hyatt Regency in downtown Minneapolis. I try to keep a change of clothes for myself in a small duffle in the Pilot. So I was set for tomorrow. Beth needed a new outfit.

Fortunately, some of the department stores downtown were still open. Beth insisted that I remain at the hotel and get some rest while she found herself some appropriate attire for tomorrow. I was not a good shopping companion under the best of circumstances. I would be worse in my fatigued condition. I reluctantly acceded to her request. I hate not being chivalrous; but sometimes it's just the right thing to do.

Beth struck out on her shopping excursion.

I felt the need for a shower. There's something about hanging around a hospital that always makes me feel that way. Seems like a hospital should be a place to go when you want to get sick, instead of when you're sick already. The shower was warm and relaxing. Afterwards, having no pajamas in my duffle, I crawled into the king bed, au naturel, and had no difficulty falling asleep.

The next thing I remember is Beth kissing my forehead. She was holding several, colorful paper shopping bags with twine handles. I realized that I hadn't moved an inch while I slept.

"What time is it?" I asked, still not moving.

Beth was busy depositing her new clothes in the closet and dresser drawers.

"Nine-thirty," Beth said, deftly folding, hanging and stowing her things.

"Are we going to Europe tomorrow?" I asked, eyeing the number of bags. The clothes kept coming out of them, like scarves out of a magician's sleeve.

"As long as I was in Saks, I thought I might as well pick up some items that I can't find in Red Wing. You do want me to look presentable, don't you?" she asked.

Turning to face me, she modeled a pink satin teddy, holding it across her chest by the delicate spaghetti straps.

"I suppose you can't very well go out in your Cinderella garb every day," I managed with a swallow.

"I was sure you would feel that way. Now, it's my turn for a shower."

She had finished putting clothes away and carried just a small pink handful of satin into the bathroom with her.

Suddenly, I wasn't sleepy anymore. I fluffed the bed pillows and sat in bed with the sheets strategically placed to assure modesty. I heard the shower start, and then stop, flowing. A moment later the hair dryer hummed.

Beth emerged from the bathroom wearing the pink teddy and matching tap pants. I could hardly breathe.

"Those pieces look like they were a good value," I said, as nonchalantly as I could manage.

"I don't recall telling you the price," Beth said, crossing to the bed.

"Don't believe you did."

I slid across the bed, making room for Beth to join me. I couldn't very well stand up in my current condition. She slipped in next to me, lying with her silky blonde hair floating on a pillow.

I rolled onto my stomach, and bringing my face above hers, gave her a long, deep kiss. All of the stress of the day flowed out of my body. And the tension in my shoulders melted away.

"Do those pajamas look as good when you're not wearing them?" I asked.

Beth smiled. "Shall we see?"

"Definitely."

CHAPTER 32

After we had been enjoying our hotel retreat for a little more than an hour together, my cell phone buzzed. I rolled over and retrieved it from the bed stand. The caller ID said "United States Government." It was Special Agent Dupont.

I composed myself and answered, "Beck."

"This is Special Agent Dupont," she said. "I've got your Affidavit ready if you'd like to review and sign?"

"Can you email it to me? Then I can make sure it is completely accurate before I show up to put pen to paper. I can proof it on my phone. It'll save time."

"No problem." I gave her the necessary contact info and a moment later the text of the Affidavit was on my cell phone screen.

I read it thoroughly. If something screwed up the legality of Dr. Allister's bust, it was *not* going to be an error in my Affidavit.

After reading, I called Agent Dupont with several small corrections. "Where do you want me to come to sign the original?" I asked.

"How about the Field Office on Washington Avenue in say . . . fifteen minutes?"

I looked at my wife. She lay on her back with one hand carelessly resting, palm-up on the pillow next to her face. Her eyes shone and her cheeks glowed. I wanted to stay here with Beth.

"Sure. No problem," I heard my voice say to Agent Dupont. I clicked off the cell.

"Duty calls, my sweet."

"I'll be here when you get back, Señor Feliz. Maybe I'll just rest up a bit until then." She rolled onto her side and closed her eyes.

Beauty incarnate.

I put on the clothes I had worn earlier that day. I would shower again when I returned anyway.

"Beth?"

"Level Three East," she said, giving the location of the Pilot.

"Thanks."

In the truck on the way to Washington Avenue, about fifteen blocks, I tried to think of anything else that would need to be done to prepare for tomorrow. Then I remembered Sam. It was already after 11:00 p.m.; but I needed to speak with Sam.

I punched up his speed-dial on the phone.

A sleepy voice answered. "Hello?"

"Sam. This is Beck. I'm sorry to wake you, but it's sort of an emergency."

"Okay," he said, still sounding half-asleep. "What's going on?"

"We've found Dr. Whitson and she is okay."

"That's awesome!"

Now he was awake.

"I figured you might think so. But Sam, I still need some favors from you."

I explained what I needed and he agreed to do his best. How could I ask for more?

The Affidavit was waiting for me at the front desk on Washington Avenue. I reviewed it again and a uniformed officer notarized my signature.

"Is Special Agent Dupont still here?" I asked.

"Yeah. You want I should call her?" the officer asked.

"Please. Tell her it's Beck and I just need two minutes."

He punched in an extension. "There is a Mr. Beck here to see you. Says he just needs two minutes."

There was a pause.

"Okay, Agent Dupont. I'll tell him." Then turning to me, "She'll be right down. Have a seat." He gestured to some tired wooden chairs with upholstered seats. The springs under the upholstery looked shot.

"I think I'll just stand."

I was becoming somewhat of an *aficionado* of police waiting room furniture. In lieu of sitting, I paced the reception area, looking at framed black and whites of uniformed former FBI greats. I kept looking. I was sure J. Edgar would be here somewhere.

"Mr. Becker." It was Agent Dupont.

"Please," I said. "Everybody calls me Beck."

"Okay, Beck. What's up?"

"Shall we sit?" I asked, indicating the sad chairs.

"Are you kidding?" she said. "Those things'll kill ya. Come up to my office."

I followed her toward the elevators in the middle of the building. She was slim and in very good condition, judging by her gluteal muscles. And I'm a pretty good judge of female glutes.

Agent Dupont's office was on the tenth floor of the twenty-eight story building. Her office wasn't actually an office at all. It was a cubicle in a large room of similar cubicles. But she had a side chair that looked comfortable. She sat and motioned for me to do the same. The chair was adequate.

"So what do you need to discuss?" Dupont asked.

"I thought we should coordinate the serving of the search warrant with Katherine's availability and location in the morning."

"I do have a plan for that." She wasn't offended.

"Does it include access for Katherine to appropriate equipment so she can review the code and test the chipset functionality at the same time?"

"I s'pose that makes sense. Once she figures out what the chipset does, she'll want to test it to make sure. I'll amend the application for the warrant to include hardware and software necessary to test the routers, as well as a couple routers themselves."

"Excellent," I said. "And I know precisely where you can serve that hardware and software warrant for maximum efficiency."

She gave me a confused look.

I filled her in on the situation. Then we talked a while longer, finally settling on all the details and timing.

She escorted me back to the elevator. On the ride down she told me, "Director Trew said you'd be a decent guy."

"And?" I said.

"He was right, so far. And thanks for the additional info for tomorrow's warrant. It'll make things a lot smoother."

"You would have thought of the same things if you were as familiar with the case as I have become over the last ten days," I said.

We continued down. The elevator was slow by modern standards.

"Dan was right about you, too," I said. "Professional. Very competent. Nice person, to boot."

We exited the elevator on the main level and I followed her toward the door.

"I'll call you at 7:30," she said.

"Until then," I said, nearly doffing my imaginary hat again. But then, remembering I had promised not to pursue further doffing activities, I converted the aborted gesture into a wave.

When I got back to the hotel room, Beth was sleeping soundly. I showered and then slipped into the far side of the bed. Morning would come early. I should catch some winks. I kissed Beth on the cheek, rolled over and immediately drifted into oblivion.

CHAPTER 33

Very early Monday morning.

While most of the world slept, the FBI Agent kept watch over Katherine Whitson's hospital room. He had obtained a fairly comfortable chair from a waiting area, placing it strategically in the hallway. To stay loose, he alternated between standing and sitting. But regardless of his posture, he always maintained a vigilant guard over Katherine's room.

Well . . . almost always. He did have to urinate every few hours.

At around 2:30 a.m., he put down the magazine he had been scanning and rose to take a bathroom break. But before leaving the hallway, he would walk its entire length, searching for anyone who might be a threat to his charge.

As he walked, he checked out the family waiting area, about fifty feet down the hall from the Whitson room. It was presently occupied by a black-haired man. The Agent could only see the back of the man's head as he lay huddled under several, navy-blue hospital blankets. Scrunched up on the short sofa, the man was snoring noticeably.

The Agent hadn't seen the man enter the room between bathroom breaks. But then, the waiting area was not his primary focus. And the sleeping man didn't appear to constitute an imminent threat.

Continuing down the hallway, all the other common areas were vacant – save only the nurses' station, which was staffed by the same redheaded matron he had seen sitting there, reading a romance novel, all night long.

After checking on the sleeping man one more time, the Agent decided it was safe to quickly relieve himself. So he entered the sixth floor Men's Room.

The door closed behind him. It was dark. For some reason, the automatic light had not turned on. He fumbled for a manual wall switch. As he did so, he heard running footsteps inside the restroom. He turned to address the threat. Something hard smashed into the side of his head. His eyes flashed, then went dark.

*   *   *

With the lights back on, a man in a white lab coat and teal surgeon's pants exited the sixth floor hospital Men's Room, leaving the FBI agent sprawled out in a stall. He headed immediately down the hall toward Room 622.

Arriving outside his destination, he peered briefly through the window into the darkened room. There was enough illumination from the outside windows for him to see a slight figure lying in the bed, covered neatly by the spread. No one else was present. And no one was visible in the hall either.

Withdrawing a policeman's night stick from the cinched waistband of the surgeon's pants, the man shouldered the door slowly, and silently, open.

There was no movement in the bed as he crept closer. Nearing the bedside, he raised the nightstick above his head and brought it down brutally across the victim's chest – smashing her torso again and again with all his might. When he had finished the beating, he pulled back the bed linens to make sure the job was done.

To his dismay, he discovered that the figure in the bed had been a stuffed doll. A dummy. As he stood in disbelief, a mannequin's head rolled off the bed and cracked on the hard floor.

What had happened?

But the man in the lab coat had little time to consider his situation. For when he turned to leave the room, he found Bull's hulking frame standing between him and his exit strategy.

To say that an altercation ensued would not be remotely accurate. It is true that the man attacked Bull with the nightstick. But Bull caught the wooden weapon in one hand, wrenching it from the man's grip, and tossing it to the floor.

After that, the man in the lab coat had had a brief encounter with a poured-concrete wall, and had ended up, rather quickly, on the floor. Still dazed from the wall collision, and with Bull's mass pressing his face and chest into the institutional tile, it was all the man could do to breath. He was no longer even trying to fight.

On his way to Room 622, Bull had alerted the desk nurse of the probable injuries to the Agent in the Men's Room. Doctor's should be aiding him already. Now Bull took out his cell phone and called the local FBI office on Washington Avenue. They needed to know that their man was hurt, and that Bull held another criminal for them to take into custody.

Having made the required contacts, Bull tied his captive to the hospital bed, using several lengths of twine he had brought with him for just such a purpose. Leaving Lab Man writhing on the bed, Bull took up guard duty outside Katherine's Whitson's real hospital room – Room 625, across the hall.

When he looked through the window into her room, he could see that she was sleeping soundly. Apparently, the bad guy hadn't even disturbed her rest.

It wasn't long before additional FBI agents arrived to take over.

When they were set, and Lab Man had been removed from the premises, Bull returned to the family waiting area, and went back to sleep.

CHAPTER 34

Monday, October 26th, Early Morning.

My cell phone alarm was set for six o'clock. As seems to often happen, I awoke just before it went off. I deactivated the alarm and rolled as smoothly as possible out of the bed, trying not to disturb Beth. She would be getting up soon enough. I headed straight for the bath and did my best to replicate my usual morning routine. The duffle from the Pilot contained an abbreviated Dopp Kit. So I had pretty much everything I needed.

Emerging from the bathroom ten minutes later, showered, and etc., I saw that Beth was beginning to stir. She propped her lovely head on one hand, resting on an elbow, and blinked. I hadn't yet had a chance to dress.

"Now there's a picture," she commented. I feigned modesty, using my duffle to cover certain areas, and walked backward into the bathroom to dress.

When I re-emerged fully clothed, Beth was on her feet and ready to take her turn at the shower.

Those PJs were definitely a buy!

At six forty-five, we went down to the Hyatt coffee shop for a light breakfast. As we stood nibbling on scones and sipping coffee at an elevated café table, we discussed plans for the day.

"Once we have everything Katherine needs from ComDyne," I said, "we have to find a place for her to work. The FBI has a tech center on Washington Avenue. It may turn out to be adequate. But would you mind contacting Rosa to see if there is any chance we can use her computer lab?"

"Actually, that's an excellent idea. Rosa did offer any further assistance we might need. What time do you suppose we'll be needing the facilities?" Beth asked.

"Timing is somewhat uncertain. Dupont needs to get a federal judge to sign the warrants. Then we need to execute them at ComDyne – both at the data storage facility in Eden Prairie and at the main offices in Maple Grove. Katherine will be at the data site to help locate the right . . . program thingy."

"The ASIC code for the chipset design," Beth said.

"Yes. That's the thingy to which I was referring. Anyway, I don't know how soon Katherine will be able to locate and copy the code once she has access to the storage site. She hasn't actually been there before herself. Then there's travel time from the storage site in Eden Prairie to the U of M computer lab.

So if I were to guess at a time we might need Rosa's help," I concluded, "I would say no sooner than ten o'clock, but possibly beginning as late as noon – or maybe later. I hope not."

"I'll call Rosa's cell when we get back to the room," Beth offered. "She seems such a kind soul, I can't believe she'll mind being awakened early on a Monday to help catch Katherine's abductor. Actually, she'll probably be up already. Her daily schedule is long, and she seems the sort to get an early start. Regardless, I'll make the call."

"Terrific," I said. "The FBI tech lab will be our backup."

We returned to our hotel room, taking coffee refills with us. Beth called Rosa and our luck held – she would cancel her appointments and classes for the entire day and place herself at our disposal. She really was a kind soul.

At precisely 7:30 my cell buzzed. It was Agent Dupont.

"Beck," I answered.

"Good morning, Beck. I've got the warrants."

"That was quick."

"I found a judge that was an early-riser," she said. "Dr. and Mr. Whitson are with me and one of my colleagues on the way to the storage site. Another team is on the way to ComDyne HQ."

"Beth and I will leave here right away to rendezvous with you at the storage facility. Do we know where Allister is?" I asked.

"My baby-sitters say he has been at his office since six o'clock. He'll know something is happening as soon as he hears about the warrants. That sort of news moves pretty fast through corporate offices. But I'd still like to watch him for a while to see if he contacts any additional suspects. We've got taps on all his phones. He might make a call."

Agent Dupont had been very thorough, and her plan to give Allister some rope to hang himself made sense.

"Thanks for the update," I said. "We will see you as soon as possible. Maybe Katherine will have already found what you need before we arrive. If so, we have arranged for Katherine and Dr. Rosa Mendez to both take a look at the evidence at the U of M Center for Technology Development." I paused. "I hope that's not a problem. Dr. Mendez is already familiar with the chipset and she has the finest computer lab facilities money can buy."

I wondered if I had overstepped my boundaries. Damn. I should have talked to Dupont first.

"No. That's not a problem."

Whew!

"You really have some kind of big shot connections if you have gotten Rosa Mendez to work on this with you," she said, sounding surprised.

"Is that a big deal?"

"Every computer geek in the country . . . probably in the world . . . knows of Rosa Mendez. You really aren't a computer guy, are you?"

"Guess not," I said.

"Oh and Beck . . . seems your friend was involved in some extra-curricular activities at HCMC last night. Everybody's okay. I'll fill you in later."

"See you soon," I said, wondering what the hell Bull had been up to while I slept.

Beth and I gathered our things and were in the Pilot and on the road in less than five minutes. While we drove the twenty minutes or so to Eden Prairie, I told Beth what Agent Dupont had told me about Dr. Mendez.

"Did you know she was such a big deal?" I asked.

"Of course."

Okay. I felt a little stupid for not picking up on Rosa's notoriety earlier. I needed to reclaim some dignity.

"Agent Dupont calls computer goddesses, computer geeks," I said defensively.

"Maybe she's a geek and not a goddess," Beth replied nonchalantly.

Oh, well. Computers were not my strong suit. I might as well admit it. Maybe I would yet have a chance to display some other talent today. I kept driving without challenging Beth's response. She probably had a good point.

"Do all computer goddesses look hot in their jammies?" I asked.

Beth gave me a backhanded whack to the abdomen. I smiled and glanced over at her. She was smiling, too.

*   *   *

At 7:45 a.m. on the dot, a Caucasian woman, dressed in a black suit with white shirt and black soft-soled shoes, picked up the phone and pressed the Information button on the security entrance panel at ComDyne corporate HQ.

"How may I help you?"

"I am here to collect a package for Renee Dupont," the woman said into the speaker. "It should be waiting for me at Reception."

"Please enter and follow the signs to the reception area to your right."

The door buzzed and the woman entered the building. As she approached the reception area, she saw a man standing at the counter. Next to him, on the counter-top, was a smallish, white banker's box. As she got closer she saw "Renee Dupont" written in black marker on the box's cover.

She slid the man a business-sized white envelope and simultaneously grasped the box by both handles, removing it from his reach, then headed toward the exit.

"Just a minute, ma'am," he tried. "I need a receipt or some ID or something."

"Check the envelope," she said, not bothering to look back as she passed through the exit. She put the box in the back seat of a black four-door sedan and climbed in the front passenger side. The sedan squealed its tires as it left the ComDyne parking lot.

The reception man was hopelessly behind the woman as she departed. The car was just pulling away as he reached the glass doors. Shit! He thought. What in the hell was that?

He looked at the white envelope; then opened it. Unfolding the official-looking documents inside, he was suddenly aware of what had just occurred. What the hell should he do now?

*   *   *

Simultaneously with the incursion at ComDyne headquarters, a dark-suited woman approached ComDyne's Eden Prairie off-site computer storage facility. She pressed a similar button on the entrance console.

A voice came through the speaker, "How may I help you?"

"FBI. We have a warrant to search these premises. If you do not open this door in three seconds we will break it down."

The door buzzed open. Agent Dupont stepped inside and held the door for her companions. Behind her, Katherine and George Whitson and an additional male FBI agent entered the building. Agent Dupont approached the woman who had apparently run to the entry hall. The Agent held out the leather wallet containing her badge and identification. Then put it back on her belt.

"Here's the search warrant," Agent Dupont said, handing the stunned woman an envelope. "We need to find the backup copies of ASIC code from Wednesday, October 14th pertaining to the AS-246C-01 chipset design. If you don't know where they are, get us someone. Now!"

"I will take you to our facility manager. He should know where you can find what you are looking for," the woman said, obviously frightened.

"Let's go find him. Hurry it up!" Agent Dupont presented a force to be dealt with.

Ten seconds later, the woman knocked on the door of an office displaying a sign: "Manager."

Before the office's occupant could respond to the knock, Agent Dupont forced her way past the woman, opened the door, and strode into the office.

"What the hell?" the man behind the desk asked, standing up and facing the intruder. The woman from the entry hall had also entered and now transferred the warrant to her manager.

"FBI," Agent Dupont said, again showing her credentials. Before the manager had a chance to read the warrant, Agent Dupont demanded the location of, and access to, the necessary backup drives.

"I will need to call Dr. Allister to get his permission," the manager said, trying to sound managerial. He picked up the phone on his desk.

Agent Dupont placed her right index finger on the deskset, cutting off the dial tone. "No. You will not. He is the person we are investigating."

A look of shock crossed the manager's face.

"You will take us to the appropriate drives now, or we will dismantle every last box in this building and analyze all the pieces at headquarters."

More shock.

"Your choice," she said. The look on her face told the manager that she was prepared to carry out her threat.

"Of course," the manager said. "P-p-please f-follow . . . ." He completed the sentence with a hand gesture that the group should accompany him. He hurried out of his office and down the hall.

Reaching a large metal door at the end of the hallway, he produced a key card, slid it through the wall console and punched in a code. Then he led the entire procession inside the data vault.

*   *   *

Beth and I had arrived at the ComDyne data backup site. As we pulled into the facility, it struck me how small the building was. I had assumed that backing up data for a huge company like ComDyne would require a commensurately huge building.

In the entry alcove, I pressed the Information button on the security panel.

"I'm sorry. We are presently closed to all non-employees," a female voice said.

"We are with the FBI," I stated with authority. "Agent Dupont is expecting us. God only knows what she will do if you deny us access. She's sort of unstable," I added.

"She seems a bit on the edge," the voice said.

I stifled a laugh.

The buzzer sounded and we entered the building. A woman directed us toward a room at the far end of the hall. "She is in the data vault with the manager."

"Thank you," I said.

Beth and I proceeded promptly to the indicated room. It had a locked metal door. I knocked firmly.

A male FBI agent opened the door.

"I'm with Agent Dupont," I said. The agent stepped aside so Dupont could see me.

"They're okay. Let 'em in," she said.

As I entered the data vault, I could feel that the air was somewhat cooler and dryer here than in the hallway. The room was only about forty feet square. The center twenty by twenty foot area was filled with rows of black metal racks. Each rack held eight rows of black metal and plastic boxes. The boxes were the size of my 1990s vintage stereo receiver, but devoid of any visible controls. A few red and green lights occasionally blinked through their tinted plastic fronts.

"These are racked RAID units," Beth explained, as if I would understand. "A Redundant Array of Independent Disks."

She could tell I was still in the dark.

"Each black box contains several disk drives totaling maybe ten or fifteen terabytes of disk storage space."

I still looked ignorant. Beth gave up.

As we got closer to the group, I could see that a man was typing furiously on a keyboard at one of the workstations on the room's periphery. Everyone else was watching him work.

"Here is the backup information described in your warrant," the manager said finally.

The male agent dug into a black satchel he had been carrying. From it he withdrew two aluminum boxes and some wiring.

"Please copy it to these two external drives," Agent Dupont directed. "I assume you can connect using either USB or Firewire?"

"Of course," the manager replied, accepting the equipment from the male agent and beginning to connect it to some boxes adjacent to the workstation.

Then he returned to the keyboard. A few keystrokes later he had given the copy command.

"It will take just a minute or two for the copy process to complete."

As he finished the statement, an error message appeared on the screen. The manager looked surprised.

"What's the matter?" Agent Dupont asked.

"It's impossible," he said.

"What?" Agent Dupont persisted. "What's the matter?"

"Someone else is accessing this data and I can't make a copy right now."

"Why would someone else be accessing the data?" I asked.

Maybe a stupid question. But I took a shot anyway.

"No reason I can think of," the manager said. "But it has to be someone inside this building. We have no computer connections to the outside world.

I don't know what to do. It looks like they're erasing the data." He sounded panicky. "This isn't possible."

"Where is the data physically located?" I asked. "And is there another copy? You computer guys always have spare copies of stuff."

"Original data is in Unit B-46. The copy is on D-46."

"Where is that? Exactly?" I urged.

"In the RAID storage area behind us," the manager said.

"Show me," I said.

The manager hesitated.

"Now!" It was Agent Dupont.

The manager quickly located one of the black boxes.

"What happens if I unplug this thing?" I asked.

"Hard to say," Katherine answered. "Probably most data would survive."

Using both hands, I grabbed the metal racking adjacent to the drive box. Applying counter-leverage with one foot, I pulled hard. The racking buckled. Now I could get behind the drive box. Reaching through the rack frame, I unceremoniously ripped all of the wires from the back of the drive unit.

The manager gasped.

"Now go get the one with the original data – the one that you were trying to copy," I directed. "But before you do that, tell me where there are computer access points to this array. The locations that are outside of this room."

"Only in the system administrator's office. Far end of the hall."

He paused.

"Get the damned drive!" I shouted at him, then broke for the door. Agent Dupont raced after me.

As we approached the system administrator's door, I drew my Beretta. Seeing that I had my gun out, Agent Dupont did the same. The system administrator's door was locked. But it was wood. I kicked it in and we both entered with our weapons drawn.

The only person in the room was facing the window, away from us. He was sitting at a computer and typing frenetically on a keyboard. His hair was long and unkempt. His attire, bordering on 1960s love child. He had ignored our violent entry.

"FBI. Stand up and step away from the computer," Dupont ordered.

The man kept typing.

I holstered my weapon and rushed forward, pulling him forcibly from the chair. As I jerked him to his feet, the long hair slid off his head.

I stepped back, freeing the man.

"Well, well," I said. "Aren't you *Mr.* Allister?"

He scowled at me.

"Allister, this is Special Agent Dupont of the FBI. I believe you and she have some business to conduct."

"On the ground," she commanded.

He reluctantly complied, still glaring up at me.

I covered the Agent with my Beretta while she applied handcuffs to the formerly prestigious computer genius. She pulled him to his feet. In his present attire, I thought he strongly resembled a Willie Nelson wannabe.

Beth came running down the hall.

"It looks like he succeeded in erasing the original backup information."

Allister smiled.

"But we can hope that the secondary backup is intact."

His smile faded a bit.

"Okay," Agent Dupont said. "We've gotten all we can from here. I'll send the scumbag downtown with some colleagues. They'll explain to me later how he escaped their surveillance. Then the rest of us can meet Rosa at the U of M."

She stared directly at Allister as she said the last sentence. All trace of his smile disappeared.

"You are making the biggest mistake of your life," he said to both Agent Dupont and me, trying to muster a threat. "Neither of you is ever going to work again."

"You've been watching too much television," she said, jerking him toward the door.

CHAPTER 35

While we waited for the FBI surveillance team to arrive to take custody of Allister, Beth, Katherine, George and the male agent took the computer gear I had ripped out of the backup rack and headed off to the offices of Dr. Mendez. I sure hoped I hadn't wrecked the unit. 'Air-gapping' the drive had seemed like the only safe solution at the time.

The agents on Allister-watch-duty hung their heads as Agent Dupont transferred custody of our prisoner to them.

"Do you think you can safely see him downtown to central booking?" she asked, displaying no small amount of sarcasm.

"Yes ma'am." They loaded Allister in the car.

"To start out with, we'll book him on the kidnapping of Dr. Katherine Whitson," Agent Dupont said to the other agents. "We'll probably be adding to that later today. Be sure you read him his rights again. I did so. But he pretended not to listen."

Agent Dupont dismissed them and they drove off.

Turning to me she said, "It seems my vehicle has departed. May I hitch a ride to the U?"

"Absolutely. Right this way." I motioned gallantly toward my waiting chariot.

After we had both climbed into the Pilot, I sat there for a moment without starting it up.

"What are you waiting for?" Agent Dupont asked.

"Don't you have any portable lights or a siren I could use?"

"Oh yeah," Dupont said. "There was one more thing Director Trew said about you. You're a smartass."

"He knows me better than I thought," I said, turning the ignition and putting the Pilot in Drive.

CHAPTER 36

By the time Dupont and I reached the University Center for Technology Development, everyone else was already in attendance. We crowded into the back of the lab to observe as Drs. Whitson and Mendez worked their magic. We could overhear their discussions. But most of it didn't make much sense to me.

"I hope you don't mind, Katherine," Rosa was saying. "But I took the liberty of connecting your chip testing hardware to our system. I thought it might come in handy once you had deciphered the ASIC program."

"Not at all, Rosa. That's perfect," Katherine replied. "Let's pray we get that far. I hope you will assist me with this situation. I think I can do it. But I would, nevertheless, appreciate your consultation."

It appeared that the first hurdle was connecting the RAID drive to the University system. It probably would have been easier if I hadn't shredded all of the connector cables. But with a little soldering and some spare parts that Rosa seemed to have lying around, the two computer goddesses had succeeded in achieving a physical connection to the system.

"Here goes," Katherine said, clicking an icon with the mouse pointer.

Lights flashed on the RAID drive. Maybe it was going to work after all.

"It doesn't look like our system is able to access any of the data," Rosa said in a moment. "I have some diagnostic and repair software I could try?"

"Please do," Katherine offered. She rolled her chair to one side so Rosa could take control of the keyboard.

The process was painstakingly slow. Each test seemed to take an eternity to run. And nothing Rosa had tried thus far had succeeded in unlocking the data stored on the RAID drives.

After more than two hours of trials and failures, Rosa turned to face Katherine. "Do you have any more ideas?"

"I think you've tried everything I can think of," Katherine responded, clearly disappointed.

I figured this was a dumb idea, but I opened my mouth anyway.

"Sometimes when my TV isn't working right, I give it a thump on the side."

It sounded even dumber when I heard myself say it.

Everyone in the room looked at me blankly – except Beth.

"You know," Beth said, "given the violent circumstances under which we obtained this unit, it is possible that a hardware issue is at the root of the problem. I have some experience with RAID hardware," she offered.

Katherine and Rosa looked at each other. They agreed it was worth a shot. And neither of them really wanted to mess around with the drive's guts. Rosa unplugged the RAID unit and placed it on a static mat at a hardware work station.

I watched as Beth sat down and confidently began removing screws and taking apart the unit. There were a number of layers of protection around the drive's working parts. Beth removed each in turn until she reached the parts she wanted to inspect.

"Rosa. Do you have a magnifier?" Beth asked.

"Certainly," Rosa said. She stepped across the room and returned holding a large magnifying glass with its own light source.

"Thank you," Beth said. She oriented the magnifier so she could examine the unit. As she worked, she would periodically touch the drive with her fingers, or with a small metal probe. Each time, before she touched the device, she would reach over to a metal, half-sphere that had a green wire attached to its base. The wire ran to a metal plate mounted to the wall, where it connected to one of many identical screws.

Noticing that I appeared intrigued by the metal sphere routine, Agent Dupont whispered in my ear: "She needs to make sure she isn't carrying any static electrical charge when she touches the drive. One small shock could destroy all of the circuitry. The metal ball is connected to ground wiring."

"Ah." I nodded comprehension.

Presently, Beth said to Rosa and Katherine, "Does this actuator connection look weak to you?"

Rosa and Katherine took turns looking at the essentially microscopic connection.

"I believe you may be correct," Rosa agreed.

Katherine nodded.

"I will try reinforcing it with a bit of solder," Beth said. She picked up the smallest soldering tool I have ever seen, and with a surgeon's steady hand, touched it to the drive. Then she looked through the lens again and pronounced it, "Much better."

"The weak connection may have caused the actuator arm to move unpredictably," Beth commented as she reassembled the drive unit. When the drive was all put back together, she pushed back her chair. "Care to give it a try, ladies?"

Rosa reattached the RAID drive to the system and attempted to access data. I think everyone in the room held fingers crossed. Maybe toes, too.

Momentarily, a menu appeared on the screen. Rosa looked at Katherine.

"My turn again," Katherine said, smiling.

It seemed that Beth's patch job had succeeded.

The first order of business was to make multiple copies of the necessary files to multiple drives – some of which were then totally disconnected from the system and encased in padded metal boxes.

"I've located and opened the ASIC design program," Katherine announced. "It will probably take Rosa and me a while to figure out what superfluous function the chipset is capable of executing. Maybe the rest of you would like to get a bite to eat or something?"

Beth and George wanted to stay – Beth to watch, and George to provide moral support. The other three of us left the two geniuses to work their magic. The male FBI agent remained on guard just outside the lab. Never hurts to prepare for every contingency possible. Allister might still have partners in the wind.

That left just Agent Dupont and me. There was a sandwich shop a short walk down the street. A small bell above the door tinkled as we entered. Taking our turns moving along the counter, we each ordered a cold hoagie and a drink. She had iced tea. I had a Diet Dew.

When we got to the cash register, I offered to pay.

"Sorry. I can't accept gratuities. Company policy," Agent Dupont said. "Thanks for the offer, though."

We sat on either side of a Formica booth near the front window and unwrapped the paper from our first real meals of the day. For a while, neither of us spoke. We focused, instead, on getting something in our stomachs. Someone once said that an army runs on its stomach. If you don't eat, you can't operate at peak efficiency – physically or mentally. This is true whether you are in the army or not.

All of a sudden Agent Dupont started laughing, nearly spitting out a bit of sandwich. She finally managed to swallow and shook her head.

"What's so funny?" I asked, genuinely interested in some good humor.

She looked at me. "Give it a thump on the side." She laughed again.

"Hey! Look where it got us," I said, feeling a bit wounded. "Just goes to show that some principles are universal. You don't need special knowledge or education to apply them."

"And thumping falls into that category?"

Now I had to laugh, too. "Okay. Dumb luck triumphs again."

"Oh, I'm sorry," Dupont said seriously. "It wasn't dumb luck. Your instincts and experience clearly played a part in solving the problem just now. It's just the 'universal principle' idea I question."

"Maybe a little grandiose," I conceded.

We both had finished our sandwiches before there was any more talking.

"You're a computer person, right?" I asked Dupont.

"Yeah. But not like those three we just left."

Beth would like that Dupont had included her in the same category as Rosa and Katherine.

"So tell me," I said, "does it seem to you like technology is becoming an uncomfortably black box?"

"How do you mean?"

"Well.   We've got machines, giving instructions to machines, to build machines to be tools for mankind.   Just seems like the human element is conspicuously absent in the whole process.

Guys like Allister pull the strings on one helluva lot of mechanical puppets.   And even our very best computer minds struggle to decipher what it is, exactly, that this tiny computer chip is up to.   Just seems scary to me – like letting a computer decide when to pull the trigger."

"I don't think we've reached Armageddon yet," Dupont responded. "But I do see your point. You're wondering whether humans are the carpenters or the tools?"

"Precisely."

"I suppose a good argument could be made that we are some of each.   Humans start the process.   But once it gets rolling, we are, to a degree, at the mercy of our creations.

Do you have suggestions for improving the human vs. machine equation?" Dupont asked.

"I'm afraid I don't have any answers," I said. "But I'd like to see a few more technology folks asking some of these philosophical questions.   A very bright young Stanford grad I chatted with recently seems to think the status quo is the way of the world – as if the future is set in stone."

"Beck.   You are an interesting specimen," Dupont conceded.

"And I can bench press 350 easy." I displayed a bicep.

"Your interest factor is diminishing," Dupont said.

"Geez. If I can't brag about strength, or doff imaginary hats . . . ."

"What's that about hats?" she asked.

"Nevermind. I'm still refining my twenty-first century persona. That's all.

Hey. What happened last night at the hospital?"

"It seems your suggestion to relocate Katherine to a different room, and to post the guard outside her former one, paid dividends. Somebody ambushed our man when he went to the men's room about 2:30. The perp had whacked the living daylights out of our dummy before he realized it wasn't Katherine.

And she still might have been in danger if your friend, Bull, hadn't come to the rescue and collared the creep."

"That's Bull," I said. "He's a 'come to the rescue' kinda guy."

"From what I am told, he's quite an interesting fellow. You'll have to introduce us sometime."

"I'm not sure that Bull's really dating material," I said with a smile.

"Keep working on that persona," Dupont replied.

My cell phone buzzed. It was Beth.

"Hi there," I answered. "Get tired of code-spotting?"

"Actually, Rosa and Katherine are done with their analysis. I think you'll find it intriguing."

"We'll be right there." I pocketed the phone. Then to Agent Dupont, "They're all done. Let's grab a sandwich for your muscle," I said, referring to the agent who remained at the lab.

"Again . . . more work on that twenty-first century thing," Dupont said with a smile.

Dupont bought the extra hoagie and we hiked briskly back to the lab.

CHAPTER 37

As Dupont and I approached the Computer Lab, she called to the agent who had remained on guard. "Take a break. I'll cover security while you get some nutrition." She tossed him the plastic bag containing the paper-wrapped sandwich.

"Thanks," he said. "Okay if I step outside and stretch my legs?"

"Go for it," she replied, opening the door and entering the lab waiting area. I noticed that she now kept her hand on the butt of her service weapon. She took her security role seriously. That was good.

I followed her inside the waiting room. Then we both continued into the lab proper, where the rest of our group sat around the conference table chatting. It sounded like a mutual admiration society.

This is what I heard:

"Oh, we could never have found it without your such and such."

"But it was your blah-blah-blah that really cracked it open."

"And we would never have even gotten to first base without your yada-yada-yada."

Agent Dupont seemed content to let them blather. I was a bit more anxious.

"So what's new? Have we revived Ms. Pac Man?"

Beth rolled her eyes. I could see them through the back of her head. I'm becoming skilled at that.

Rosa was the first to speak. "Ladies, I think a demonstration is in order."

"Quite," Katherine chimed in.

"Absolutely," Beth agreed.

Rosa beckoned Agent Dupont and me to join them at the conference table. I did so, but Dupont declined. Determined to play her security role to its fullest, she stood near the door to the lab and kept watch.

Rosa stood and procured a laptop computer from the nearby counter. She placed the computer in front of me.

"This computer runs a recent Microsoft operating system. Are you able to get on the internet?" she asked, trying not to sound condescending.

"I should be able to manage, assuming that I have an outside connection," I said.

"The ComDyne router with the aberrant chip is plugged into our system computer on the counter over there." She indicated with a thumb toward a computer along the wall to her right. "The wireless capabilities of the laptop and the router should allow you to connect."

The laptop was already open and powered up. The pressure on my performance was palpable. Even though I frequently connected to the web with a very similar computer, for some reason having the three computer goddesses in the room really put the pressure on.

I slid the mouse cursor over the Internet Explorer icon and gave it a double-click. An hourglass appeared and soon the program was open. A University of Minnesota welcome screen popped onto the display.

I changed the URL to Google.com and hit enter. The Google search screen appeared.

Success. I was on the web.

"Very good, Beck," Rosa said, again with sincerity. "Now, do you have any websites that you visit where you use a credit card."

"Sure. I buy lots of stuff online."

"Good. Then if you would be so kind, please access one of those sites and login."

I logged in to exquisite_jewelry.com. With all these women around, I wasn't about to appear the thoughtless husband.

"Please navigate to your Account page and check your credit card information," Rosa continued.

I did so.

"Now please add a new credit card and type in the credit card number I have written on this paper – it's a Visa number." She handed me a piece of yellow lined paper with the number. "Then save the new card information," Rosa directed.

I had no problems creating the new credit card payment option. I know all of this stuff is really basic computing; but I was pleased to be totally competent at these minimal tasks.

"Now, please logoff from this site and proceed to your online banking page."

Damn. Beth did all of the banking. I looked at her.

"I'm the one who handles the petty details at our house," she offered in my defense. Beth leaned over my shoulder and pulled up our bank account information.

"Please open your checking account register," Rosa asked.

Beth clicked on our checking account number.

"Please note the balance, and then, if you would be so kind, logout of the bank site."

I moved the cursor to the word "Logout" at the top right of the screen and clicked it. See. I wasn't a complete idiot.

"Please close your browser."

I clicked on the little "X" box in the top right corner of the banking window. The screen now displayed the same desktop as when I had started.

"Was this just a test to see if I can run a keyboard?" I asked, only half-joking. For a moment, no one said anything.

"That's right, Babe. Well done!" Beth wasn't going to leave me hanging.

"One moment please."

Rosa stood up and went to the other computer on the side counter – the same location where, just a short time ago, the router hardware problem had flummoxed the brilliant women.

She sat at the remote keyboard. The rest of us waited at the table in silence. It only took about five minutes; but it seemed a lot longer.

Rosa returned to the conference table, retaking her original seat.

"Beck, please check your account status at exquisite_jewelry.com. In particular, look for recent transactions."

I re-opened Internet Explorer and checked my jewelry purchasing account. I was surprised to find that my new credit card had just been used to purchase a $5,000.00 tennis bracelet. The delivery address was not my house, though.

"Impressive," I said.

"Now Beth, if you would please check your bank account balance?"

Beth punched up our online accounts. The checking balance showed $1.00.

"Wow! If you can make our balance smaller, would you mind making it really big?" I asked Rosa.

"Sorry. That would be criminal. I just transferred money from your checking to savings. You may put it back in your checkbook whenever you wish."

I thought I had seen everything when Rosa asked that we gather around her at the other computer screen. We did so, with Rosa at the controls. She punched a few keys and then sat back, spectating along with the rest of us.

The University Welcome Screen appeared on the display. Then without further input from the keyboard, the screen switched to Google.com. Then to exquisite_jewelry.com. The computer continued to retrace every keystroke Beth and I had entered moments ago, and paged through the exact same web screens.

Rosa punched a couple more keys and the web pages vanished, to be replaced by Beth's and my faces, as viewed from the laptop's built-in camera. She was leaning over my shoulder entering the banking info into the laptop.

"Please open your checking account and check the balance." Rosa's voice came from the computer speakers.

Without our knowledge, the laptop had turned on its own video camera and microphone.

Holy crap! If that chipset could do everything I had just witnessed, what else was it capable of?

Rosa clicked off the program, returning her computer to its desktop display. She turned her chair to face the group.

"What you have just witnessed is a small portion of the functionality possible behind the open gate on the AS-246C-01 chipset. Anyone with knowledge of the open gate, and the ability to write the code, could do exactly what we have just demonstrated. And they could do it with each and every computer connected to a network using any of ComDyne's new routers," Rosa explained.

"This sort of functionality is not, and could not be, accidental," she continued. "Furthermore, the portion of Dr. Allister's ASIC design program that Katherine and I dissected today contains detailed instructions directing the chip manufacturer's computer to build the chipset in this precise way."

"And the manufacturer probably didn't even know what they were building," I stated.

"Correct," Rosa said. "Of course, it is theoretically possible that the chip manufacturer might have known. But unless they were let in on the game from the start, there is only a remote chance the manufacturer had any such knowledge."

Machines building machines, I thought to myself. No element of human involvement once the ball gets rolling.

"It's fortunate you were able to catch the corrupt chipset before it reached the world markets," I said to Katherine. "Had that router been widely disseminated to corporations and governments around the world, God only knows what havoc it could wreak. Certainly, with easy access to credit card data and bank accounts, someone on the other end of that chip could have made a mess of international banking."

But I knew from keeping up on international espionage events, that much worse was certainly possible.

As recently as March of this year, the Tibetan government had asked an international consortium of computer security experts to investigate suspected cyber-spying activities at its embassies and government offices. Upon completing its work, the consortium had declared that it had discovered a large-scale cyber-espionage operation – an operation they had termed, "Ghost Net."

Based on over ten months of monitoring Ghost Net activity, the consortium had determined that Ghost Net had infiltrated high-value Tibetan political, economic and media locations in at least 103 countries. Computer systems belonging to Tibetan embassies, foreign ministries and other Tibetan government offices around the world had been compromised. Ghost Net had also accessed sensitive computer data belonging to more than a dozen other countries. It had even infected a NATO computer system.

Although Ghost Net's internet servers were physically located in the Peoples Republic of China, there was no way to say conclusively that the Chinese Government was behind this espionage effort; but that was what many governments believed. Really . . . who else would care about Tibetan government affairs?

All of the highly damaging espionage that Ghost Net had achieved – and the full extent of the damage was still not known – had been accomplished solely through software infiltrations. Mainly, through email attachments.

Ghost Net's primary weapon was a "trojan horse" virus, termed "Ghost Rat." Ghost Rat would enter the targeted computer as an email attachment. Once on board, the virus would access the Ghost Net internet servers and install additional software on the infected computer, ultimately allowing attackers to obtain complete control of the victimized system.

The effect was much the same as I had just witnessed in today's demonstration of the ComDyne chip. Keystrokes would be recorded, passwords and codes would be copied, even computer microphones and cameras would be set to transmit without the knowledge of the computer operator.

But Ghost Rat could only enter the targeted system if a human let it in — usually by opening the tainted email attachment. In a very real sense, Ghost Net was at the mercy of its target. If the target was vigilant, it remained safe. If the target was less careful, Ghost Net got in.

However, if the gateway into the target computer system were somehow installed in that system's own hardware — for instance, in a microchip onboard the system's ComDyne network router — someone like the operators of Ghost Net would have unrestricted access to all computers on the network. Password protection, anti-virus software, human vigilance and data encryption would no longer be obstacles.

And even though many essential government computers are either air-gapped or run their own proprietary operating systems, the same is not the case for other high-value targets, such as defense contractors, public utility companies, state and local law enforcement and many other entities.

What might Ghost Net-type operators do with information they collect from such sources? Misdirect smart bombs. Restore jammed enemy communications. Reprogram cruise missiles to alternate targets. Monitor, or even revise, encrypted U.S. military communications.

Much more was certainly possible. The extent of the potential damage would be limited only by the creativity and skills of the attackers.

If such information should fall into the hands of a country like North Korea or Iran, we could well be looking at the beginning of World War III!

Holy crap, again!

I turned to agent Dupont.

"Considering the Chinese kidnap muscle, the Korean manufacturer and this analysis of the chipset, we've got to have enough to get Homeland Security involved."

"We certainly could. But I'd like to take a run at Allister before we turn things over," she said. Then turning to Rosa and Katherine, "You've made copies of your findings?"

"Multiple," Rosa said.

"I'd like to send an agent up here with a video camera to have the two of you explain all of this on tape, if you wouldn't mind? Maybe do another demonstration for the camera?"

Katherine and Rosa looked at one another. Katherine spoke first.

"I'm a little concerned about the camera adding ten pounds." She smiled. Then, "Of course, we'll help."

"Great! I'll get that video team over here right away. They'll make sure everything is properly documented and understandable to any juror who sees the tape.

In the meantime," Agent Dupont said, "I'm going to leave my colleague outside your door to make sure you are not disturbed. And Beth, would you mind staying to explain the hardware fix you executed for the videographer? I don't want some defense lawyer claiming that you somehow reprogrammed this thing."

"Sure, my pleasure. I love listening to these two incredible ladies talking computers."

"And George?" Dupont asked, turning to Whitson. "Will you stay as moral support for your wife?"

"Wild horses could not drag me from my Katherine's side," he said, placing a hand on her shoulder. "I just got her back. I'm not going to lose her again."

"Okay." Agent Dupont turned to me. "I suppose I am going to regret this invitation. Do you wanna watch?"

"Absolutely!" I said, rubbing my hands together in anticipation. "But do I have to just watch? Or do I get to play, too?"

"Regretting it already." She turned and made for the door.

I hastened after her.

CHAPTER 38

This time I left the Pilot behind for Beth's use, and Agent Dupont was at the wheel of one of the generic, dark FBI sedans. It was getting close to five o'clock on Monday afternoon. The heavy downtown traffic between the University Lab and the FBI Field Office attested to the fact that most workers were on the road and headed home. It took us more than a half hour to traverse the two-mile distance between origin and destination. The difficult traffic precluded all but trivial conversation.

Agent Dupont had arranged for Allister's detention in one of the holding cells on her floor of the FBI building. But we went to her office first.

"I want to make sure we're both on the same page before I question Allister," Agent Dupont began. "You and your incredibly adept ad hoc team have all but solved these crimes."

That was nice to hear.

"But closing the deal is my specialty. I don't want to have Allister sitting around for years – maybe even out on bail – awaiting a trial. I want him to confess tonight. And I hope to put his whole corrupt gang of cyber-crooks out of business in the process."

She continued speaking with confidence, eyes fixed on mine. "I am going to allow you to watch the interrogation from behind the mirror; but I don't want any interruptions. Are we clear?"

She had cleverly detected that I might be the type of loose cannon to whom she needed to express herself with the utmost clarity.

And I was – both clear, and a loose cannon.

"Understood," I said.

She raised an eyebrow in question of my commitment.

"Completely," I assured her.

"Good. Shall we get to it then?"

"Please," I said, motioning for her to lead the way.

Agent Dupont handed me off to a male agent who escorted me to the observation space behind the two-way mirror of a small interrogation room.

The door to Interrogation opened, and a uniformed officer showed Allister, and a man I assumed to be his attorney, into the room. The officer directed them to straight-backed wooden chairs on the far side of the table from me.

Allister's arms were cuffed behind him. He looked uncomfortable. The officer left. Allister's attorney asked him to sit quietly because this room would be wired for sound and video. He complied.

They waited in the room for a long fifteen minutes before the door opened again. This time the same uniformed officer ushered in Agent Dupont. As soon as she saw Allister's handcuffs, she said to the uniform, "The cuffs won't be necessary officer. He's no common thug. I think we can trust his good behavior. If it doesn't work out, we can always restrain him further."

That was pretty slick. She had become his buddy by relieving his pain; but she had also subtly reminded him that she held the key to whether his discomfort would be returning. Very nice.

I wondered how she planned to get a confession out of Allister with his attorney in the room.

The attorney stood.

"Thank you on behalf of my client for having the handcuffs removed," he said. "My name is Brown, with Brown, James and Harrison. And you are?"

"Renee Dupont, FBI," she said shaking the lawyer's hand.

The interplay was fascinating. He took apparent control of the conversation, while she diminished her own authority by using her first name. Parry and riposte.

"I have advised my client not to answer any questions, Renee. So I'm not sure what we are doing here. Why not just have him arraigned on the bogus kidnapping charge and we can all be on our way?"

"That may be where we end up," Dupont appeared to concede. "But I've got my job to do. It wouldn't look good upstairs if I didn't at least take a shot." She opened her arms, palms up. What choice did she have?

"Understood," Brown said. "How may I help you get this whole mistake behind us?"

"First of all, let's have a seat, shall we?" Dupont indicated for Brown to sit, and she did likewise.

"I'd like to go over some things that I understand to be true about your client, and if you feel you can do so without compromising his legal position, I'd appreciate any corrections or clarifications you might offer."

Brown motioned for her to proceed.

"Okay. First of all," she said, consulting her notes clumsily. "Your client holds a number of postgraduate degrees from prestigious educational institutions."

She proceeded to recite a complete history of Allister's educational background.

"Have I missed anything?" she asked Brown, who looked at his client. Allister shook his head.

"Good. Then there are also a large number of professional accolades, honors and achievements."

Dupont launched into what seemed an endless litany of Allister's professional accomplishments. Looking at Allister, I could tell he enjoyed hearing about himself.

Every once in a while, Dupont would intentionally get something slightly wrong. At first Allister made corrections by whispering them to his lawyer. But after a few attempts at the three-way communication, Allister started making the corrections directly to Dupont.

Brown told Allister he should not answer the questions directly. Allister responded that he "damn well" knew his own background and saw no reason he shouldn't answer the questions himself. Brown threw up his hands in defeat and allowed Allister to continue. By the time Dupont had finished confirming Allister's professional achievements, he was talking quite freely.

"And then you came to ComDyne," she said. "And your position was, and has always been, that of Systems Architect."

Allister was nodding.

"Wow! I know a little about computers. That kind of makes you the big man on campus at ComDyne," Dupont feigned awe.

Allister shrugged . . . trying to play Mr. Humble.

"And it looks like while at ComDyne, you personally designed the architecture for numerous systems that have, in effect, built the company into the technological giant it is today."

Allister continued nodding, his arms crossed proudly on his chest.

"It says here that, as ComDyne's ambassador, you have traveled to many centers of high technology worldwide: Japan, South Korea, Taiwan, Germany." She looked up at Allister.

"Don't forget the Republic of China," he said.

"Oh, yes. My apologies. China was inadvertently omitted from my list."

I surmised that, in fact, she had no information at all about Allister's international travels prior to the interview. The first few countries were probably educated guesses. His mentioning China was the answer she had hoped for.

Dupont shuffled some more papers. The longer Dupont and Allister discussed his illustrious career, the more difficulty his attorney was having concentrating.

"Can we wrap this up tomorrow?" Brown asked.

"I was hoping we could get through it now and maybe Dr. Allister could sleep in his own bed tonight," Dupont said, looking up from the stack of papers.

"Yes. For Christ's sake. Let the woman finish so I can get out of here!" Allister scowled at Brown.

Brown leaned back in the wooden chair, getting as comfortable as possible. It was starting to appear that Brown disliked his client more and more as time went by.

In theory, whether an attorney likes his client or not shouldn't really make a difference to the quality of legal representation. But contrary to popular belief, lawyers are humans, too. If Brown disliked Allister, the attorney could not help but feel less inclined to zealously defend the asshole.

Apparently sensing that timing was right, Dupont prepared to strike.

"Well, that's almost everything. I just need to pose one hypothetical situation, and if you're so inclined, get your thoughts on the subject?"

There was nothing that Allister would enjoy more than pontificating on an area of his expertise. His lawyer again advised Allister against answering any further questions. Allister turned to Brown.

"Would you just shut the hell up!"

Brown stood up and paced the room, clearly trying to control his temper and to remain professional.

"Your hypothetical, my dear woman?" Allister asked Dupont.

"Okay. Let's suppose that at a large technology company – like ComDyne, for example – the computer programmers and QA flunkies came up with a software problem that was too tough for them to solve. They had asked all of their supervisors, but no one could seem to resolve the issue. Who would they go to for help?"

"Ultimately," Allister said, "the Systems Architect, of course. He would be the best programmer and have by far the most complete understanding of all of the company's software."

"And once the problem reached the Systems Architect's venue . . . ?"

"Either he would resolve it, or it would have to be something other than a software issue. Perhaps a hardware defect of some sort."

"And if that were the case? There was a hardware problem?"

"The Systems Architect would contact the hardware manufacturer and resolve the issue. If it couldn't be satisfactorily resolved, the company would reject the manufacturer's hardware product and find a more reliable supplier."

"Is that how you would resolve this hypothetical situation if it arose at ComDyne?"

She was getting very close now.

"Of course."

It had popped out of his mouth too quickly. Allister looked like he was beginning to feel uncomfortable.

"So when Dr. Whitson brought a hardware defect in the AS-246C-01 chipset for ComDyne's newest router to your attention, that is what you did? You contacted the Korean manufacturer and demanded that it be fixed?"

"I don't know what you're talking about," Allister stammered. "There's nothing wrong with the AS-246C-01."

"Please, Dr. Allister," Brown pleaded. "Don't say anything further."

This time Allister considered Brown's request. But egomaniac that he was, he refused to be outwitted by this mere public servant.

"I see," Dupont pondered. "So if that is true – there is nothing wrong with the chipset – why did you personally escort two Chinese gentlemen to Dr. Whitson's apartment, stage her seemingly voluntary departure, pack a bunch of useless clothing and toiletries, and forcibly remove her to a dungeon in Ottawa County, holding her there for nearly ten days against her will?"

"None of that is true. I deny it completely!"

Allister's voice was cracking a bit. But he remained defiant.

"Then maybe you can explain why those two Chinese gentlemen have described your involvement in just such an act?"

The trap was closing.

"No. I can't explain it. They must be mistaken . . . or . . . or lying."

"And Dr. Whitson . . . is she mistaken as well?" Dupont pressed on.

"The woman is not only incompetent, but a shameless liar," Allister tried. "Surely you can't take her word over mine."

"Perhaps that might be true without the corroborating testimony of the two Chinese men and . . . oh, yes. Did I mention the unusual subroutine built into the ASIC design software for the AS-246C-01, which by the way, I personally witnessed you trying to delete?"

Allister tried to look oblivious. Dupont wasn't buying his pitch.

"Dr. Allister," Dupont said incredulously. "Surely you know the portion of the design program to which I refer . . . the lines of code that would allow the Peoples Republic of China to spy on all users of the ComDyne router?"

Allister was speechless.

Dupont turned to face Brown. "Am I correct counselor, that espionage is a capital crime in the United States?"

Brown was still standing, shaking his head in disbelief. "May I have a moment with my client, unmonitored?"

"Certainly," Agent Dupont said, flipping off two switches on the side of the table and pulling a screen over the mirror. "Let the officer outside know if you need me."

And she left.

Ten seconds later she entered the observation room where I stood in silent admiration. I applauded emphatically.

"Brava! You are, indeed, an exceptional interrogator, Special Agent."

"Thank you." She accepted my compliment with a small bow. "But it's not over yet. Right now his attorney is trying to get him to flip on his contact from the government of China. Even with the death penalty as a bargaining chip, that may not be an easy sell. China is notoriously unforgiving."

"There's always Witness Protection," I said. "For whatever that's worth. They don't publish their failure statistics.

And I suppose the U.S. Attorney may not be inclined to give Whitson a free pass, when the U.S. doesn't have jurisdiction over China to impose a penalty. A political slap on the wrist might be all the U.S. can actually do to China. Hell, we're probably doing some similar espionage against China at this very moment. International diplomacy is so messed up."

There was a knock at the door and the uniformed officer poked his head inside. "You're wanted in Interrogation."

Already? That was quick.

"We'll find out something soon," Dupont said. "Keep your fingers crossed."

"And toes," I added.

As soon as Agent Dupont had raised the screen from the mirror, she returned to the table and flipped both switches back on. She remained standing, leaning forward with knuckles on the tabletop.

"Do you have an offer?" Brown asked. Allister looked like a child's punching clown with most of its air sucked out.

"We take the death penalty off the table and your client tells us everything he knows about the whole spying and kidnapping scheme – names, contact information, financial transactions, everything. And he forfeits any gains from this conspiracy.

If he complies completely and truthfully, instead of the needle, he gets life without possibility of parole on the espionage charge, and twenty-five years for kidnapping, to run concurrently."

I wondered how anything but "concurrently" might be possible.

"My client would want to be isolated in a secure facility and offered protection from potential assassins," Brown continued.

"What . . . you want the prison system to protect him from fucking China? We can give him a secure cell, but no guarantees."

Brown looked at Allister. He nodded weakly.

"Done," Brown said.

Agent Dupont removed a pen and pad of yellow paper from the table drawer and tossed them in front of Allister. "Start writing," she said, and headed for the door.

CHAPTER 39

While Allister composed his statement of confession, Agent Dupont and I had an opportunity to discuss the day's events in the FBI sixth floor conference room.

"I have to give you credit, Agent," I said. "You possess a unique finesse in the interrogation room. I especially enjoyed how you got Allister talking about himself."

"That was the easiest part. The man is a legend in his own mind, to borrow a phrase."

"I hadn't heard about the confessions of the co-conspirators in Ottawa County Jail. That tidbit certainly helped," I commented.

"Which confessions would those be?" Dupont asked with a smile.

Never trust the word of a law enforcement official during interrogation.

"And evidence on the chip connecting it directly to China?" I asked.

"A logical assumption," Dupont responded. "Or an educated guess."

"You should play poker."

"Now I have a couple questions for you," Dupont said. "That is, if you don't mind?"

"Go for it," I said.

"When the agents served the search warrant at ComDyne HQ, they seemed to have a particularly easy time locating every single item identified in the warrant. It was all in a box with my name on it. Who arranged this coup?"

I tried to blush. "I guess that would be my doing."

"I hope there wasn't anything in your . . . ah . . . process that might have violated Dr. Allister's rights. Such activities could have tainted the evidence necessary to obtain a conviction in court, in the event a trial was necessary."

"I'm fairly certain . . . and I am an attorney, mind you . . . that there was nothing improper in the way the evidence was dealt with prior to coming into FBI hands. I enlisted the help of a ComDyne insider in assembling everything into a convenient package.

I was only trying to minimize the inconvenience for ComDyne that a clumsily executed search warrant might have caused. Since the employee, whom I would prefer to remain nameless, was authorized to access, handle and move all of the boxed items around the ComDyne facility, I don't think there is anything illegal about him, or her, doing so.

And he or she never actually removed anything from ComDyne's complete control – your agents did that, with a legitimately-obtained warrant. Last I heard, cooperating with law enforcement in executing a search warrant wasn't a no-no."

"I have to agree with your analysis," Dupont said. "But I envy your ingenuity and resourcefulness in assembling such a diverse and complicated list of items as were contained within the box. Someday I'd like to hear more details of how, exactly, you managed it."

"Of course," I said. "Someday."

"I also have to confess to harboring a bit of jealousy at your creative solutions to complex problems today," the Agent continued.

"For instance?" I asked. I honestly wondered what she was taking about. I had felt relatively useless since the dawn raid on the Ottawa County "bunker."

"While the computer experts fretted over ways to block destruction of the ASIC code data by using their analytical and technological abilities, you forcibly bent the RAID storage rack, and tore the drive assembly right off its wires. Quick. Decisive. Pragmatic. Maybe not elegant. But most definitely effective. If you hadn't prevented Allister from erasing the files on that RAID unit," Dupont continued, "we might never have been able to prove the dangers of the chip, and the routers might be shipping all over the world by next week."

"Once a soldier, always a soldier" – then to clarify – "I'm an Annapolis grad. When I see something I need, I just go get it, any way I can."

"And I loved your idea of 'thumping' the RAID unit when the computer queens were stumped." Dupont laughed again.

"My father once told me that there isn't much a good whack can't fix," I said. "You just need to be sure of what, or whom, you're whacking. If you think about it, Dad's theory might just fix a lot of what's wrong with politics in the world."

"Novel approach," Dupont conceded.

A uniformed officer appeared at the open conference room door. "Your guy's done writing," he said.

"I better get back to that business," Dupont said. "You're leaving, I presume."

"Not much left to see. And it's been a long day. I'd best find my wife and see if we're heading home or staying another night in the Cities."

"I'll have someone run you over to the U if you like."

"No thanks. It's time for Beth to be leaving the computer goddess club anyway." I offered Agent Dupont my hand. "It's been a pleasure Special Agent."

"Likewise, Beck. Hope to work with you again sometime."

Dupont headed for the interrogation room while I made my way to the elevator.

CHAPTER 40

Beth had decided that another night at the hotel wasn't a bad idea. So after she picked me up at the FBI offices on Washington Avenue, we drove the fifteen blocks through downtown and parked in the Hyatt ramp.

Since we had already picked up overnight sundries for the previous night's stay-over, no further shopping was needed. And frankly, Beth was too tired anyway.

For at least several minutes, we lay silently in bed beside each other. It was a comfortable silence. But I felt the need to disturb it anyway.

"Beth?"

"Um hmm?" Her eyes were closed.

"Did you have a nice day with the other computer goddesses?"

"Um hmm."

"Are they unbelievably intelligent and amazing to behold?"

"Um hmm."

I waited a moment until Beth was drifting off to sleep.

"So are you," I whispered, softly kissing her cheek.

CHAPTER 41

By the time Allister finished writing his confession, he had made it sound like he was some sort of hero-genius-patriot. But the facts were all there – everything necessary for successful prosecution of all persons involved. And his confession ensured that Allister would remain confined in a Federal Detention Facility for the remainder of his self-absorbed life.

His writing had identified the two Chinese gentlemen as co-conspirators in the kidnapping of Katherine Whitson. Allister denied, however, that they had any knowledge of the espionage arrangement. They were hired muscle – nothing more, nothing less.

Allister had also implicated Chinese President, Hu Jintao, himself, as being the driving force behind the spy operation. Of course, he hadn't actually spoken with the President; but his confession narrative insisted that he had dealt directly with the President's "Special Envoy." It turned out the man he had identified as his contact was a low-level intelligence operative stationed with the Chinese diplomatic mission at its embassy in Washington. Ironic.

The bottom line concerning Allister's Chinese handler (Allister would have hated that term) was that he had diplomatic immunity, and the U.S. couldn't touch him without permission from the Chinese government. Not surprisingly, China declined to allow the Americans to prosecute its agent. The U.S. did its best under the circumstances. The "Special Envoy" was summarily expelled from the country – forever to be considered *persona non grata* on U.S. soil.

The world Press picked up the story of the Chinese spy – dubbing the AS-246C-01 the "Ghost Chip." But China simply denied the charge as capitalist propaganda. It had weathered fiercer storms regarding its human rights record, nuclear proliferation, environmental devastation, etc. A spying charge was a mere gadfly – easily deflected.

The good news for Allister was that, with the entire plot out in the open, China's motive for eliminating him had decreased substantially. There really wasn't anything more he could say or do to harm them. He might yet survive to enjoy a long incarceration.

Ottawa County authorities turned the two kidnapping accomplices over to the custody of the BCA. The Minnesota Attorney General would want as much press coverage as possible concerning this high-profile bust.

Each kidnapper ultimately received a fifteen-year prison sentence in a widely-publicized trial – where the Attorney General, again, garnered significant camera time. The expectation was that the kidnappers would be returned to China upon their release from U.S. captivity – though, their prospects of surviving their prison sentences were far less favorable than Allister's. China did not tolerate poor performance – translated as "getting caught" – from its operatives. Most of the law enforcement folks I knew expected that violent encounters with prison shivs lay somewhere in their futures.

As for ComDyne, the U.S. Attorney General reported in a televised press conference that the company had "cooperated fully" with the federal government's requests for further information regarding the near disaster involving the new line of routers. Needless to say, the new routers never hit the market, and ComDyne stock plummeted.

Through its internal investigation, ComDyne confirmed that Allister had apparently acted on his own in designing the Ghost Chip. Until Dr. Whitson's discovery that something was unusual about the chipset, no one at ComDyne had had any inkling that anything surreptitious was going on.

Furthermore, ComDyne's investigation cleared the South Korean chip manufacturer of any knowledge of the improper chip design. As expected, the manufacturer had relied on Allister's design program to determine the chipset layout and construction parameters. The manufacturer would have had no realistic method to determine that part of the chipset was capable of performing unauthorized functions, or what those functions might be.

In the manufacturer's case, it was strictly a matter of computers building computers. There was no human involvement other than assuring that manufacturing equipment was operating with its own design specifications.

The other interesting development at ComDyne was that it had hired a new Systems Architect – Dr. Katherine Whitson. The hiring was not only a smart business decision, because of Katherine's technical talents, but also a savvy political move. When your company has just been the subject of an espionage investigation, who better to place in charge than the whistle-blower herself?

Katherine harbored no animosity toward ComDyne and was pleased to accept the promotion. But she did so with one condition – that her loyal and capable intern, Sam, continue to work with her in her new capacity. It was an unprecedented request in the high tech world. For a Systems Architect to tutor an intern in the complexities of product design, was unheard of.

To say that the career opportunity for Sam was extraordinary would be a substantial understatement. Given his obvious intelligence and computer expertise, Sam's ability to hang onto Katherine's coattails until he was ready to move on to greater responsibilities portended well for his professional future. He was ecstatic at his good luck – though once he had had a chance to think about it, he was sure to realize that his unwavering support for, and devotion to, Katherine had more to do with the promotion than the winds of fortune.

CHAPTER 42

Winter had settled on Red Wing. It would be a white Christmas this year – nearly a foot of snow already blanketed the yards along Jefferson Avenue. December temperatures hovered in the single digits. Mornings came late and darkness early.

On this particular evening, Beth and I were enjoying a dip in our backyard spa – though in Minnesota, we usually call them hot tubs. The brisk northern air hung clear as glass around us. And the black sky displayed its shimmering jewels for all to see.

Beth and I cuddled in the corner of the warm pool, where the water was deepest.

"Beth," I said, the cloud of my breath mingling with vapors from the hot tub.

"Yeah, Babe."

"How come I always get to be the one to shovel a path to the hot tub and open the top?"

"You're the man," she replied.

"You don't feel in any way diminished by my hogging all of the hot tub access procedures?"

"Not in any way," she said sweetly.

I thought for a moment.

"What do you think Katherine and George Whitson are doing right now?" I asked.

"Probably working. Maybe reading a book," Beth said. "Why do you ask?"

"George Whitson is so fussy about having everything around their condo just so," I said. "I'm not like that."

"No, you're not like that."

"So if . . . just for example . . . someone else wanted to shovel the path and open the hot tub during the wintertime, I wouldn't ever complain about how it was done, or whether the path was wide enough, or anything like that."

"No, you wouldn't," Beth agreed.

"Do you think anyone is ever going to offer to do those things at our house?"

"Besides you?"

"Besides me."

"I don't think so."

"I didn't think so either," I said. "And I really wouldn't have it any other way."

Beth looked up and gave me a smooch on the lips. "You really wouldn't, would you."